THE POOLE HARBOUR MURDERS

Rachel McLean writes thrillers that make your pulse race and your brain tick. Originally a self-publishing sensation, she has sold millions of copies digitally, with massive success in the UK, and a growing reach internationally. She is the author of the Dorset Crime novels and the spin-off McBride & Tanner series and Cumbria Crime series. In 2021, she won the Kindle Storyteller Award with *The Corfe Castle Murders* and her books regularly hit No 1 in the Bookstat ebook chart on launch.

ALSO BY RACHEL MCLEAN

Dorset Crime series

THE POOLE HARBOUR MURDERS

THE DORSET CRIME SERIES
BOOK 10

RACHEL MCLEAN

ACKROYD
PUBLISHING

Ackroyd Publishing

ackroydpublishing.com

Printed and bound in the UK by CPI Group (Uk) Ltd, Croydon CR0 4YY

AUTHOR'S NOTE

This is the tenth book in the Dorset Crime series, and it sees Lesley being expected to behave more like a 'proper' DCI and oversee two teams, instead of getting stuck into the work of the MCIT. Whether she manages to do as she's told remains to be seen.

The two teams are:
Major Crimes Investigation Team (MCIT):

- DI Hannah Patterson, transferred from Devon (who appeared in *The Fossil Beach Murders*)
- DS Nathan Strunk, former professional standards officer who appeared in *The Ghost Village Murders*
- DC Tina Abbott, MCIT member since *The Corfe Castle Murders* (currently on maternity leave)
- DC Meera Vedra, MCIT member since *The Blue Pool Murders*

Cold Cases Team (new team):

- DI Jill Scott, recently returned from parental leave
- DC Mike Legg, formerly of the MCIT
- DC Katie Young, who briefly joined the MCIT in *The BluePool Murders*
- DC Stanley Brown, MCIT member since *The Monument Murders*

Both teams are based out of Dorset Police HQ in Winfrith near Wool, which has recently relocated to a shiny new building on its existing site (to great consternation in the local press, both in the books and in real life).

Happy reading!
Rachel McLean

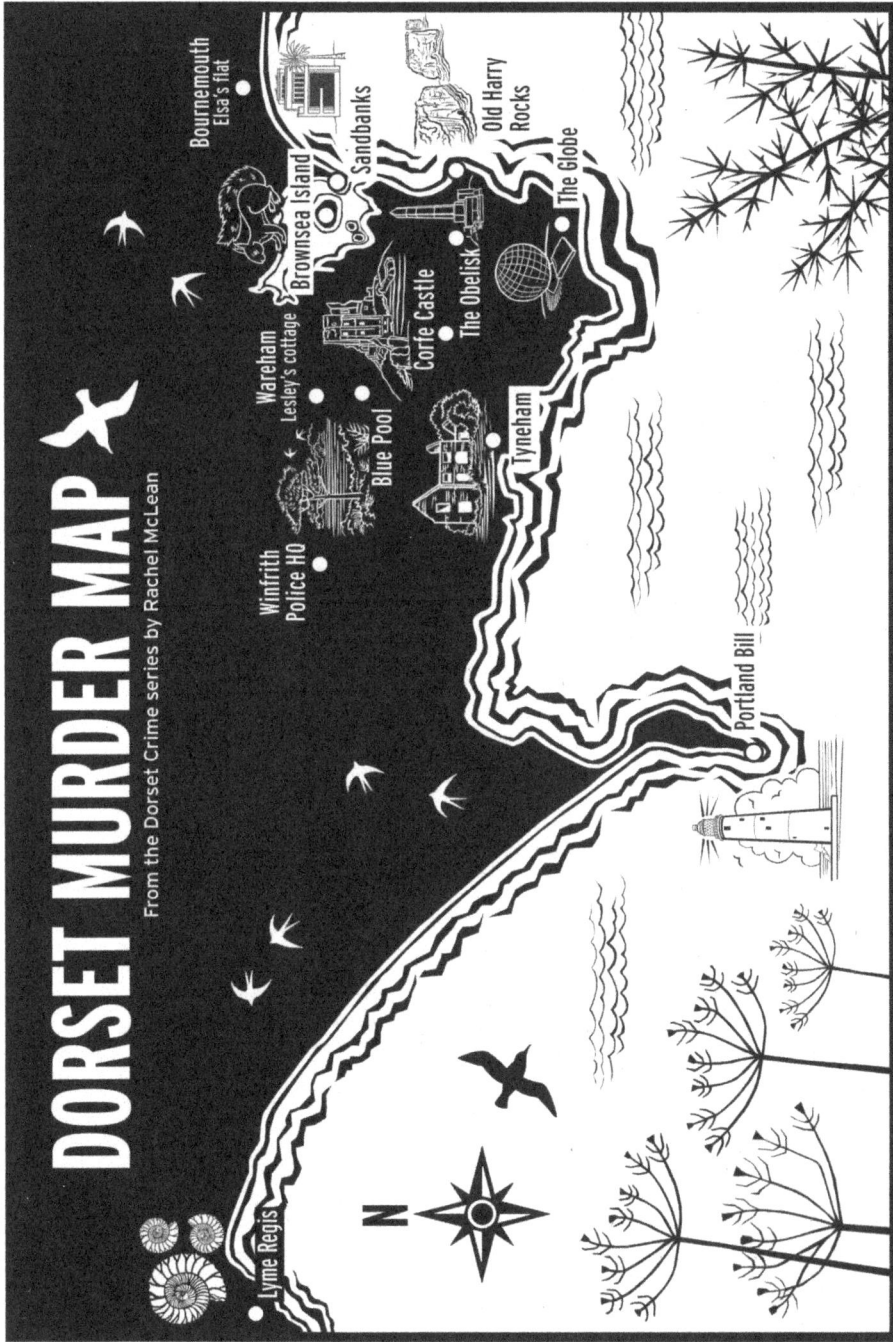

DORSET MURDER MAP

From the Dorset Crime series by Rachel McLean

Lyme Regis

Winfrith Police HQ

Wareham
Lesley's cottage

Blue Pool

Tyneham

Portland Bill

Bournemouth
Elsa's flat

Sandbanks

Brownsea Island

Corfe Castle

The Obelisk

Old Harry Rocks

The Globe

N

Illustration by Maria Burns

rachelmclean.com

CHAPTER ONE

JULY 1973

Izzy Davison sat at the reception desk of the Sandbanks Hotel, her eyes heavy. The clock read 2am.

She leaned back, listening to the soft hum of the intercom system and the background swoosh of the sea beyond the windows. The baby-listening service was part of her job, and usually, she didn't mind it. But tonight was different.

The baby in 204 – Ellie, her name was – had been crying for the past hour. Her wails echoed through the intercom, piercing the quiet of the hotel lobby.

Izzy sighed, looking around. The place was deserted. She picked up the phone and dialled the duty manager.

"Yeah?" His voice was gruff, tired.

"Mr Thompson, it's Izzy. On baby-listening. It's Room 204. The baby's been crying for ages."

"Parents not back yet?"

"No sign of them."

He grunted. "I'll check it out."

Izzy put the phone down, her fingers tapping the desk. She

listened. The crying had stopped. She hoped the manager had sorted it.

The minutes dragged. She flicked through the other intercoms, devices the hotel lent to parents so they could go out for the evening without having to take small children with them. She rubbed her eyes, yawning, and tried to focus on her work, but her mind kept drifting back to Ellie.

At 5am, the crying started again.

Izzy straightened, her heart sinking. She listened, bending towards the intercom. She waited for someone to shush the baby.

Nothing.

She checked the guest log. Mr and Mrs Sharp. Surely they'd be back by now?

By 6am, she couldn't take it anymore. She stood, smoothing down her skirt, and headed for the lift.

She rode up in the lift, listening to its creaking and the sounds of the hotel coming to life. Distant toilets flushing, the hum of pipes in the wall. She stifled another yawn and tried to picture the baby in her cot. Alone in that room.

Surely not.

Room 204 was at the end of the corridor. She hesitated outside the door, then knocked softly. No answer.

She knocked again, then used her pass key to enter. The room was dark, the curtains drawn. Ellie's cries were louder now, desperate.

Izzy opened the curtains just a crack and moved to the cot. The baby was red-faced, her tiny fists clenched. Izzy lifted her, cradling her gently.

"It's alright, lovey," she murmured. "It's alright."

She looked over towards the bed. It was empty, the sheets unruffled. The little slabs of chocolate from turndown service were untouched on the pillows.

She looked down at the baby. "Where are your mum and dad, eh?"

A voice made her jump. "What are you doing?"

She turned. A man stood in the doorway, his expression hard.

"Mr Sharp," she said, pushing her shoulders back. She reminded herself she had a right to be here. "Your daughter... she's been crying for hours."

He frowned, stepping into the room. He took Ellie from her, yanking the little bundle from her arms.

Izzy looked from the baby to him. "Where's Mrs Sharp?"

"Rowena?" He cast about the room, only now spotting the neat bed. "I don't... I don't know." He turned back to Izzy, his eyes dark. "You can leave now."

"Are you sure? You don't need help?" She looked at the baby, wriggling in her father's arms.

"I said you can leave."

Izzy swallowed. She gave a little bob, feeling foolish, and made for the lift.

Why had they left that poor baby alone all night? And where was her mother?

CHAPTER TWO

JUNE 2025

TONY PATEL STOOD on the edge of the quay, watching the dredger move slowly through the water. They were dredging silt from Upton Lake, an area of Poole Harbour that protruded to the north above Hamworthy, a quiet spot with little of the beauty of places like Brownsea Island or Arne. Behind him was a railway bridge, passenger trains chuntering past every fifteen minutes or so and up ahead was Upton Country Park, separated from the harbour by a high fence.

This work was part of a conservation project that didn't make a lot of sense to Tony, a project that was giving his team hundreds of hours of work and would supposedly save one very local species of grebe from losing its summer habitat.

The early morning light cast a grey hue over the water, the air cool and damp. He pulled his jacket tighter, wishing he'd brought a warmer one.

"Tone!" one of the crew shouted from the boat. "You might want to see this."

Tony frowned. He'd been overseeing the dredging operations for weeks now, and he was thoroughly bored of it. It wasn't unusual for the crew to call him over, but there was something in the man's voice.

He walked over to the edge, peering down at the water. "What is it?"

The crewman pointed. "There. Near the bucket."

Tony squinted, trying to make out what he was seeing. At first, it looked like a bundle of clothes. But as the dredger's bucket lifted, he realised it wasn't just debris.

"Bloody hell," he muttered, then turned and shouted. "Stop the dredger!"

The crewman signalled to the operator, and the machine came to a halt. Tony's heart pounded as he leaned closer, trying to get a better look.

"Is that...?"

"Looks like a body," the crewman said, his voice low.

Tony swallowed. "Get the police. Now."

The crewman nodded, pulling out his phone. Tony stayed where he was, eyes fixed on the water. He'd been with the Environment Agency for years, but he'd never come across anything like this.

The body, or the remains of one, floated just beneath the surface, tangled in reeds and debris. A woman, by the long hair. There were scraps of clothes hanging from her, and...

He swallowed back bile. She'd been there a while. If he didn't want to risk losing the Egg McMuffin he'd had for breakfast, that was all his brain could process on the matter.

He put a hand over his mouth, muttering to himself. This part of the harbour had been silted up for decades. She looked... she looked in a bad way.

"Police are on their way," the crewman said, returning to his side.

Tony nodded, avoiding looking down at the woman. "Good. We need to keep the area clear. No more dredging till they get here."

He lowered himself to the damp ground. A little way off, more crewmen were talking between themselves. He allowed himself a glimpse at the woman. Just a glimpse.

Red. That was the colour of her clothes, wasn't it? Or was it something else in the water? And her hair...

It fanned out around her. She bobbed and dipped, moved by the water. Her head... her head was deformed somehow. Had that been caused by the dredger hitting her?

He closed his eyes and looked away.

Poor woman. And her poor family, when they had to see the state she was in.

CHAPTER THREE

DCI LESLEY CLARKE sat at her desk, the early morning light filtering through the blinds. It was June, the summer heating up and the grockles descending on Dorset.

None of them were anywhere near Police HQ in Winfrith, though. This was the back of beyond, as far as the tourist trail was concerned.

Her office was quiet, the only sounds distant movements from somewhere along the corridor. When Superintendent Carpenter had put her in charge of the new Cold Cases team in addition to her own Major Crime Investigations Team, he'd also insisted she move office, so she wasn't distracted by being right in the middle of them. And then, of course, there had been the move to the shiny new office just across the way from the old one. She'd still not got used to either of those changes, but at least this building had aircon that actually worked.

She sighed and sipped her coffee, trying to shake off the remnants of a restless night, just as the door swung open without a knock. DI Hannah Patterson stepped in, her expression unreadable.

"Morning, boss."

Lesley frowned and put her mug down. "Hannah. What is it?"

"Just had a call from Uniform, in Poole, boss."

"And...?"

"The Environment Agency have been dredging Upton Lake. It's a bit of Poole Harbour that sticks out to the north, near—"

Lesley put up a hand to stop her. "I'm sure that's all very interesting, but how does it concern us?"

Hannah's shoulders dipped. Her mid-length mousy hair was greasy; how long had she been up for?

"Right. Yes. OK, so they've found a body. Got caught up in the dredging equipment."

Lesley winced. "Badly damaged?"

A shrug. "Not sure."

"What exactly are you sure of? Any information on the body yet?"

Hannah looked down at the notepad in her hand and shook her head. "Long hair, so they reckon it's a woman."

"Doesn't necessarily follow."

"I know. And..."

Lesley waited, tapping her fingertips on the table. She'd tried to get along better with Hannah since the DI had become head of the MCIT. But she couldn't forget the run-in they'd had in Lyme Regis a couple of years earlier, and she hadn't been exactly pleased to hear the woman was going to be joining the team.

"Who's going over there?" she asked.

Hannah pursed her lips. Her eyes were bloodshot. That had better not be a hangover.

"I am, boss. I'll take Meera."

"Good." DC Vedra was a thorough detective, still inexperienced but learning fast.

Hannah nodded. Lesley leaned back in her chair. Her stomach growled.

Hannah flicked a look down towards Lesley's stomach and Lesley arched an eyebrow. Hannah, to her credit, blushed.

Lighten up, Lesley told herself. *You've got to get along with the woman.*

"OK," Hannah said. "I'll keep you posted."

Lesley sighed, wishing it was her heading out there to stand at the edge of the water and confer with Forensics and Pathology. Gail Hansford, Dorset's best crime scene manager, would be there already. Gail had a way of getting to crime scenes faster than the speed of her CSI van seemed to allow.

"Right. Keep me updated."

Hannah eyed her. "Updated. Does that mean you need to know everything we're doing, or... Only, I do know what I'm doing, boss."

Do you? Hannah had always exuded confidence, that was certain. Right from when Lesley had clashed with her over operational boundaries between Dorset and Devon police. But how much did she actually know?

Lesley nodded. "I'll attend the first briefing. Then we'll play it by ear, yes?"

Hannah's left eye twitched. "Of course." She turned away, her movements stiff.

The door closed behind her, leaving Lesley alone again. She picked up her coffee, staring at the wall.

Why was this not getting any easier?

CHAPTER FOUR

DC MEERA VEDRA stood a little way back from the water, shivering despite the sun climbing in a clear blue sky. The marshland stretched out before her, reflecting the sun and the birds wheeling overhead. Beyond it was the harbour, or at least a section of it, and beyond that were the ugly buildings that flanked the water on the Poole side. She watched as Gail Hansford, the crime scene manager, directed her team, their figures moving carefully around the exposed remains.

DI Patterson stood beside her, arms crossed. "It's not pretty, is it?"

Meera shook her head. She'd seen one of the Environment Agency guys throwing up behind a bush when she'd arrived.

"Poor woman," she said. "If it is a woman." The body had long hair, but it was far too decomposed for them to have any idea from here what its sex might be. Much less to attempt to identify it.

Gail approached, her expression grim. "We've got the body partially uncovered. There's a lot of mud, and not only on the outside."

The DI nodded. "What can you tell us?"

"Not much yet. The remains are skeletal, but there's some clothing. Looks like a coat, maybe. Hard to tell."

Meera glanced at the DI, who was gazing past Gail towards the body.

"Any personal effects?" DI Patterson asked.

Gail shook her head. "Nothing obvious. We'll have to be careful with the excavation. The mud's preserved some of it, but it's fragile."

The DI turned to Meera. "Have you spoken to the pathologist?"

Meera nodded. No one had asked her to call Dr Bamford, but she'd known the question would be coming. That was what it was like, working for DI Patterson. You had to second-guess her. "He's on his way."

Gail returned to the body, her team working methodically. Meera watched as they used small tools to gently remove the mud. It was painstaking work.

The DI shifted beside her. "You've worked with Gail before, haven't you?"

"Yes. She's good. Thorough," Meera said.

A grunt. "We need thorough."

A van pulled up, and Dr Gareth Bamford stepped out, pulling on a pair of gloves as he approached.

"Morning," he said, nodding to Meera and the DI.

"Dr Bamford," the DI said. "Thanks for coming."

"Wouldn't miss it," he replied, throwing Meera a wink.

Meera liked Bamford. He was efficient, but he had a way of putting people at ease. She'd heard about his predecessor, Henry Whittaker, who'd been quite the opposite. Old-fashioned to the point of Victorian. God knows what he'd have made of her.

The pathologist joined Gail at the body, crouching down to examine it. Meera looked to the DI for a nod, then edged forward with her.

"Right, let's see what we've got," he said, turning his head from side to side. Somewhere to their left a heron squawked, a rasping, guttural sound that made Meera jump.

The doctor and Gail conferred quietly. The body was a mess, the flesh stained dark from the mud. Meera tried to imagine who this person had been, how they'd ended up here.

Bamford straightened up, turning to the detectives. "It's going to take time to get anything definitive. But the preservation's not bad, considering. It's hard to untangle the extent to which the mud has preserved the body, in which case this is an old case, or to which the water might have damaged it, in which case, I just don't know..."

Tony Patel, the Environment Agency foreman who'd reported the discovery of the body, was behind Meera.

"There's been a fair amount of pollution in that part of the harbour, in recent years," he said.

The DI turned to him. "What kind of pollution?"

"2021. There was a spillage. Sewage and other stuff. Nasty."

"You think she's been here that long?"

He eyed the DI. "With respect, DI Patterson, I've got no idea. It's my job to manage the cleanliness of the waterways around here, not to pronounce on how long bodies have been hanging around."

Meera resisted a smirk.

"But...?" the DI said, folding her arms and giving Tony a sharp look.

"It took a good while to clean up," he said. "If that body went in here any time up to around... last year, I'd say, then there would still have been substances in there that could have affected it."

"Last year," Meera muttered. "Jackie Kendall?"

Jackie Kendall was an estate agent who'd gone missing the previous summer. The investigation had been closed six months earlier when charges against the main suspect, her ex, had been dropped in the face of a solid alibi.

The boss shook her head. "Let's not go getting ahead of ourselves, Meera. Gareth, I assume you can do some analysis into the substances that have entered the body, what might have come into contact with it?"

He nodded. "Any help Tony here can give me on identifying them would be helpful, though."

Tony gave him a grim nod. He looked towards the body then put his hand to his mouth and quickly looked away.

"Good." The DI wrinkled her nose. "Cause of death?"

The pathologist barked out a humourless laugh. "Give me a chance."

"But...?"

He frowned. "Much too early to say. We'll need to get the remains back to the lab. But there are some signs of trauma."

Meera frowned. "Trauma?" The DI gave her a look.

Bamford threw her a smile of sorts. "Possibly. There's plenty of damage. Could be post-mortem, though. No knowing what might have happened to her in the water. Boats, fauna. We'll need to analyse the body properly."

The DI nodded. "Keep us updated."

"Of course."

Meera watched as Bamford returned to the body. Tony left them too, summoned by one of his crew. She felt a mix of fascination and unease. She'd seen bodies before, but this was different. This wasn't someone bleeding out in their bedroom after a domestic incident, or a drugs overdose in a back alley somewhere. It wasn't even one of those cases with a body found in a beauty spot. This spot had a certain beauty to it, alright, but of all the parts of Poole Harbour to be working in...

The DI turned to her. "There are a couple of businesses over there. And the park behind us." She jerked her head backwards towards the fence behind them, then gestured across the water, where there was a McDonald's and a Premier Inn. A railway bridge passed over the water. Meera wondered if anyone in a train between Poole and Hamworthy might have seen something.

But then, with the body so decomposed, who knew when it might have gone into the water? Or even if it had gone in around here?

What with the tides, and the passage of time, it might have come from almost anywhere.

"I'll speak to them," Meera said. "Just in case." She sighed. She didn't exactly have anything specific to ask them.

"Good. And keep me informed. I want to know everything."

Meera bristled. Micro-managing. But maybe on a case like this, it was justified.

"Of course, Ma'am."

Hannah gave her a sharp look. "Please, Meera. I've already said this. Call me Hannah."

Meera nodded. "Hannah."

She hated having to use the DI's first name. No one called their DI by their first name, not unless they'd worked with them forever and were not just colleagues but friends. And 'Hannah' wasn't someone Meera could imagine being friends with.

"Good." The DI strode off, heading for her car.

Meera turned back to the scene, watching as Gail and Gareth continued their work. She'd been in this team for far longer than the DI, since before the DCI had been placed in charge of Jill's team, too.

She knew what she was doing. She could handle this.

CHAPTER FIVE

LESLEY SANK INTO THE SOFA, feeling the day's tension ease from her shoulders. The living room was finally starting to feel like home. Pictures hung on the walls, a new rug lay beneath the coffee table, and the soft glow from the lamp gave the room a cosy warmth.

Elsa sat at the other end of the sofa, legs stretched out. "I'm glad we got this room sorted," she said, looking around.

Lesley nodded. "I think it was all your work, love." Truth was, she'd never really been one for interior design. Elsa's flat in Boscombe had been a bright modern space, all leather sofas and gleaming quartz worktops. This house was older, built in the 1930s, a bit more homely. Cosier than both the flat and the high-ceilinged Victorian house she'd lived in in Edgbaston before moving down here.

"You picked that cushion." Elsa pointed.

"Only because you stood right next to it in John Lewis and kept looking at the damn thing."

Elsa smiled. "It is nice, though."

Lesley shrugged. Truth was, she didn't know a nice cushion from a not-nice one. But she did know that this house made her feel at ease. When she opened the bedroom window, she could hear the sea from two streets away, and it was only a ten-minute walk to Hengist-bury Head. But if they needed civilisation – something Lesley frequently did – Bournemouth was on the doorstep.

"If you say so." Lesley picked up the remote and flicked through the channels until she landed on the news.

The familiar face of Sadie Dawes appeared on the screen, standing by a dual carriageway near Hamworthy. Lesley's jaw tightened.

"Bloody Sadie Dawes," she muttered.

Elsa smiled at her. "You wouldn't have solved DCI Mackie's murder without her."

Lesley grunted. "That's debatable."

Elsa picked up the glass of beer she'd put on the coffee table and sipped. "You've got to admit, she's good at what she does."

Lesley didn't respond. She watched as Sadie spoke, her voice clear and authoritative.

"Speculation is mounting over the identity of the body found during dredging operations in Upton Lake. Although nothing has been confirmed, sources suggest it could be Jackie Kendall, the Bournemouth estate agent who disappeared last summer."

Lesley's grip on the remote tightened. "What makes her think that?"

Elsa shrugged. "People are still talking about Jackie. My friend Fran, she knows the woman who—"

Lesley turned to her. "You've got connections to Jackie Kendall? Why didn't you tell me?"

Elsa held out a hand. "Whoa, slow down there. I've got a conveyancing solicitor friend who has been known to act on properties sold by Pritchard & Locke."

"The firm Jackie worked for."

"Works. She's not dead yet."

Lesley sucked her teeth. Jackie Kendall had been missing almost exactly a year. Chances were slim that she'd turn up alive.

"If it is Jackie," she said, "then we'll have to reopen the case."

Elsa shifted, sitting up slightly. "You'll figure it out. You always do."

Lesley sighed. For a moment she remembered the Elsa she'd first met in the Duke of Wellington pub in Wareham, days after she'd started her job in Dorset. Her wife was still as striking now as she had been five years ago. But the assertion that Lesley would 'figure it out' stirred something uncomfortable in her. Was 'figuring it out' even her job now?

"Thanks," she muttered.

Elsa smiled. "Besides, you've got a good team. Even if you don't always see eye to eye."

Lesley felt her chest tighten. The team. Both of them. The body was decomposed, from what she'd been told. What if it wasn't Jackie, but something for DI Jill Scott's cold cases team?

Sadie's report continued, with footage of police vehicles and forensic tents at the site. Lesley knew she'd have to deal with the media circus that would inevitably follow.

"Do you think it's her?" Elsa asked.

Lesley leaned back, staring at the ceiling. "I don't know. At least we have her details on file, so we can establish that quickly."

Elsa reached over and placed a hand on Lesley's arm. "You'll get to the bottom of it."

Lesley nodded, feeling the weight of the case pressing down on her. "Yeah. We will."

The news moved on to another story, but Lesley's mind was still on the body at Hamworthy. If it *was* Jackie Kendall, they'd need to find out what had happened to her. And why.

Not to mention why the facts hadn't been uncovered a year ago.

CHAPTER SIX

LESLEY STOOD at the front of the briefing room, waiting for her two teams to settle. The MCIT and Cold Cases team filled the seats, their chatter a low hum.

They didn't do this in her office anymore, not with two teams. Instead, there was a separate room near the two team rooms, which they used for briefings and for larger investigations, where other officers had to be brought in. The room had a lock, which reminded her of the investigation into Fran Dugdale's death at Tyneham and how they'd avoided using a board in case any of DC Dugdale's Professional Standards colleagues had wandered by.

She shuddered, then glanced at the clock. Time to get started.

"Right, folks," she said, her voice cutting through the chatter. "We've got this body found at Hamworthy. No ID yet, but we do know it's a woman. Our priority is to identify her."

Hannah Patterson leaned back in her chair, arms crossed. "The media are already speculating it's Jackie Kendall."

Lesley nodded. "You saw the body. Do you think it's been there a year?"

"Possibly less," Meera said. "She went missing a year ago. Might have died more recently."

Lesley nodded; she had a point. She looked at Hannah, eyebrows raised.

Hannah shook her head. "I'm no expert, boss. But that amount of damage..."

"The Environment Agency said there were chemicals in the water, from the pollution incident in 2021," Meera said.

Hannah gave her a look. "Two years before Jackie went missing."

Meera lowered her voice. "Harry Patel did say the chemicals had lingered. I've done some research. This dredging operation is also supposed to clean up the last of that."

Lesley nodded. "OK, so we have to consider that it is Jackie, but the conditions accelerated the deterioration of her remains." She wrinkled her nose, thinking of the poor family having to identify her. There was an ex-husband, she remembered. A violent man, currently serving time which made for the most solid of alibis she could think of. And a new partner, who'd only been a suspect for all of about five minutes.

She turned to Jill Scott, the DI leading the Cold Cases team. "Jill, given the state of decay—"

Jill straightened in her chair. "You want us to check if any of our mispers might match."

"Please."

Jill glanced at DC Mike Legg, the most experienced member of her team. "We've already been having a look. Mike?"

Mike cleared his throat. Normally he'd be sitting next to his wife, DC Tina Abbott. She was in the other team, currently on maternity leave. Lesley had two married couples in her two teams, and she'd made damn sure that both couples were split between the teams.

"There's the Rowena Sharp case," Mike said. "She disappeared from the Sandbanks Hotel in 1973. Booked the baby-listening service, went out, and never returned. Her husband, Donald Sharp, was tried but found not guilty. No body was ever found."

Lesley noted the way the room shifted at the mention of a baby. "That's a lot earlier than 2023. Or 2021, for that matter."

He nodded. "I saw the photos of the body. I thought, with that level of decay..."

She nodded. "Go on."

"Rowena was last seen at the hotel on the evening of 16 June 1973. Her husband claimed they'd argued, that she'd walked out on him and the baby. There were suspicions, evidence of an argument the night of her disappearance. Enough to get him charged. But not enough to convict. The case went cold after the trial."

"How old would she be now?" asked DS Nathan Strunk, the newest member of the MCIT. Lesley was trying not to let his last job bother her: Professional Standards, a colleague of the man who'd killed DCI Mackie.

Jill turned to him. "She was born in 1950, so she'd be in her seventies."

Nathan whistled.

"Could be her," Jill said. "If the body's been there a while." She flashed Mike an encouraging look.

"Or it could be someone else entirely," Meera added. "We shouldn't jump to conclusions."

Lesley spotted the frown cast Meera's way by Hannah, and made a mental note to check things were running smoothly in that team. She'd hoped that Hannah only punched upwards when she was being a pain in the arse.

"Exactly," she said. "We need to keep an open mind. But it's worth looking into, Jill. See if there's anything in the case files that might help."

Jill made a note. "Will do, boss."

Lesley turned to Hannah. "Hannah, we're going to assume this is an MCIT case for now. It's more likely, by my reckoning. You're SIO. I want your team to focus on the forensics. Work with Gail and Gareth. We need that ID."

Hannah flashed Jill a triumphant look then gave a curt nod. "Already on it."

"Good. And Jill, keep going through the Rowena Sharp file. Anything that might link her to Hamworthy, I want to know."

Jill exchanged murmurs with her team. "We'll get on it."

The two teams turned inwards, talking between themselves and making plans for their next steps. Hannah was giving orders to her team while Jill was asking questions. Lesley watched, trying not to feel like a spare part.

She raised a hand. "Quiet down, everyone."

The room fell silent. She looked at the faces around her. The MCIT and Cold Cases teams were a mix of experience and fresh perspectives. They needed to focus.

"The body's in a bad state," she said. "It's likely been there a long time. That could point to a cold case, even to Rowena Sharp. But the media's stirring up interest in Jackie Kendall."

Hannah leaned forward. "You said Jackie's ex-husband was alibied?"

"Yes," Lesley replied. She'd led the case herself, before Hannah had joined the team. It had frustrated her not to get anywhere with it. Not to even know if a crime had been committed. "He was in prison, up north. And there was no reason to suspect her current partner. But the media loves a mystery."

"Are we reopening that case, boss?" Meera asked.

Lesley shook her head. "Let's not get ahead of ourselves. Our focus is on identifying this body. If it turns out to be Jackie, we'll deal with it then."

Hannah folded her arms. "We'll get you that ID."

"Good." Lesley looked around the room. "This is a high-profile case. The media's already sniffing around. We need to be thorough and careful. Let's make sure we don't talk to journalists, OK? Don't let anything slip."

Nods and grunts of agreement all round.

"Good. Then let's get to work."

CHAPTER SEVEN

SEBASTIAN SHARP SAT on the edge of his mother's bed, surrounded by boxes. The room felt cold, even though the heating was on. He hadn't been back here since her death, and now he was alone with her things.

He opened another box. Papers, mostly. Old bills, letters from friends. He picked up a notebook, pages soft with age. The paper was yellowed, the ink faded.

He opened to the first page. It was a diary. 1973.

He swallowed, his hand going to his chest. He glanced towards the door, but he knew no one was coming,

This felt... was it OK for him to read this?

He'd take a quick look. There was no name on the opening page, no indication of whose diary it was. It didn't look like his mother's writing.

He took a breath and turned to the next page.

The handwriting was neat, precise. He read the first few lines, then stopped.

He'd been right; this wasn't his mother's diary.

It was Rowena's. Ellie's mother. His father's first wife.

He read on, his eyes widening. He put a hand on the mattress to steady himself.

He looked at the first page again, squinting. He didn't have his reading glasses with him, but...

She'd written it as a letter. To someone called Peter.

Sebastian didn't know a Peter. He didn't think Ellie did, either.

He sighed and heaved himself up from the bed. His glasses were downstairs, in his briefcase. He found them, came back upstairs, put them on and picked up the pile of letters.

He read another page. And another. They were all the same. Rowena had been writing to this Peter, pouring her heart out. And they weren't just friendly letters.

Peter, I can't keep doing this. Donald suspects something. I know he does. But I can't stay away from you. I need you. I love you.

Sebastian dropped the book onto the bed and rubbed his eyes.

His father had never mentioned a Peter. Neither had Verity, his mother. Rowena hadn't had the chance: she'd disappeared years before he was born.

He flicked to another page.

I hate lying to him. But what choice do I have? I can't leave him. Not yet. Not with Ellie so young.

He swallowed hard. *Ellie.* Did she know?

The room felt uneven, like he might topple off the bed. Sebastian leaned back, his arms out behind him. He looked up at the ceiling.

Ellie's mother had kept this. And then his mother had, too. Why? Had she known about the affair? Had his father?

He flicked through to the end. There were at least a dozen separate entries, all in the form of letters. Maybe more. He didn't want to count.

Ellie. He needed to talk to his sister. She deserved to know. But how could he tell her? *Not with Ellie so young.*

What if she already knew?

He stood up, the notebook clutched in his hand. He had to get out of here.

He hurried downstairs and shoved the book into his briefcase. He'd call Ellie. She'd want to see this.

And maybe she'd know who Peter was.

Back in his car, he took a few breaths, then pulled out his phone and dialled her number. She picked up after a few rings.

"Sebbie. What is it?"

He licked his lips then looked down at his palms; sweaty.

"I'm at Mum's house," he said. "Going through her things."

"Right." Her tone was grim. "How's it going?"

He hesitated. "I've found something. You're not going to like it."

"What d'you mean?"

"A diary. Written by Rowena. Your mum."

He'd never met Rowena. She'd died, or disappeared at least, five years before he'd been born. But he'd seen photos, read the old newspaper reports. He knew how her memory haunted Ellie, just a baby when it had happened. Ellie had moved from Norwich to Poole after their father's death, so she could be near where her mum had last been seen.

Just in case.

Was that *just in case* about to happen now? Was this the breakthrough Ellie had been looking for?

Ellie's voice was small. "Mum? What? I don't understand."

"It's in the form of letters. And it's old, El."

"Letters? What do you mean, letters?"

"They're addressed to someone named Peter. But she wrote them for herself, I guess. They're... personal."

"Personal how?"

He swallowed. "She was having an affair, Ellie. With this Peter."

"Where did you find them?" Ellie's voice had sharpened.

"They're in a diary. A notebook. In Mum's things. She must've known about them."

Silence. He could hear traffic on the main road two streets away. Someone emerged from a house opposite his mum's and waved: a neighbour he knew by sight but not name. He returned the wave.

"Ellie?"

"Why didn't she tell me?"

He shrugged. "I don't know. Maybe she thought it wasn't her place."

"Or maybe she wanted to protect Dad."

"Maybe."

Her breathing was quick and shallow. "I need to see them."

"I'll bring them to you."

"Today. Please, Sebbie."

"I will."

"Thanks."

He hung up and slumped back in the car seat. What else had his parents kept from them?

CHAPTER EIGHT

MEERA STOOD BESIDE DI PATTERSON, waiting for Yiannis Kallias to answer the door. The house was modest, tucked away in a quiet cul-de-sac. The front garden needed weeding, and there was rubbish piled up next to the bins.

The door swung open. Yiannis, unshaven and wearing a creased shirt, frowned at them.

"More questions?" His voice was weary. "I thought you'd given up on Jackie."

The DI stepped forward. "Mr Kallias, we're here to talk about your partner's disappearance. May we come in?"

He hesitated, then stepped aside. "Fine. But I don't know what more I can tell you."

Inside, the living room was cluttered. Papers and empty coffee mugs littered the table. A suit hung from a coat hanger on the back of the door, and a laptop was open on the sofa, displaying a missing persons website.

Yiannis gestured to the sofa. "Sit, if you can find space."

The DI remained standing. Meera followed her lead.

"Mr Kallias," the DI said, "you've been running an online campaign to find Jackie. Can you tell us about it?"

He pushed back his shoulders, meeting her gaze. "I had to do something, didn't I? The police weren't exactly helping." He shrugged, his gaze dropping to the laptop. "I thought it might get people talking, maybe remind someone of something they'd seen."

Meera glanced at the screen. "Has it brought any leads?"

"Nothing useful. Just trolls and conspiracy theorists." He rubbed his eyes. "It's exhausting."

The DI's tone sharpened. "We did investigate, Mr Kallias. Thoroughly."

"Then why's she still missing?" His voice cracked. "You questioned me, searched the house, my car. You were convinced I did something to her."

Meera watched him closely. His frustration seemed genuine.

"We're not here to accuse you," the DI said. "We just need to revisit some aspects of the case."

"Why now?" He looked between them. "What's changed?"

Meera looked at the DI, who was nodding.

"A body was found recently," DI Patterson said. "We're exploring all possibilities."

Yiannis's face paled. "The body in Upton Lake." He scratched his stubble, making Meera wince. "You think it's Jackie?"

Meera felt for him. A year, he'd been going through this. His partner missing, her ex at first suspected, then cleared. And now, they were dragging Yiannis into it again.

"We don't know yet," she said. "But we wanted to let you know we're considering it a possibility."

He sank into an armchair. "I just want to know what happened to her. She wouldn't just leave."

"Did Jackie ever mention feeling threatened?" the DI asked. "Anyone she was worried about?"

He shook his head. "There was the ex, Brian. But he was out of the picture, she wasn't scared of him anymore. And you know he had a solid alibi."

The DI nodded. Meera made a mental note to check the case files, remind herself of what had happened with Brian Kendall.

"But she was stressed about work," he said. "Kept talking about some viewing she'd done. How she shouldn't have done it."

"Why did she think she shouldn't have done it?" Meera asked.

He shrugged. "She wouldn't tell me. A few times she came close to it, but then she shut down. I don't know. It was almost like she was scared. Of what, I've no idea."

The DI frowned. "Why didn't you mention this before?"

"I did. But you were too busy tracing Brian, and then when you discounted him, trying to pin it on me."

Meera shifted, trying to push back feelings of guilt. It wasn't like she'd even worked the case. "Mr Kallias, anything you can tell us might help. Even if it seems small."

He sighed. "She worked for a high-end estate agency. You know all that. Sometimes she'd come home, and I could tell something was off. But she wouldn't talk about it."

"Did she ever mention names?"

"No. But... she wasn't happy. I could tell."

"Mr Kallias," the DI said, "I really hope you didn't withhold information—"

"I didn't withhold *anything*!" He stood, jabbing a finger towards her. "I told you everything I knew. You just didn't listen."

Meera stepped in, holding up a palm. "We're listening now. If you remember anything else, please let us know."

Yiannis nodded, his anger fading to resignation. "I just want her back."

The DI turned to Meera. "We should go."

Outside, Meera took a breath. "He's scared."

The DI's eyes narrowed. "He's hiding something."

"Or he's just frustrated. We still haven't found his partner."

The DI's voice was low. "Don't get too sympathetic, Meera. It clouds judgement."

Meera swallowed her immediate reaction. "We need to keep an open mind."

"Just do your job."

Meera watched her boss walk to the car, wondering what made the DI so cold. It might not even be Jackie they'd pulled from the harbour. But if it was, would Yiannis be able to help them discover how she died?

CHAPTER NINE

ELLIE SHARP STEPPED off the train at Norwich station, the chill of the air biting through her coat. She hadn't been back here in years. Not since her dad's funeral. Now she was here for Verity's.

She'd never got on with her stepmother. But she'd come for Sebastian. He'd been the one constant in her life, even if they had different mums. Very different, from what she'd managed to learn about her own mum.

As she made her way to the taxi rank, her phone buzzed.

"Ellie, you here yet?" Sebastian's voice was tense.

"Just got here. Heading to yours now."

"Good. We need to talk."

She nodded. "I know."

The taxi ride was short. Norwich hadn't changed much. The same grey buildings, the same winding streets. She stared out of the window, her mind on the notebook, those letters in it. Rowena's letters. Her mum's letters.

Sebastian was waiting outside his flat when she arrived. He looked older. Tired.

"Els." He pulled her into a hug.

"Sebbie." She held him tight. "How are you holding up?"

He shrugged. "It's been... a lot."

She hugged him again. She knew what it was like to become an orphan.

They went inside. His flat was cluttered, boxes everywhere. Verity's things, she assumed.

"Tea?" he asked.

"Please."

They settled in the small kitchen. Sebastian handed her a mug, then placed a notebook on the table between them.

Ellie stared at the book. It was old, the paper yellowed and fragile. The cover had a repeated pattern; daisies. Inside, her mum's handwriting was neat, almost too perfect.

"Where'd you find this?" She kept her voice steady.

"In Mum's bedroom. She'd hidden them in a box, under her bed."

"Are there more?" He shook his head. "This is the only one."

Ellie nodded. "You read them?"

"Some. Enough to know it was written by your mum. She addressed it to someone called Peter."

"Peter." She frowned. "Do you know who he is?"

Sebastian shook his head. "No idea. But they were... intimate."

Ellie opened to a random page. The paper was yellowing and the ink faded, but she could still make out the words. She cleared her throat.

"'Dear Peter'," she read aloud. "'I can't stop thinking about our last meeting. The way you'..."

She stopped reading, her cheeks burning. She closed the book.

"Shit."

Her brother nodded. He put a hand on her wrist. It was warm. She looked into his eyes, then down at the letter.

"Why would Verity keep these?"

Sebastian shrugged. "I don't know. Maybe she didn't want anyone to know about the affair."

"Or maybe she was protecting Dad."

"Maybe."

Ellie took a few breaths then opened to another page. This entry was longer, more detailed. Her mum talked about work, about her life as a new mum. About her love for this Peter. And...

"She mentions Dad," Ellie said. "Says she feels guilty."

"Does she say anything about you?"

Ellie smiled. "She does." She put the notebook down. "I need to read it all."

Sebastian nodded. "I thought you'd say that."

"Do you mind?"

"Of course not. It's yours, really."

She gave him a small smile. "Thanks, Sebbie."

He squeezed her hand. "I'm sorry, Els. I didn't know about any of this."

She felt hollow, like the world had turned on its axis. "Neither did I."

They sat in silence for a moment. Ellie wasn't sure how to feel. Angry at her mum for the affair. Angry at Verity for keeping the diary. And confused about what it all meant.

"Do you think Dad knew?" she asked.

Sebastian frowned. "I don't know. He never mentioned anything."

"Maybe that's why he took us to Sandbanks that time. Maybe he knew Peter would be there, wanted to confront him."

"Or maybe it was her idea, so she could see him."

Ellie sighed. "I need to find out who Peter is."

"How?"

She shrugged. "I don't know yet. But what she wrote... it might help."

Sebastian nodded. "I'll help you, Els. Whatever you need."

She wiped her cheek. "Thanks, Sebbie."

He gave her a small smile. "We're in this together, yeah?"

"Yeah."

She looked at the book again. It was a link to her mum. A mum she'd never really known.

"Why didn't you read all the entries?" she asked.

"It felt more appropriate for you to have them. She wasn't my mum."

"She was only mine for a few months." She felt the familiar tightness well up in her chest when she thought of her mum's disappearance. Her father had been reluctant to talk about it, but she'd dragged it out of him, over the years. Left in a hotel room. She still didn't know why her father had gone too. And then... then found by a girl from the hotel. And her mum gone.

She swallowed. "This Peter? You ever heard of him?"

Sebastian shook his head. "Mum never mentioned him. And you know what Dad was like."

She grunted.

Ellie stroked one of the daisies on the notebook's cover. Her mum had handled this. She picked it up and held it to her nose. It just smelt of age.

"Dad was suspected, wasn't he?" she said. "Of Mum's murder."

Sebastian looked away. "Yeah. But he didn't do it, Ellie. He couldn't have."

"I know." She sighed. "But these letters... They change things."

"Do they?" His voice was sharp. "We don't know who this Peter is. We don't know anything."

He was right. "I need to find out who he was. What he meant to Mum."

Sebastian frowned. "You think he could've...?"

"I don't know what to think. But I need to find out."

He nodded slowly. "What do you need from me?"

"This notebook, for one. And any other information you might have."

"I'll help. Whatever you need."

Ellie smiled. "Thanks, bro."

They sat in silence for a moment, the weight of what they'd discovered between them.

"When's the funeral?" she asked.

"Day after tomorrow. Small service. Mum didn't have many friends."

Ellie nodded. She'd never formed a bond with Verity, despite the woman becoming her stepmother when she was just five. "I'll be there."

"Thanks."

She picked up the book, skimming the contents. "She mentions Bournemouth a lot. And Sandbanks."

"That's where she... where it happened, isn't it?"

"Yeah. She was on holiday with Dad. And me."

Sebastian looked at her. "You don't remember anything, do you?"

"I was a baby, Seb. I don't remember a thing."

He sighed. "Sorry. Stupid question."

"It's not. I wish I did remember. Maybe it'd help."

They sank into silence again, the only sound the gurgle of Sebastian's dishwasher running.

"Do you think Verity read these?" Ellie asked.

Sebastian shrugged. "She never mentioned them. But she was... private."

"Yeah. She was."

Ellie picked up the diary and stuffed it into her bag. She should take more care, she knew. But it had been in the back of a wardrobe for forty years. "I'll go through this tonight. I'm at the Premier Inn in Duke Street."

"You can always stay here."

She gave her brother a smile. "I've grown out of kipping on your sofa."

He shrugged. She'd always bedded down in Sebastian's living room on her visits after their father's death, despite Verity's large house being only a five-minute drive away. "Fair enough," he said. "Call if you need company."

"I'd rather do it on my own... if you don't mind."

"It's yours, Els. Of course I don't mind. But let me know if you find anything."

"I will."

Sebastian stood. "I should... I've got stuff to sort for the funeral."

"Of course. Can you give me a lift to the hotel?"

"Yeah. Just give me a minute."

She nodded and he left the kitchen.

Ellie looked down at her open bag, the diary clearly visible. Her mum's words. Words she'd never thought she'd see.

But who was Peter? And what did he have to do with Rowena's death?

She was going to find out.

CHAPTER TEN

MEERA SAT ON THE SOFA, her fingers tapping lightly on the armrest. The house was quiet, save for the occasional creak of ancient floorboards. Suzi was finally asleep upstairs, giving her and Jill a moment to talk.

Jill emerged from the kitchen, a mug of tea in each hand. "Here," she said, handing one to Meera.

"Thanks." Meera took a sip, the warmth soothing her. "How was your day?"

Jill sat on the sofa, the weight making Meera slide towards her. This sofa had seen better days, but it had belonged to Jill's grandmother, and it wasn't going anywhere.

"Fine," Jill said. "I'm hoping that body in Upton Lake turns out to be one of mine."

Meera nodded. "You mentioned a Rowena Sharp, in the briefing."

Jill sipped at her tea and shifted in her seat, making Meera almost bounce beside her. "Forty years she's been missing, though. How do I even start to pull together a case, with that kind of time span?"

Meera put a hand on her arm. "You're good at piecing together evidence. That's why they hired you."

"Let's hope so." Jill leaned into her wife. "How about your day? I suppose you're hoping the BBC are right, and the body's Jackie Kendall?"

Meera sighed. She wasn't sure what she was hoping.

"We went to see Jackie's partner today," she said. "Yiannis Kallias." She'd looked Yiannis up when she'd got back to the office. He hadn't always surrounded himself with squalor. He'd been a successful business owner when Jackie had disappeared. She remembered the suit on the back of the door.

"I bet he wasn't happy, bringing it all up again."

Meera shook her head. "He was pissed off with the police. But still obsessed with Jackie. He's running an online campaign to find her."

"Poor bloke. D'you reckon he's got anything to do with it?"

"They suspected her ex, at first. He was violent, she had a restraining order. But he was in prison when Jackie went missing."

"Quite an alibi."

Meera nodded. "Not one you'd fake."

"No." Jill looked at her. "You seem down. Worried about it?"

Meera shook her head. "It's the DI. Hannah, as she insists we call her. She's... I can't make her out."

"You don't have to make her out. You just have to work with her."

"That's the thing. She snaps at me at the slightest thing, treats me like I'm some kind of idiot. She was clearly rattled by Yiannis's attitude to the police today, and she took it out on me."

Jill leaned forward and put down her mug. "What happened?"

Meera sighed. "We were interviewing him at his house. Well, if interview is what you'd call it. He was... difficult. Hannah was impatient. She snapped when I asked a question she thought was irrelevant."

Jill nodded. "She's under pressure. The DCI's not exactly her biggest fan."

"I know, but it's not fair to take it out on us."

"True. But you can't control her behaviour, only how you respond."

Meera frowned. "I was hoping for a bit more sympathy."

Jill raised an eyebrow. "Sorry, love. Grumpy colleagues are an occupational hazard. Best just to be practical about them. "

Meera sank into the sofa. Her back would be hurting by the time she went to bed. "I just wanted her to have my back."

"She's not Dennis," Jill said. "You need to adjust your expectations. Have you spoken to Nathan?"

Meera shook her head. "DS Strunk? No chance. I'm not... I'm not making this formal."

"OK. So you'll have to find a way to work through it, then. Or around it. Which I wouldn't recommend."

"I know." Meera looked down at her tea. "It's just... frustrating."

Jill rubbed her shoulder. "Try not to take it personally. Focus on the work. If she snaps, let it roll off you."

"Easy for you to say."

"Not really. I've had my share of difficult bosses." She raised an eyebrow. "The DCI isn't exactly a walk in the park."

"But you know where you are with the DCI."

"True."

A small cry came from upstairs. Jill rubbed her eyes then stood. "I'll check on her."

Meera watched her go, feeling a mix of gratitude and irritation. She knew Jill was right, but it wasn't what she'd wanted to hear.

She leaned back, closing her eyes. The case was a mess. Two missing women, one body. The media were circling, and her senior officers were on edge. Hannah's attitude wasn't helping.

She thought about Yiannis. He'd been scared, defensive. Was it just the pressure of the investigation, or was there more to it? And what about Jackie? Had they missed something the first time around?

Jill returned, settling back into the armchair. "She's asleep again."

"Thanks."

Jill studied her. "You OK?"

"Yeah. Just... thinking."

"About the case?"

"About Hannah."

Jill smiled. "You'll figure it out. You always do."

Meera nodded. *You always do.* This time, she wasn't so sure.

CHAPTER ELEVEN

JULY 2024

Jackie Kendall pulled into her driveway, the familiar crunch of gravel under her tyres doing little to ease her nerves. She sat for a moment, listening to the news and trying to forget about work.

The election was two weeks away, and the news talked of nothing else. She was bored of it.

I don't want to listen to politics. She switched off the radio and leaned back, taking in sea air through the open window. She knew it should calm her. But right now, it didn't.

She grabbed her phone, which she'd put on silent, and got out of the car. Her bag was heavy; piles of particulars for an open house in the morning. She shouldered it and walked up her driveway, looking around her with tight, agitated movements.

The street was quiet, the usual hum of suburbia. Nothing out of place.

Until she reached her front door.

It was ajar.

Jackie's heart thudded. She hadn't left it like that. Of course she hadn't. Even now, with the stress, she remembered to lock her house every morning. Every night, too.

She pushed it open, the hinges creaking. The hallway light was off. She flicked the switch. Nothing.

Shit.

"Hello?"

Her voice echoed back at her. Silence.

She took a deep breath, stepping inside. Her hand fumbled for her phone, but she stopped herself. No point calling the police. Not yet.

The living room was untouched. Sofa, TV, the pile of magazines on the coffee table. All as she'd left it.

She moved to the kitchen. The door was open, the back garden visible. She hadn't left that open either.

She checked the cupboards. Plates, glasses, tins. All there.

Upstairs. She hesitated at the bottom of the stairs, listening. Nothing.

She climbed, each step slow, careful. The landing was dark. She reached for the light switch. Still nothing.

Her bedroom door was open. She pushed it wider, peering in.

The bed was unmade, but she'd left it like that, and Yiannis wouldn't have made it. The wardrobe doors were shut. She opened them, checking inside.

Clothes. Shoes. Her jewellery box on the shelf. She opened it. Earrings, necklaces. All there.

Yiannis's side: all his suits there, his cufflinks, rings. Nothing missing.

She moved to the spare room. The door was shut. She opened it, the door catching on the carpet.

Boxes. Old files. The stuff she hadn't got round to sorting.

She checked the boxes. Nothing had been disturbed.

Doesn't make sense.

Back on the landing, she leaned against the wall, trying to calm her breathing.

Nothing's missing.

But someone had been here. They'd got in, looked around, and left.

A warning.

She went back downstairs, shutting the front door properly this time. She checked the lock. It wasn't broken. They'd used a key, or something.

She went into the kitchen and stared at the back door. She'd locked it last night. She hadn't even opened it this morning. Why would she?

The sound of a car pulling up made her tense. She glanced at the clock. Yiannis.

The front door opened, and she heard his footsteps. She stared out at the garden, at the wood pigeons in the tall trees at the end.

"Jackie?"

"In here."

He appeared in the doorway, his face creasing with concern. "You look like you've seen a ghost."

"Someone's broken in."

"What?" He scanned the room, clearly trying to reconcile her statement with the tidiness of the kitchen.

She walked towards him and grabbed his hands. Hers were sweaty. "The front door was ajar when I got home. And the back door was open."

He looked around, his eyes narrowing. "What's missing?"

"Nothing."

"Nothing?"

She shook her head. "I've checked. Everything's here."

He frowned. "We should call the police."

"No."

"Jackie—"

"There's no point, love. Nothing's gone. They'd just say it was me being careless."

He put a hand on her shoulder, lowering his voice. "So why'd they break in?"

She shrugged, trying to feign calm. "I don't know."

His expression softened. "You're sure nothing's missing?"

"Positive."

"OK. I still think we should—"

"No. You know how overstretched they are. What's the point?"

He nodded, unconvinced. "Right. Well, we'll get the locks changed. First thing tomorrow."

"Yeah." There was no point claiming on the insurance; the cost of a locksmith was less than their excess.

He moved to the kettle, filling it. "Coffee?"

"Please."

She watched him, grateful for his presence. She hadn't told him everything. She couldn't.

But she hated keeping secrets from him.

They drank their coffee and then switched to deciding what to cook for dinner. Jackie wasn't hungry, but she went through the motions; cooking, eating, a late-night glass of Port. She even managed to feign arousal when he instigated sex, although her heart wasn't in it.

She slept fitfully, startling at every creak of the floorboard or hum of the boiler. At 5am she finally gave up and heaved herself out of bed, yawning.

She grabbed her phone from the bedside table, slipped on her dressing gown and stepped onto the landing, suddenly scared.

What if they'd come back?

What if they were down there now, waiting for her?

She knew what they were capable of.

Her phone buzzed, in her dressing gown pocket. She took it out, dry-mouthed.

A text from an unknown number.

Stay out of it, Jackie.

Her stomach twisted.

They know my name.

They'd seen her for, what, no more than ten seconds? But they knew who she was and where she lived.

And she didn't dare even talk to Yiannis about it.

CHAPTER TWELVE

JUNE 2025

HANNAH STOOD at the front of the briefing room, her gaze sweeping over the team. DS Nathan Strunk and DC Meera Vedra sat around the table, their expressions a mix of anticipation and wariness. Tina was still on maternity leave, leaving them shorthanded. Hannah would need to speak to the DCI about that, if the body turned out to be an MCIT case.

She still wasn't sure what she made of this lot, or of the way she'd inherited them, or at least a subsection of them, when she'd taken the transfer to Dorset. Had she made the right choice, moving from Devon?

Too late to worry about that now.

"Right," she began, "we need to dig further into the Jackie Kendall case. The media interest's picked up, and we can't ignore it, even if this doesn't prove to be her body."

Nathan leaned back in his chair. "We went through this last summer. Her ex-husband's got an alibi, and her current partner—"

"Yiannis Kallias," Meera interjected.

"That's the one. He doesn't seem involved."

"He's still looking for her," Meera added. "Poor bloke."

Hannah nodded. Jackie Kendall had disappeared three months before she'd started in this job. Maybe she could prove herself by making some kind of breakthrough where the DCI hadn't managed it.

She'd have to walk a careful line if she was going to do that.

"I know," she said. "But don't we owe it to Jackie's family to try harder?"

Nathan narrowed his eyes. "She's a grown woman. The hypothesis last year was that she'd simply walked out of her life voluntarily. No crime in that."

"You really think that's what she did?"

He shrugged.

She continued. "Let's go over what we have, either way. See if we can uncover any more." She ignored the grunt from Nathan. "I want to know more about what Jackie was doing before she disappeared. Her work, her personal life. Everything."

"We did that whe—"

She held up a hand. "As you'll recall, Nathan, I wasn't here last June. So I, at least, need filling in. Humour me."

He twisted his lips and nodded. She gave him a smile that covered her frustration.

Nathan was a good copper, or so she'd been told. He'd solved the murder of the man dumped in a wheelie bin in Lyme Regis a couple of months earlier, although she'd heard a rumour that Tina had breached the terms of her maternity leave to give him a hand, and some meddling locals had played their part, too. But he could be insubordinate. She didn't like it.

Hannah tapped her pen on the table. "Yiannis mentioned she was stressed about work. Maybe we should start there."

"Good. I want you to look into her work at the estate agency. See if there were any issues, any clients she was dealing with that might have—"

"You think someone wanted to kill her because she didn't get the right price for their house?" Nathan asked.

Hannah narrowed her eyes at him. "I'm not speculating as to motive, Nathan. But her job would have brought her into contact with a lot of people. We need to know if there were problems with any of those interactions."

He grunted.

Did she have to take him to one side after this, have a word? She shook her head.

Meera shifted in her seat. She kept looking from Hannah to the sergeant, her expression uneasy.

"What is it, Meera?" Hannah said. "You look like you have something to say."

"Oh." Meera hesitated. "Yes. We interviewed Yiannis in detail, at the time. Once the alibi for her ex had been verified, he became a person of interest. But there was no evidence, no sign of problems in their relationship. He did tell us she'd been jumpy in the weeks leading up to her disappearance, though."

"Jumpy?"

"Um. I can't... Hang on." Meera flicked through her notepad. "It doesn't go back that far. Sorry, boss."

"Hannah. How many times—"

"Hannah. Sorry." Meera was looking down at the cover of her closed notebook. "If I dig out my notes, I'll be able to find more."

"Surely you transcribed your notes onto the system?"

"Yes. Of course. So... I remember him mentioning a break-in, or at least... Yes. He told us there was a break-in, about a week before she went."

"About a week, or exactly a week?"

Meera reddened. "I'd have to check my notes."

"You do that."

Nathan gave the DC a nod. They didn't like her, she could tell.

But this was the police, not the social club the MCIT seemed to have been before she joined, what with people marrying each other and going out to the pub after work. Their job wasn't to get on. It was to solve serious crimes.

"Check your notes on the system," she said. "Tell me what Yiannis told you. And I want sightings. Check online, social media. See if anyone saw her after she disappeared."

Nathan frowned. "It's been months. If there were sightings, they'd have come forward by now."

"Not necessarily," Hannah replied. "People might not have realised it was important. And if there's anything on social media, then that will still be available to us."

"Hopefully."

Meera nodded. "We could try local forums, Facebook groups. See if anyone mentioned anything at the time."

"Not to mention good old-fashioned door-to-door," Hannah said. "And check with local businesses. CCTV, if there is any."

Nathan sighed. "We did door-to-door, in—"

"I don't want to know what you did last summer. I want to know if there's anything that was missed. Truth is, Jackie Kendall disappeared, and the police still haven't found her. I think we owe it to her and her family to keep trying, don't you?"

He licked his lips. "Of course. But..."

"But what?" Hannah folded her arms and cocked her head, watching his face.

"This is a long shot."

"I'm not denying that," she admitted. "But we don't have a choice. I want to find out what happened to her."

Silence settled over the room. Hannah could sense that the two detectives were desperate to share some kind of confidence, to talk about her behind her back.

Let them.

"Anything else?" she asked.

Both of them shook their heads. *Just the two of you.* She really needed to speak to the DCI, see if she could get someone brought over from the cold cases team. Surely new cases were a priority?

"Right," she said. "Get to it. I want updates by the end of the day."

The team began to gather their things. Meera lingered, her expression thoughtful.

"Something on your mind, Meera?" Hannah asked.

Meera hesitated. "It's just... when we spoke to Kallias, he seemed scared. Not of us, but of something else."

Hannah raised an eyebrow. "You think he knows more than he's letting on?"

"Maybe. Or maybe he doesn't know what he knows."

"Keep an eye on him," Hannah said. "If he knows something, I want to find out what it is."

CHAPTER THIRTEEN

ELLIE SHARP STOOD outside the Dorset Police HQ, glancing up at the sleek, modern building. The glass and metal facade reflected the blue sky and white clouds shifting across it, giving it an imposing look. She shifted her weight, feeling a chill which was nothing to do with the weather.

Sebastian stood beside her, clutching an envelope containing the notebook. "You sure about this?" he asked, his voice low.

Ellie nodded. "We've got to, Seb. If what she wrote means what we think it does..."

He sighed. "Yeah, I know. Just... let's get it over with."

They entered the building, the automatic doors sliding apart with a soft hiss. Inside, the reception area was bright and open, with floor-to-ceiling windows and a polished stone floor. A few officers moved about, their footsteps echoing quietly.

Ellie approached the front desk. "We're here to see DI Jill Scott," she said, trying to keep her voice steady.

The receptionist nodded, picking up a phone. "Name?"

"Ellie Sharp. And this is my brother, Sebastian."

"Take a seat. I'll let her know you're here."

They took a bench near the windows. Ellie watched as a couple of officers passed by, their expressions focused. She wondered what they'd think if they knew what was in the envelope.

After a few minutes, a woman approached them. She was in her late thirties, with short blonde hair and a no-nonsense demeanour. "Ellie Sharp? I'm DI Jill Scott. This is DC Katie Young."

Katie, younger and with a friendly face, gave them a nod.

Ellie stood. "Thanks for seeing us."

Jill gestured for them to follow. "Let's find somewhere to talk."

They were led down a corridor to a small meeting room. It was plain, with a table and a few chairs. The windows looked out onto the landscaped grounds.

"Take a seat," Jill said, closing the door behind them.

Ellie and Sebastian sat opposite the two officers. Sebastian placed the envelope on the table.

Jill frowned at it. "You mentioned something about a diary?"

Ellie took a breath. "My mother, Rowena Sharp, went missing in 1973. We found this in our stepmother's belongings after she passed away. It's a diary, of sorts. In the form of letters from my mum to a man named Peter."

The two detectives shared a look. Ellie knew a body had been found in Poole Harbour in recent days. Did they think it might be her mum?

Katie leaned forward. "Peter?"

Ellie nodded. "We think she was having an affair. We don't know who Peter is, but..."

"But you think it might be relevant to your mother's disappearance," Jill finished.

Sebastian shifted in his seat. "We've seen the news. The body found at Upton Lake."

Ellie shot him a look. "We're not saying it's her. But if it is..."

Jill exchanged a glance with Katie. "We'll need to take a look at that diary."

On a nod from Ellie, Sebastian pushed the envelope across the table.

Katie picked up the envelope, handling it carefully. "We'll need to log this as evidence."

Ellie watched her, feeling a mix of relief and anxiety. She'd been torn about bringing the notebook in, but it felt like the right thing to do.

Jill leaned back in her chair. "If what your mum wrote in here suggests a possible motive or lead, it could be significant. I head up a team looking into cold cases, and your mother's disappearance is one of them."

Ellie felt a flicker of hope. "You'll reopen the case?"

Jill pursed her lips. "If there's enough to warrant it, yes."

Katie looked at Ellie. She smiled. Her eyes were large, almost too large for her face. "You've done the right thing, bringing this in. We'll do everything we can to find out what happened to your mother." She looked at the DI, who gave a small frown.

Ellie drew in a shaky breath, feeling Sebastian's hand on her arm. She hoped they were doing the right thing. Her father, and Verity... they'd chosen to hide this.

But it was hers now. She didn't have to make the same choices as them. She just had to hope that, whatever the police uncovered, it wouldn't open too many wounds.

Jill stood. "We'll be in touch. If you think of anything else, anything at all, let us know."

Ellie and Sebastian got to their feet. "Thank you," Ellie said.

As they left the building, Ellie looked back at the sleek modern structure. She felt like they'd taken a step forward, but she wasn't sure where it would lead.

"You alright?" Sebastian asked as they reached the car.

She felt her shoulders slump. "Yeah. I just hope this helps."

He gave her a reassuring smile. "It will. We'll find out what happened to her, Els."

Ellie looked out at a seagull perched on a low wall made of caged blocks of stone. She hoped he was right.

CHAPTER FOURTEEN

Meera parked the car outside the Pritchard & Locke office in Sandbanks. The building was modern, with a glass front and elegant signage. It screamed money.

DS Strunk dipped his head to look out of the passenger window, glancing at the surrounding properties. "Nice spot for an estate agent."

"High-end clientele," Meera replied.

He grunted. "You sent her that email, filled her in on what we're here for?"

Meera nodded. They had no reason to suspect anyone from this firm, no reason to withhold the reason their interest had been piqued.

"Come on, then." He sighed and heaved himself out of the car, stretching his arms out as he surveyed the surrounding buildings. Meera could hear the clang of ropes against masts on the harbour. It was a sound that always made her smile.

"You think there's something to it, Sarge?" she said. "The link?"

He shrugged. "No idea. But there's no harm in finding out."

Truth was, they were here to find out about Jackie, more than about Rowena. Rowena wasn't their case.

She nodded. "Let's see what Carys Pritchard has to say."

Inside, the office was all polished surfaces and minimalist decor. There were far fewer photographs of properties than Meera had expected, but at these prices, you wouldn't need to sell many.

A young receptionist looked up, her smile professional.

"We're here to see Carys Pritchard," the DS said, flashing his badge.

"Of course. She's expecting you." The receptionist gestured towards a glass-walled office at the back.

Carys Pritchard stood as they entered. She was sleek, but a little less understated than the office: blonde hair set in place, expensive suit, and a scent of perfume that was almost overpowering.

"Detectives," Carys greeted them, extending a hand. "Please, sit."

Meera took a seat, the DS beside her.

"Thank you for meeting with us, Ms Pritchard," he said. "I'm DS Nathan Strunk, this is DC Meera Vedra."

Carys's gaze lingered on Meera for a little longer than felt appropriate, but then she smiled and turned her attention back to the DS. She gave him a simpering smile.

"Call me Carys. I understand you're looking into the history of Locke & Co?"

"That's right," Nathan said. "We're trying to establish any connections between your firm and two women, Rowena Sharp and Jackie Kendall."

Carys's expression didn't change. "I know all about Jackie's disappearance. A tragedy. But Rowena Sharp? That was before my time."

"She worked here in the seventies," Meera said. She'd spoken to Mike before coming out, got what information she could. He'd thought they were chasing down a blind alley. "What can you tell us about the firm's history?"

Carys leaned back, crossing her legs. "Locke & Co was established in the sixties by Edward Locke. It was a family business, really. His son, Geoffrey, was involved too."

"And Rowena?" the DS asked.

"She was one of the early employees. She'd just finished her training when... well, you know. Geoffrey was also training at the time."

Meera made a note. "And Jackie Kendall?"

"Jackie joined much later. She was experienced, came from a firm in Southbourne. I took over the firm in 2012 when Geoffrey retired. Rebranded it to Pritchard & Locke."

"Any reason for keeping the Locke?" Nathan asked.

Carys smiled. "I wanted to modernise, attract a different clientele. But I didn't want to let go of the past completely. And the firm, well it had a reputation..."

Meera looked at the DS. "Going back to Jackie. Did she ever mention feeling stressed or pressured at work?"

Carys shrugged. "Property is a high-pressure job, Detective. Especially at this level. But Jackie was good at what she did. I never had any issues with her performance."

That wasn't what I asked.

"Did she ever mention feeling threatened?" Meera pressed.

Carys's eyes narrowed. "Not to me. But then, she wasn't one to share personal matters."

The DS leaned forward. "What about the firm's reputation? Any controversies we should know about?"

Carys gave a sharp laugh. "Controversies? No, Detective. We're a reputable firm. We deal with high-end properties and high-end clients. We can't afford controversy."

Meera studied her. "What about Edward and Geoffrey Locke? Any... family issues that might have affected the firm?"

Carys's smile faded. "Edward was a businessman. Geoffrey... well, he had his moments. But nothing that might have impacted the firm. Not in my time, anyway."

Meera nodded, making more notes. "And your relationship with Jackie? How would you describe it?"

Carys's mouth was tight, her eyes hard. "Professional. She was one of my top agents. I valued her work."

"Did you know she was behaving strangely before she disappeared?" the DS asked. "Her partner—"

"Yiannis. Lovely fellow." Carys pulled on that smile again.

He nodded. "He told us she was being... 'jumpy', I think he said. Nervous. Was she like that at work?"

Carys frowned. "Jumpy? No. As I said, she didn't share personal matters with me."

The DS looked at Meera. She shrugged. They weren't getting anything new. And the link to Rowena... it was too old, too vague.

"Thank you, Carys," he said. "You've been helpful."

The estate agent stood as they did. "If you need anything else, don't hesitate to ask. I want to see this resolved as much as you do."

Outside, the DS let out a breath. "She's a piece of work."

"She's got a firm to protect," Meera said. "But I don't think she's hiding anything. At least, not about Jackie."

"Or Rowena," he added. "Seems like that was before her time."

Meera nodded, glancing back at the office. "Looks like we're back at square one, Sarge."

CHAPTER FIFTEEN

LESLEY PARKED outside Dennis Frampton's house, a 1930s semi with a neat front garden. She stopped to check her mascara hadn't smudged in the vanity mirror and yawned.

She'd been visiting Dennis every month since his retirement eighteen months ago. At first, it had been a welfare thing; she felt bad that he'd been injured saving her daughter, and that the injury had forced his retirement. But now, she'd grown to look forward to these evenings.

Dennis might have driven her insane when he'd worked for her, but the truth was, she missed him.

Pam answered the door, her face lighting up. "Lesley! It's good to see you. Come in, come in."

"Thanks, Pam. I hope I'm not intruding."

"Not at all. Dennis'll be pleased. He's been driving me a bit potty, to be honest. The heat gets to him, you see."

Lesley followed Pam into the living room. Dennis sat in a high-backed chair, a newspaper folded on his lap.

"Boss," he said, his eyes sparkling. "You're not due until next week."

She rolled her eyes. *Every time.* "You've retired, Dennis. It's Lesley now."

"Of course." He pursed his lips and removed his glasses, placing them on a side table. "But what brings you here?"

"Just thought I'd see how you're doing, Dennis."

He frowned. "You're busy next week, is that it? Going to Exeter, to see Sharon. How is she?"

Lesley shook her head. "It's nothing to do with Sharon. And I'll come next week too, if you'll have me. But there's something I'd like to get your input on."

In recent months, Dennis had become her sounding board. The only person she felt she could talk to as an equal. The only one she could be honest with. If anyone had told her this would be their relationship five years ago when she'd first joined Dorset Police, she'd have laughed in their face.

Pam was hovering at the door. "I'll make us some tea. And there's parkin, if you're interested."

Lesley smiled. She only drank tea here. Normally hated the stuff, but Pam made it properly, and it wasn't so bad. "Sounds lovely."

Dennis shifted in his chair. "Leg's all healed, if that's what you're wondering. I'm fine, physio has signed me off."

"Glad to hear it. How's retirement treating you?"

He shrugged. "It's... different. Pam's got me playing golf. Never thought I'd be doing that."

"Good to keep busy."

He eyed her. "This isn't a social call, is it?"

Lesley leaned back. "We've got a couple of cases. One might interest you."

"Oh?"

"Rowena Sharp. You remember her?"

Dennis winced. "I wondered if you'd want to know about her."

"You've seen the TV reports, then?"

"Is it her?"

"We're not a hundred percent yet, it's not like we have her DNA on file, it wasn't a thing back then. But..."

"But you want to keep your options open. And your new cold cases DI wants to prove herself."

Lesley arched an eyebrow. "Who says—"

He chuckled. "I know how it is. So what can I help you with?"

"What do you remember about the case?"

"I wasn't on the force then, but everyone talked about it. Estate agent, vanished. Never found."

"It's not just the body," Lesley said. "Why we're reopening the case."

He looked at her, waiting for more.

"Her son and daughter came to HQ. You'd hate the new building, by the way. All glass and metal."

He wrinkled his nose. "Sounds like I retired at the right time."

She smiled. "Rowena's kids. Not kids any more, in their forties. Ellie, her daughter, she was there when it happened."

"Left alone in that hotel room," he said with a wistful look. "Poor little mite."

Lesley licked her lips. "They found a diary. Turns out she was having an affair."

Dennis raised an eyebrow. "Rowena Sharp? Who with?"

"That's what we're trying to find out. The diary's in the form of letters addressed to someone named Peter. Ring any bells?"

He shook his head. "Not off the top of my head. But it's been a long time."

"Thought you might have heard something, back then."

"Like I said, I wasn't on the force. But I remember the talk. She was a private person, wasn't she?"

"That's what her daughter says. Didn't want people knowing her business."

Dennis nodded. "So, this Peter... he could be involved?"

"Possibly. Or he might know something. Either way, we need to find him."

Pam returned with a tray, clanking it loudly so they would be aware of her approach. *Good old Pam, always discreet.*

"Here we are," she said. "Tea and parkin. I made it this morning. I tried to teach Dennis to bake, but he was having none of it."

Lesley suppressed a laugh and took a slice. "Thanks, Pam."

Dennis picked up his cup. "So, what do you need from me, boss?"

Boss. "Just your thoughts. Anything you remember about the case. Or about Rowena."

He sipped his tea. "I'll have a think. But like I said, I wasn't involved."

"Anything you can recall would help."

He nodded. "I'll let you know if I remember anything."

Lesley surveyed the room. It was cosy, old-fashioned. Dennis seemed settled here, despite his grumbling.

"Thanks, Dennis. I appreciate it."

He waved a hand. "No problem. It's nice to feel useful."

Pam smiled. "See, Dennis? I told you you'd miss it."

He grunted.

Lesley finished her tea. "I'll keep you updated on the case. If you want."

He nodded. "I'd like that."

She stood. "See you next week. Thanks for the tea, Pam. And the parkin. It was delicious."

"Anytime, Lesley." Pam gave Dennis a look. "You're welcome here."

Lesley headed to the door, feeling a bit lighter. Dennis might be retired, but he was still a part of her team.

CHAPTER SIXTEEN

MEERA and the DS entered the meeting room at HQ. DI Patterson was already there, tapping away on her laptop.

"Alright, guv," the DS said, standing a bit straighter.

The DI looked up, rolling her eyes. "Nathan. Meera." She pointed to herself. "Hannah."

Meera winced. She just couldn't get used to it, calling a DI by her first name. Maybe it was a Devon thing.

"Hannah." DS Strunk's voice was tight. The DI shook her head and frowned at him.

Meera took a seat. The DS followed, looking uneasy.

"How did it go with Carys Pritchard?" Hannah asked.

The DS cleared his throat. "Not much to report, I'm afraid. She was... guarded."

Meera frowned. She wasn't sure *guarded* was the word she'd have used for Carys. Not towards the DS, at least. "She didn't give us anything useful," she added. "Just the usual spiel about how professional the firm is, no issues with Jackie or Rowena. She didn't remember anything about Rowena's disappearance. She'd have been a child at the time, long before she started working there."

Hannah's gaze shifted to the DS. "Nathan, did you pick up on anything else?"

He hesitated. "She seemed quite... polished. Maybe too polished. But nothing that would cause us to suspect her of hiding anything. Meera went over the files from last summer and there was nothing of interest in the interview the DCI did with her."

The DI grunted. "Good observation, Nathan. It's often the polished ones who have something to hide."

Meera resisted the urge to roll her eyes. "We asked about any controversies, any issues with clients or staff. She said there was nothing she was aware of."

The DI eyed her. "Of course she did. Did she mention the break-in at Jackie's house?"

Meera shook her head. "No, b... Hannah."

"That's interesting."

The DS frowned. "Do we know if Pritchard knew about the break-in?"

Meera shook her head. "We don't. If the two of them were close, she should've known."

The DS looked at her. "You think they were close?"

"To be honest, no."

Hannah leaned back in her chair. "Nathan, I want you to dig into Carys Pritchard's background. See if there's anything between her and Jackie I might be worried about."

Meera frowned. "You think...?"

A sigh. "I don't *think* anything right now. We're just keeping options open. Nathan?"

He nodded. "On it."

Meera clenched her jaw. "I can help with that. I've got some contacts who might be able to—"

Hannah shook her head. "You're fine, Meera. You've got paperwork to do from the Marco Callington case, haven't you?"

She hadn't even worked on the Marco Callington case. That had been the Sarge, and Tina unofficially.

She forced a smile. "Of course."

Hannah stood. "Good work, Nathan. Keep me updated."

The DS glanced at Meera then looked up at the DI. "Of course."

Meera stayed seated as Hannah left the room. She turned to the DS. *"Good work, Nathan?"*

He shrugged. "She's the boss, Meera. We've got to play the game."

Meera bit back a retort. *Since when did you play the game?* Only this morning in the briefing, it had been like he was sparring with the DI.

She hated this. Not knowing who was in favour from one hour to the next. Not even knowing if she'd be brought in on a case.

"And we really do need to dot the i's and cross the t's on the Callington case," he added.

She frowned. "OK."

He gave her a sympathetic look. "Let's just focus on the case, yeah? We'll get there."

Meera eyed him. He'd get there, sure, but would she be allowed to join him?

CHAPTER SEVENTEEN

LESLEY PUT DOWN THE PHONE. "Thanks, Gareth, I'll update my team."

She leaned back in her chair, staring at the ceiling. The news from Bamford was a relief, but it also complicated things. She took a bite of the sandwich she'd picked up half an hour earlier from the canteen, chewing slowly. Tuna and red onion. Why did they put raw onion onto sandwiches? Bloody stupid idea, as far as she was concerned.

She sent identical messages to Hannah and Jill in turn: *Come to my office. There's been a development.*

A moment later, Jill arrived, closely followed by Hannah. The two of them didn't speak to each other as they came in, and each took a seat on the other side of the desk. As usual, Lesley thought of Dennis, the neat way he had of occupying the chair in front of her desk. It had been good to see him this afternoon.

She eyed the two DIs. Hannah looked as if she'd rather be anywhere else. Jill seemed curious.

She took another bite of her sandwich, waiting to see if anyone would speak.

Nothing.

"I just had a call from Gareth Bamford," she said. "Pathology's ruled out Jackie Kendall," she said. "DNA from her toothbrush, which we've been holding in the evidence store since she went missing." She watched Hannah for a reaction. "It's not her."

Jill nodded. "There's no sample for Rowena. Her disappearance was too long ago."

Hannah stared at the floor, her gaze blank. Her mouth was moving like she was chewing gum, but she said nothing.

Lesley turned back to Jill. "No. But there's her kids, who came to bring the diary."

Jill shook her head. "Daughter. Ellie. Sebastian's her widower's son, but from his second marriage."

Of course. "Right. Well, can you get a sample from Ellie?"

"A female descendant's better anyway," Jill told her. "Mitochondrial DNA. Only passes down the female line."

Lesley raised an eyebrow.

Jill smiled. "I know it sounds niche, but it might be useful, for cold cases. I was watching a documentary on Richard III. When they found him in a car park, they used—"

Lesley held up a hand. "I'll stop you there. If you can use this mito—"

"Mitochondrial DNA."

"That's the fella. If you can use this to find out if our body is Rowena, then that would be extremely helpful. Apparently it's harder than it sounds to work out how long she's been in the water."

"I'll speak to Pathology. And call Ellie, see if she can come back in."

"If she's still around," Lesley pointed out. "If not, I'm sure we can get local police to obtain a sample."

"She lives here."

"Not in Norwich?" Lesley frowned. She'd been about to pick up the sandwich for another bite but then thought better of it. "I thought that was where..."

Jill shook her head. "She moved down here, after her father died. I'm wondering if she hoped she might bump into her mother or something. Lives in a flat in Poole."

"Good. Go and see her. Explain your mitochondrial DNA and get a sample from her."

"Will do." Jill wrote in her notepad with a flourish. She seemed to be enjoying the cold case brief.

Lesley turned to Hannah. "Obviously, with this not being Jackie—"

Hannah leaned forward. "With respect, boss, I don't think that makes much difference."

"You don't?"

"Uh-huh. Jackie's still missing, it's only been a year. As you know, the media have picked up interest again. It'll be the one-year anniversary of her death in a few days. The Echo are leading up to it with a series of articles dredging up the original case."

Lesley felt her jaw clench. "That's all we need."

"I think if we reopened the case, it might show we're listening to public opinion. And maybe we could even find her."

"Alive, even," Jill put in. Hannah shot her a look.

Lesley looked at Hannah. *Since when did you care about public opinion?* The two of them had worked together on a case in Lyme Regis, over two years earlier. It had been crawling with locals desperate to offer an opinion, and Hannah had treated them with little more than contempt.

"It doesn't work like that, Hannah," she said. "We have limited resources, and—"

"There is a chance that by reopening this investigation, we could save a woman's life."

Lesley leaned back in her chair. "How so?"

"Her partner, Yiannis. He told us she'd been acting strange. Her manager, Carys Pritchard. She seemed off."

"Off?"

A nod. "Nathan Strunk visited her with Meera." Hannah cast a glance at Jill. "They thought she was hiding something."

"Is that enough to reopen a missing persons investigation?"

Hannah's face was set, her eyes boring into Lesley's. Lesley wanted to look away, even if it meant eating more of that godawful sandwich. But she wasn't going to let the DI intimidate her.

"Yes, boss," Hannah said. "I believe it is." She leaned back again, wrinkling her nose. "I have a theory. I think something happened to Jackie, maybe something to do with her job as an estate agent, that made her scared. I think she went missing deliberately."

"In which case, she's none of our concern. She's a grown woman."

"People are entitled to run away," Jill added.

Hannah threw her colleague a sharp look. Jill shifted in her chair. Lesley fought back a powerful urge to tell them to behave themselves.

Hannah looked back at Lesley. "But if Jackie witnessed something illegal, or she was the victim of a crime..."

"Then it might not be the concern of your unit at all," Lesley told her.

Hannah's nostrils flared. "Tell you what. Give me a week. If I can uncover some kind of lead on Jackie by this time next week, you'll reconsider reopening the case. If not, you can shut it down."

Lesley wanted to laugh. *It doesn't work like that.*

Instead, she held Hannah's gaze. "A week. No longer. And it doesn't affect you or your team's work on any other cases. There's still the Callington court case to wrap up."

"There is. And it won't be affected."

Lesley licked her lips. She could taste raw onion; she'd have to go to the vending machine, get some mints. "Alright," she said. "But if I see any sign of—"

"It won't affect our workload."

"Which does not mean overtime."

"No."

"Good." Lesley shifted from side to side, relieving the tension in her shoulders. "Jill, let me know how you get on with the DNA. Hannah, you can stay here a moment longer."

Jill cast Hannah a wary look, then turned back to Lesley. "Boss." She stood and left the room.

When Lesley was alone with Hannah, she stood up and walked round her desk. She perched on its edge next to where the DI was sitting. Hannah watched her, unflinching.

She'd done this with Dennis, when he started to get on her nerves. It had always made him uneasy. Not Hannah Patterson.

After a moment's silence, she cocked her head. "How are you finding working here?"

Hannah flinched. "Fine, boss."

"Not missing Devon?"

"I... Well... Of course. I'm missing my old colleagues. But this is a step up for me. Leading my own team, having my ow—"

"We work together here, Hannah. I expect you and Jill to use each other as sounding boards. To share information, even resources if necessary."

A shadow crossed Hannah's face. "I know."

Lesley sighed. "You don't seem happy."

"I'm just settling in, boss. If my performance isn't—"

Oh, it's not about your performance. It's your attitude. But Lesley wasn't quite ready for that conversation yet.

She stood up, pushing herself off the desk. She'd been walking more since moving to Southbourne; she and Elsa were even thinking of getting a dog. She could feel it in her body's ability to move more easily.

"Well," she said, pacing the office, which was smaller than her old one. "If there's something bothering you, you'll come to me, won't you? I don't like it when my team aren't open with each other."

"No, boss." Hannah was still facing the desk, her back to Lesley.

"Good." Lesley wasn't convinced, but she'd made the point. Started a process which she was hoping she didn't have to follow through. "We'll review the Jackie situation in a week. Good luck."

Hannah nodded, still without turning towards Lesley, and left the room.

Lesley walked to the back of the office and leaned against the wall, willing herself to stand upright.

God, I hate this.

Leading two teams, spending most of her working hours behind a desk. It wasn't what gave her energy. But it was what a DCI was supposed to do.

She checked her watch, cursed, and hurried out of the room. Carpenter was expecting her.

CHAPTER EIGHTEEN

Lesley stood waiting to be summoned by Superintendent Carpenter, taking a moment to gather her thoughts. The waiting area outside his office in the new HQ building was all glass and metal, a stark contrast to the old one. She wondered what he made of it.

"Enter!"

She entered to find Carpenter sitting behind a sleek desk, the floor-to-ceiling windows behind him offering a view of freshly land-scaped grounds.

"Lesley," he said, not looking up from a laptop screen. She frowned; she'd never seen Carpenter with a laptop before.

He looked up, glancing back down at the laptop with a grimace. "You're here to update me on the body in Upton Lake? I hope we know who it is."

She sighed and took a seat. "We know who it isn't, at least."

"Oh?" He shut the laptop's lid with an irritated clap and pushed it to one side.

"The body's not Jackie Kendall. Pathology's ruled her out."

He raised an eyebrow. "Disappointed?"

She frowned. *This isn't about my personal feelings.* "It means we're back to square one on identification. But Hannah Patterson's pushing to reopen the Kendall case anyway."

He smiled, placing his elbows on the desk and steepling his fingers. "And that's why we brought her across from Devon. She's a terrier, that one."

"I know."

He gave her a bemused smile. "She's giving you trouble?"

"Nothing I can't handle, Sir."

"Indeed. So, she wants to reopen it. And what might you think?"

"I don't think there's any new evidence. Nothing substantive, anyway. Hannah seems to think Jackie was hiding something, and that her manager at the estate agent knows about it."

"Knows about what?"

"That's the thing. This is just speculation." She looked across the vast desk at Carpenter. She'd been wary of trusting him when she'd first arrived in Dorset, had even suspected him of being complicit in the murder of her predecessor. But all that had changed.

She sighed. "Truth is, Sir, I've given her a week. Told her that if she uncovers anything significant in that time, I'll consider reopening the case. But if not..."

"She's that keen?"

"Sorry?"

He chuckled. "Lesley, I've never known you to take orders from a subordinate."

"I'm not taking orders."

He waved a hand: *potato, potahto*. "You know what I mean. She wants to reopen the case, you're not so sure, yet here you are giving her a week to convince you otherwise. Would you have let Dennis do that?"

"Dennis was a DS, Sir."

"You know what I mean. Would you have let one of your old DIs do it, in West Midlands? Who were they?" He screwed up his face. "Zoe Finch. The one you brought down here at considerable risk to your own career to help you investigate Tim Mackie's death."

Lesley felt her chest tighten. She'd expected to be formally repri-manded for that. To be fired even. But Carpenter had secretly wanted her to dig into Mackie's death, it had turned out.

"No, I..." She considered. "Zoe was a new DI when I managed her. So no, I wouldn't have let her. But now, maybe."

"She's more experienced now, eh? I hear she moved up to the northwest somewhere."

"Cumbria."

"Cumbria." He shivered. "Don't envy her. But anyway, my point stands. If you have a good DI in your team, and they make a sugges-tion, it's worth listening. Not necessarily doing what they suggest, but listening." He clasped his hands together. "You're not infallible, DCI Clarke."

She swallowed. Was that a criticism? Or just a bare statement of fact?

"Sir," was all she could find to say.

"You're not happy in your new role," he said. "Itching to get out there, whizzing around the back roads of Dorset, chasing leads."

She made an effort to control her face muscles. "I'm a DCI, Sir. It's my job to be—"

"We both know what your job is, Lesley. But we also know that it takes time to adjust. You're restless. That's why you're giving Hannah the chance to reopen the Jackie Kendall case, against your better instincts. You know MCIT is down a member and you might end up having to get involved."

Lesley opened her mouth to speak, then closed it again. She hadn't considered that. But he was right.

"I don't believe it'll come to that, Sir."

"You don't think Hannah will find anything."

"No."

"So why are you humouring her?"

She slumped in her chair. "It's..."

She licked her lips. Why was she allowing Hannah to do this? Then it came to her.

"There have been... tensions, in MCIT. I'm hoping that a high-profile case will give them an opportunity to pull together and achieve some coherence."

And that Hannah might be less of a mardy-arse if she's got something to do.

"That's a fair assessment," Carpenter said. "Not sure it's the best use of police resources, though."

"Hannah has assured me that it won't affect her team's performance on their caseload."

"Good. And there'll be no requests for overtime."

"No."

"So she's effectively taking this on in her own time, to prove a point."

Lesley blinked. If he was right, had she made a mistake? She shrugged.

Carpenter stood up. "On that basis. I'm happy for your team to do a little more light digging. No antagonising witnesses, though. And absolutely no interaction with the press. We do not want the anniversary of Jackie's death to become any more of a circus than it already is."

Lesley stood, knowing this meant she was dismissed. "No, Sir. I'll keep you informed."

"That you will."

CHAPTER NINETEEN

MEERA LEANED against the kitchen counter, fingertips gripping the worktop behind her. "You should've seen her, Jill. Hannah was all over the place in that briefing. It's like she thinks I'm useless. And why do I have to call her 'Hannah', anyway? She's a DI, I'm a DC. It makes my flesh crawl every time she makes me do it."

Jill looked up from their tiny kitchen table, where she was half-watching Suzi work on a jigsaw. "What did she say? Specifically?"

Meera gritted her teeth. She didn't want to explain herself. "Every time I said anything, every time I had a question, or something to say about the interview we did with Carys Pritchard, she just acted like it was all the DS. Gave him credit for everything, like I wasn't even there."

"He's your senior officer. He was leading the interview, right?"

"Yes, but I took equal part in it. We all know when you're interviewing a female witness with—"

"That's it, that one. Good girl!" Jill gave Suzi a high five as their daughter finished the jigsaw. It was one she'd done a hundred times before, but Meera knew how excited it made her to complete it.

Meera sighed. "Jill?"

Jill looked up at her. "Can this wait? Look, I know you're fed up. I know Hannah isn't the easiest to work with. But she's a copper. We're an odd lot. You just have to rub along with people."

"And I will. But I just wanted to vent."

Jill put up a hand; wait a minute. She went to the biscuit tin and pulled one out for Suzi, then gave it to her with a flourish. "Your prize, madame."

Suzi giggled and looked at Meera, who crouched down to bring herself level with her. "Well done, sweetie. You're a whizz at those jigsaws."

"I am!" Suzi shoved the biscuit whole into her mouth, making Meera wince, and ran out into the living room. In search of another jigsaw and the biscuit it would bring, no doubt.

She straightened, feeling her hamstrings twinge. "Are you sure it's a good idea giving her a biscuit every time she finishes one of those?"

Jill looked back at her. "It's a reward, love. Just a biscuit. What harm can it do?"

Meera gestured towards the door. "She's in her toy box right now, finding another one so she can get another of your 'rewards'."

A shrug. "So? Better than sitting in front of the TV."

As one, the two women looked up at the clock. It was nearly time for *Bluey*.

Suzi ran in, brandishing another jigsaw. "Mama!" she said to Jill. "Got 'nother one."

"So you have, Su-su."

Suzi giggled and tipped the jigsaw over to empty out the pieces. Meera winced and bent to pick up a piece that had fallen onto the floor.

"Thanks, Mummy."

Meera kissed her daughter's forehead. "That's OK."

She straightened, feeling that twinge again, and looked at her wife. "I've been thinking."

Jill's eyes sparkled. "Dangerous, that."

Meera scowled at her. "If Hannah isn't going to give me the credit when I do get things done, then there isn't much point making an effort."

Jill frowned. "Really?"

Meera shrugged.

Jill was shaking her head, occasionally pointing out a jigsaw piece to Suzi. Meera tightened her jaw. *Don't make it so easy for her.*

"I don't think you're even capable of not making an effort," Jill said.

"If I put my mind to it..."

Jill smiled. She crossed the kitchen to stand in front of Meera, who resisted a momentary urge to back off. Instead, she stood returning Jill's gaze as Jill pushed back a lock of hair that had been falling into her left eye.

"You're one of the most diligent coppers I've ever known," Jill said. "Look at everything you did on the Tyneham case. The way you beat yourself up when you lost those suspects around the lanes near Kimmeridge."

"They weren't just any old suspects. Day Watson was about—"

"That's not the point. You'll try not to make an effort for what, a day? Then the old Meera will kick in and you'll find it impossible."

"OK." Meera put a hand on Jill's arm. "Then I'll get on with the job, but keep a low profile. Avoid the Jackie Kendall case."

Jill raised an eyebrow. "That's the juiciest case your team has had for months."

"It might not even be a case." Meera sniffed. "The—" she glanced at Suzi and lowered her voice "—body isn't Jackie. It's probably your Rowena. You forget, I saw the state it was in."

"And you forget what that guy from the Environment Agency said."

Meera sighed. "It's your case, love."

"Maybe it is, maybe it isn't. If we can get a comparison with Ellie Sharp's DNA, we'll know for sure."

"She's given you a sample?"

"Not yet. But the woman moved to a city she hadn't visited since she was a baby, in the hope of finding some sort of connection with her missing mother. She'll help us."

Meera nodded. "Either way, I'm keeping my head down. I don't want to attract Hannah's attention any more than I have to. It'll just make things easier."

"And what about getting recognition for your work? If you want to progress—"

Meera bristled. "We've had this conversation. I'm not you, Jill. I'm happy as a DC."

"Sure, but—"

"But nothing. I'm not interested in career progression; I just want an easy life. Now Suzi's at school I'm enjoying the whole half past three thing. I've made up my mind."

Jill pulled back, exhaling loudly. "If you insist. But I think you're making a mistake."

CHAPTER TWENTY

LESLEY STEPPED out of the house in Southbourne, locking the door behind her. The air was fresh, the kind of crisp that only came with early summer mornings by the sea. She approached the new Nissan Leaf parked in the driveway, the one Sharon had convinced her to pick. It was practical, environmentally friendly, and a bloody nuisance when it came to finding charging points.

She slid into the driver's seat, setting her bag on the passenger side. The car hummed to life, and she pulled out onto the road, making for the seafront.

The view was stunning today. The sea was calm, a gentle blue stretching out to the horizon. People were already out, some jogging along the promenade, others dragging trolleys and heavy bags, ready for a day at the beach. Families with children, couples, the odd dog walker. This was why she was still living down here.

She drove along the front, pausing occasionally behind someone looking for a roadside parking space and resisting the urge to sound her horn. It got easier out of season. But then, that was something she'd known ever since her first time trying to reach Corfe Castle on a sunny day.

As she passed Fisherman's Walk, her mind drifted to the case. Not Jackie Kendall. Carpenter might have agreed to her giving Hannah a week to find something, but Lesley wasn't convinced. They'd been through it all before. Jackie's violent ex-husband had an alibi, and there was no evidence against her current partner.

So if it wasn't Jackie, who was it? Hopefully today would bring them closer to answering that question.

She turned off the seafront, heading towards Bournemouth and the A35 towards Winfrith. The roads were getting busier, the morning rush kicking off. As ever, she had to wait to get onto the Christchurch Road. One of these days, she'd manage this without traffic.

She shook her head. *You're forgetting what the traffic was like in Birmingham.*

The cars in front started to move just as Lesley's phone buzzed on the dashboard. She looked at the screen. Gareth Bamford.

She tapped the hands-free button. "Gareth. I hope you've got news for me."

"And a very good morning to you too, Lesley."

"You know what I mean." She slowed the car again; traffic lights, at the crossroads with no left or right turn signs. She often wondered what was down those roads, had never had cause to find out.

He chuckled. "Don't worry. Anyway, I have news. We've got an ID on your body from Upton Lake."

She gripped the wheel tighter. "Go on."

"The DNA matches with the sample Ellie Sharp provided over the weekend. It's Rowena."

A lump formed in her throat. She edged forward as the car in front moved no more than a couple of metres. "You're sure?"

"Positive. It's consistent with the condition of the body, too. Full post-mortem is today, I'll be able to tell you more about how long she's been in the water."

"You think she was in the harbour for fifty years?"

"It's difficult to tell. It's a vast body of water, and there are mud deposits in places that could conceivably preserve a body. Or so I reckon. I'd like to recommend we get a forensic anthropologist in, to help with the specifics."

And someone who can tell us about currents and tides. "I'll speak to Superintendent Carpenter."

"Good. At least now her next of kin can be informed."

The lights changed and Lesley grimaced. *Poor Ellie Sharp.* She'd moved to Poole in the desperate hope that she might meet her mother again.

She started at the sound of a horn behind her and waved in dismissal. "Alright, alright, keep your knickers on." She pulled forward, blowing out a long breath.

"Lesley?"

"Sorry, Gareth. Thanks. Keep me informed about the PM findings, will you? And I'll let you know if and when we get that anthropologist."

"I can send over some recommendations."

"Thanks." She hung up and tapped the steering wheel as she approached Bournemouth town centre. On days like this, rush hour traffic mixed in with holidaymakers, she wondered why she hadn't decided to buy a house right next door to HQ. But it was near Elsa's old home in Boscombe, and they were growing to love Southbourne. The drive was worth it.

Rowena Sharp. After all these years.

She had to tell Hannah. And Jill. But who first?

At St Withun's roundabout she took the right turn on autopilot, her mind racing. She picked up the phone again, glancing at it.

Jill would be relieved. She had a live case, a juicy one too. Witnesses already identified, and a body in reasonably good condition, considering. Even if it would prove challenging to dig up evidence after so long.

And Hannah... Hannah would be pissed off.

Her finger hovered over speed dial. It was another minute before she finally decided.

The call was answered on the second ring. "Boss."

"Hannah," she said. "I've got news."

CHAPTER TWENTY-ONE

JACKIE KENDALL SAT on the edge of the narrow bed, staring at the faded wallpaper. The room smelled damp, and the single window barely let in any light. She hadn't slept properly in weeks.

She pulled on a jumper, the same one she'd worn yesterday. She hadn't brought spare clothes. Washing underwear in the sink every other night wasn't ideal, but she couldn't buy any more. She'd taken as much as she could in cash when she'd left and was determined not to use her credit card.

Her stomach growled.

Breakfast. She'd have to go downstairs. She hated it, but she couldn't stay hidden in this room all day. And there was no way this place did room service.

She opened the door, peering into the dim hallway. No one. She slipped out, locking the door behind her. Not that it would stop someone sufficiently determined.

The stairs creaked as she descended. She flinched at each sound, half expecting someone to jump out at her. *Idiot.* She was in Cumbria, miles from anyone who knew her.

The dining room was small, with mismatched chairs and a

stained carpet. A couple sat at one table, speaking in low voices. Jackie kept her head down, choosing a seat in the corner.

A woman in her sixties shuffled over, notepad in hand. "What'll it be?"

"Just tea and toast, please."

The woman grunted, heading back to the kitchen. Jackie watched her go. No name badge, no smile. Not that Jackie expected one.

She glanced at the couple. They hadn't looked at her. Good. She picked at the edge of the tablecloth, trying to calm her nerves.

The woman returned, slamming a mug of tea and a plate of underdone toast in front of her. "Anything else?"

Jackie shook her head. "No, thank you."

The woman wandered off, not bothering to clear the empty plates from the other tables. Jackie sipped her tea. It was weak, barely warm.

She missed her house. Missed her bed, her things. Missed feeling safe.

She hadn't even told Yiannis where she was. She couldn't. Not after the break-in. Not after the text.

Stay out of it, Jackie.

She shivered, wrapping her hands around the mug. Yiannis. She owed it to him to tell him where she was. She'd read news reports, not long after she'd left; he was under suspicion. And Brian, of course. She'd hoped they'd just assume that Brian had turned up and killed her, that she was gone. But Brian was in prison at the time. Of course.

Yiannis. She still had his number in her phone, still looked at old photos before going to sleep every night.

Could she stay like this forever? Did she owe it to him to make contact? Or would he go straight to the police? She knew that there'd been speculation, after they'd found that body in Poole Harbour.

She had no idea who the body was, but she knew for sure it wasn't her.

Because she was in the middle of fucking nowhere, somewhere in

Western Cumbria, keeping a low profile. It was working, so far. As far as she could tell.

The couple got up to leave, the man nodding at her as they passed. Jackie tensed, waiting for him to say something. But he didn't. Just a nod. She forced herself to nod back.

She finished her tea, leaving the mug on the table. She'd have to go out today. She needed more cash.

She'd managed to get casual work in a hairdresser's in Workington, sweeping the floor and making cups of tea. They paid her in cash, assuming she was a benefit cheat. She didn't set them right. But the bus fare ate up half her wages, and it was dull, back-breaking work. Nothing like the last time she'd done it, Saturday girl in a Bournemouth salon back in the late nineties.

She stood, heading back to her room. She'd wait until the couple had left. Then she'd go out, do her shift, and come straight back. Maybe it was time to move on.

She climbed the stairs, her chest itching at the cheap soap she'd washed her t-shirt with. She hadn't brought enough clothes. She hadn't brought enough of anything.

But she couldn't go back. Not yet. Not until she knew it was safe.

If it would ever be safe.

CHAPTER TWENTY-TWO

LESLEY ENTERED the briefing room at Dorset Police HQ. She couldn't help feeling the contrast between the building's extreme, and no doubt temporary, cleanliness, and the nagging sensation in her gut that things might be about to turn ugly in the MCIT.

But for now, she was with the Cold Cases team and could at least trust Jill not to piss anyone off.

She hoped.

The team was already gathered, waiting for her.

"Morning, everyone," she said, taking her seat. "Let's get started. Jill, you lead."

Jill nodded, glancing at the screen. "Right, folks. The body at Upton Lake has been identified as Rowena Sharp. Disappeared on a June night in 1973 after leaving her baby, Ellie, alone in a room of the Sandbanks Hotel. She was there for a family weekend away."

"I remember those," said Stanley. "My parents used to call them bargain breaks."

"Bargain breaks?" said Mike. "At the Sandbanks Hotel?"

Stanley shrugged. "Not sure if they ever were a bargain. But it was the seventies equivalent of the mini break."

Jill cleared her throat and the team quietened.

"Sorry, guv," said Stanley. He'd taken to calling Jill that as he couldn't get used to addressing Lesley by anything other than *boss*.

Which suited her just fine. She still wasn't keen on the *ma'am-ing*.

"OK," said Jill. "Anyway, she was here on a family break with her husband Donald and little Ellie. But she came to the area frequently before her death. She worked for Locke & Co Estate Agents. Pritchard & Locke, it's called now."

"That's the one Nathan and Meera visited," Katie said. "Didn't Jackie Kendall work there?"

"You're right," Jill said.

"So are the two cases connected?"

Jill took another look at the board, sighing. Lesley could tell this wasn't going how she'd planned.

But the Cold Cases team – DCs Mike Legg and Stanley Green from the old MCIT, and DC Katie Young who'd worked with them on the death of Fran Dugdale – was keen to test ideas, to throw theories around. It was important not to let them get carried away, but it could lead to a breakthrough.

Lesley gave Jill a nod: *you're doing fine.*

"Everyone," Jill said, pulling back her shoulders from her position behind the board. She wasn't a tall woman, around five foot four, and she wasn't slim either. But there was something about her neat blonde hair, scraped back into a neat ponytail, and her polished clothes and make-up that gave off authority.

"We need to consider if something could have happened to Rowena on an earlier business trip," Jill said. "Something that might have led to her death. And of course, there are the love notes, in the diary."

Stanley gave a whistle. Lesley held herself back from reacting, but Jill threw him a frown and he shrugged. "They have to be relevant."

"They could be," Jill said. "But we can't assume anything.

They're a solid lead, though. She wrote to someone named Peter. From the tone of her writing, she was definitely conducting a relationship with him."

"Peter who?" Katie asked, scribbling in her notebook.

"That's what we need to find out," Jill said. "The notes suggest it was someone she worked with, but we don't have a surname yet."

Lesley leaned forward. "What about the original investigation? Her husband was the main suspect, wasn't he?"

Jill turned to her, her jaw tightening. "He was, but the case fell apart. No body, no evidence. He remarried and moved to Norwich. Died in 2022."

"Convenient," Stanley muttered.

"Let's not jump to conclusions," Jill said. "We need to look at this with fresh eyes."

"What about local witnesses from the time?" Katie suggested.

Jill checked her notes. "There's an Isobel Davison. Izzy, she was known as in 1973. She worked at the Sandbanks Hotel, she was on the baby-listening service that night. Might be worth talking to her. She can point us in the direction of any other hotel staff who might be able to help."

"She still local?" Lesley asked. "How old would she be... seventies?"

"She's running a hotel in Christchurch," Jill told her. "Boutique place, near the quay."

Lesley nodded. "Good. You won't have the same kind of evidence as when you're investigating a more recent case. No forensics, minimal pathology. So you need to build a picture of what happened back then."

"Yes," Jill said, looking just slightly irritated at being told how to do her job in front of her team. She quickly pushed it down.

"Who else can we talk to?" Katie asked. "What about her husband's second wife?"

Jill turned to her. "Check the notes with the diary."

Katie looked down at her screen. "Ah. Another one who's died."

Mike chuckled. "This is what it's going to be like, on this job."

"You knew the downsides when you joined the team," Lesley reminded him. "You relished the challenge."

"Oh, don't get me wrong, boss. I do. Just takes a bit of getting used to."

She raised an eyebrow. Would Tina have been better suited to this team? She had a knack for solving puzzles. But then, she also had a knack for liaising with outside teams, not so pertinent to the cold cases.

"Sebastian and Ellie Sharp," Jill said, bringing them back to the case. "Ellie was Rowena's daughter, and Sebastian is her half-brother. They found that diary, and they might know more about Rowena's life."

"Family stories, passed down through the generations," said Katie.

Stanley looked at her. "Stories of women going missing and turning up dead?"

Katie's arm twitched. Jill gave Stanley a look.

"There's no way of telling what Gerald might have told his children," she said.

"Not much," he replied, "if they only just found the diary."

Lesley leaned back in her chair. "You do have a point, Stanley," she said. "Gerald went to the trouble of hiding Rowena's diary, or at least that's what I assume, and then Verity – Verity, right, that's the second wife?"

"It is," Jill confirmed.

Lesley nodded. "Verity hid it too. Why would you hide your dead husband's dead first wife's diary? One that was addressed to a man you never met?"

"Unless she did meet him," Katie suggested. "Unless Peter and Verity knew each other."

Lesley shook her head, chewing on a biro. "That's too much of a stretch, I think. Verity and Donald didn't marry until...?"

"1977," Jill said.

"Right. Four years after Rowena's death. It doesn't sound to me like Verity would have been on the scene in 1973."

"It's worth checking, though," suggested Mike.

Lesley threw him a smile. She could sense the team champing at the bit, making connections, working on a puzzle.

This was a very different puzzle than the ones they were used to, but it was there for the solving, nonetheless. She hoped.

"It is," she said. She looked at Jill.

"Er, yes." Jill looked up at the screen, which was displaying Rowena's letters. "Maybe someone at Pritchard & Locke might know who Peter was. If she travelled to Dorset regularly on work, then he could have been a colleague here."

Lesley nodded in approval. "Any other sources of information?"

"There's Geoffrey Locke. He was a trainee at Locke & Co at the time, a colleague of Rowena's. He eventually took over the business from his father but he's retired now. We're trying to track him down."

"That's someone else to be speaking to," Lesley said. "Jill, you can allocate the interviews. I won't meddle, but I want to see the reports on each one."

Jill nodded. "We'll start with Ellie. She's local, so it should be straightforward."

"Good," Lesley said. "Focus on Peter. We need to find out who he is. He could be the key."

"Agreed," Jill said. She looked around the room, to a chorus of grunts and nods.

Lesley stepped forward. "This is a big case, folks. Goes back forty years, and it'll be imprinted in people's memories. We've got a body now, but that doesn't mean it'll be easy. We need to be methodical. Jill, keep me updated."

"Will do, boss."

Lesley smiled. "Right, let's get to work."

The team began to disperse, and Lesley caught Jill's eye. "Good job," she muttered.

Jill smiled. "Thanks." This wasn't Jill's first cold case; there had been Roger Gallagher, the man dragged out of Lyme Regis Harbour at Christmas. But it was the first complex one, the first that dated back decades. She looked relieved to be finally getting on with the job..

CHAPTER TWENTY-THREE

Hannah sat at her desk, staring at the phone. She needed to gather her thoughts and prepare a plan, now they knew the body wasn't Jackie. She'd been in a low mood all morning, disappointed the case hadn't turned out to be hers.

She'd sent Nathan and Meera to interview Carys Pritchard, and for what? Now they didn't have a body, chances were the case would be closed.

But the boss had given her seven days. And she'd bloody well make use of those seven days, and prove herself. Even if her team couldn't be relied on to help.

For now, the boss had told her she needed to start by reining in media speculation. Officially, the investigation into Jackie's disappearance wasn't being reopened, and the high-ups wanted the press to stop banging on about it.

In Hannah's opinion, the best way to tackle this was simply to ignore it. Don't give the vultures the oxygen of attention. Feed them titbits from the Rowena Sharp case instead – not her lookout, but she was sure someone else would manage to do it – and wait for them to calm down.

But no. The boss wanted her to deal with it.

And the obvious place to start was with that woman from the BBC. Sadie Dawes.

She dialled Sadie's number, tapping her pen on the desk as she waited for the journalist to pick up. Trying to suppress the sneer that she couldn't stop playing on her lips.

"Sadie Dawes," came a female voice, lighter than she sounded on TV.

"DI Hannah Patterson here. We need to talk about your report on the news last night."

A pause. "DI Patterson. I don't believe we've met."

Hannah licked her lips. "I'm heading up the Major Crimes Investigation Team, based out of Dorset Police HQ at Winfrith."

"That's a lot of words to tell me you've taken over Dennis Frampton's old job."

Hannah clenched a fist. *Not Dennis's old job. DCI Clarke's.*

"It's not quite like that," she said.

"I'm sure it isn't. Doesn't bother me, either way. What do you want, DI Patterson?"

Hannah straightened. "You've been speculating about the body found in Upton Lake being Jackie Kendall. That's not... helpful."

Sadie chuckled. "Speculating? I'm reporting, DI Patterson. It's what I do."

"The body hasn't been identified as Jackie. It doesn't assist a police investi—"

"Has the body been identified, DI Patterson?"

Hannah stopped short. "The body has not been identified as Jackie Kendall."

"So it has been identified as someone else."

Hannah said nothing. She closed her eyes and wondered if she should have just gone with her gut and not made the call. If the problem had gone away, then the boss would have congratulated her, even if she hadn't actually done anything to make it happen.

Doing nothing is doing something. That was what her dad had always told her.

"DI Patterson? Are you still there?"

"Sorry. The line dropped out for a moment."

"Hmm. So if it's not Jackie, then who is it?"

"We're not at liberty to disclose that."

"You do realise the press can assist you in a major investigation, don't you? You've got a body in Poole Harbour. We've got an audience of most of the population of the South West. We can help."

Hannah pursed her lips.

There was a sigh down the line. "Have it your way."

Hannah took a breath. "We need you to hold off on further speculation. It's hindering the investigation."

"Investigation? What investigation? Are you reopening the Jackie Kendall case, or is this the investigation into whoever's body it is you've identified?"

Hannah gritted her teeth. "Like I say, I'm not—"

"Not at liberty to say right now. I get it."

"Exactly."

"DI Patterson, what you don't seem to realise is that the local press has a long history of working in tandem with the police. We have access to people who might be able to provide you with information."

"You also have access to all the nutters and hoaxers."

A laugh. "That's how you see the public you serve?"

"You know what I mean. I've seen plenty of cases where a hotline's opened, the media promote it, and police time is wasted talking to people who just want a bit of attention."

"You might want to talk to your new boss, Hannah. DCI Lesley Clarke. She'll tell you that without me, she might not have solved the most significant case since she joined the Dorset force."

Hannah didn't believe a word of it. She'd seen the DCI in action, and she certainly didn't expect the woman would be bested by a journalist.

"That's irrelevant," she said.

"So you say. Well, in any event, my job is to inform the public, and—"

"Inform, not inflame."

Sadie laughed. "Inflame? That's a bit dramatic."

"You're... The media speculation is making it difficult for us to do our jobs."

"Maybe if you did your job better, I wouldn't have to speculate. Why exactly wasn't Jackie's disappearance solved a year ago?"

"I wasn't here a year ago."

"Oh, blaming your colleagues, are you? Nice touch, DI Patterson."

Hannah stared at the phone. Should she defend herself? Was it even worth it?

"Thank you for your time," she said. "I hope you'll take my request into consideration."

She hung up, ignoring the fact that Sadie was still speaking. She tossed her phone onto the desk, her heart racing.

Shit.

The boss had asked her to calm things down, and she'd only made them worse.

Was this what it was going to be like, on this case?

CHAPTER TWENTY-FOUR

Dennis Frampton sat in his living room, the hum of the fan doing little to cut through the heat. He sipped his tea, grateful for the quiet. Retirement had its perks.

His phone buzzed on the coffee table. He checked the screen: Johnny Chiles. He hadn't heard from Johnny in a while.

"Johnny," he answered. "Long time."

"Sarge. Sorry, I know I promised to—"

"It's OK, son. I know how busy you are. Two kids now, yes?"

"Yeah." Dennis could hear the smile in his former colleague's voice. "Thomas and Daniella. Dani's going to be one next week."

"Nice. How's life in the big smoke?"

A pause. "Expensive. How's retirement treating you?"

Dennis chuckled. "Quiet. Pam's got me doing more gardening than I'd like, and I've taken up golf, believe it or not."

"Golf? Really?"

Dennis smiled. "Really."

He knew it was a cliché, and he often felt like an impostor among the fancy types at the golf club, but he was growing to enjoy it. And the buggies meant he could enjoy the outdoors without inflicting too much pain on his leg.

"You planning a visit to Dorset anytime soon?" he asked. "Your dad lives in Stoborough, that right?"

"He moved to Poundbury. Closer to shops, to County Hospital."

"Ah, yes. How is he?"

"In remission. Hopefully for a while yet."

Dennis had faint memories of Johnny's dad Eric, who'd been a sergeant in the west of the county somewhere until his retirement twenty years ago. He barely knew the man, but was always pleased to hear that a former colleague's luck was turning.

"You don't see him much, do you?"

"Wish I could. I feel bad, Sarge, you know? But with the kids and everything... it's tricky."

Dennis had tried to wean Johnny off the habit of calling him Sarge for the first few months of his retirement and finally given up. It didn't help that there was a thirty-year age gap between the two of them.

"Still happy with the Met, then?" he asked, steering clear of mentioning the reason Johnny had transferred.

"Yeah. It's... different. Not quite what I expected. Tough."

Dennis leaned back. "You'll get used to it. Or you won't. Either way, you'll manage."

"Yeah. Listen, Dennis, this isn't just a social call."

Dennis straightened at the use of his first name. "Oh?"

"I need your help. I want to transfer back to Dorset."

Dennis frowned. "Back here? Thought you were settled up there."

"Not really. It's... complicated. I could do with some advice. Maybe a word in the right ear?"

Dennis glanced at the door. Pam had met Johnny a few times and liked the young man. He'd been like a second son to them back when he'd been in Dorset. Especially given that their actual son barely got in touch these days.

But there was a reason Johnny had moved to London. A reason that only Dennis and the DCI knew. And it wasn't a good one.

Dennis sighed. "Johnny, you know I'm retired. I don't have much sway these days."

"I know. But you know people. DCI Clarke, for one."

Dennis rubbed his chin. "Lesley's not your biggest fan, Johnny. You know that."

"I know. But things have changed. Arthur Kelvin's gone. His nephews are out of the picture. I've got nothing hanging over me now."

Dennis nodded; he had a point. "Look, son. I'll see what I can do. But no promises."

"Thanks, Dennis. I appreciate it."

Another *Dennis*.

"Just... make sure this is what you want, Johnny. It's not the same as when you left. The DCI has two teams now, with two new DIs."

"I know. But it's home."

Dennis smiled. "That it is. Very well, I'll be in touch."

"Thanks, Sarge. I mean it."

Dennis ended the call, staring at the phone. He'd always had a soft spot for Johnny. But getting him back to Dorset wouldn't be easy.

CHAPTER TWENTY-FIVE

JULY 1973

DONALD SHARP PACED the hotel room, his mind racing. The room was luxurious, decorated with flock wallpaper and the deepest shag pile carpet he'd ever seen. He'd been hoping to treat his wife, to give her something special.

She loved it here, by the sea. She must do; she came here often enough.

Now he knew why.

He turned to face her. "How long?"

Rowena sat on the edge of the bed, arms folded. "Does it matter?"

He waved the notebook he'd stumbled across in her suitcase. He'd been trying to find aspirin for a headache that was now only going to get worse. "Of course it bloody matters! How long, Rowena?"

She looked away. "A few months."

Donald clenched his fists. "Who is he?" He looked down at the page that he'd opened it at.

Peter. No surname. No information about who he was or how she'd met him.

But he lived down here, in Poole. He had to.

"Doesn't matter," she said.

He took a step towards her. "It does to me."

Rowena stood, meeting his gaze. "It's over, Donald. I don't love you anymore."

His chest tightened. "You don't mean that."

She swallowed. "I do."

He took a step closer. "We have a child, Rowena. A family."

Ellie was in the bathroom, crying. Rowena had shoved the cot in there as soon as he'd started shouting at her.

So she cared enough about her daughter to ensure she didn't hear this, but not enough to hold their family together.

She looked towards the bathroom door, her expression softening. "Ellie will be fine. She's young. She'll adapt."

And I'll never see her again. Donald shook his head. "You can't just walk away."

"I'm not walking away. I'm moving on."

"With him?"

Rowena didn't answer.

Donald turned, running a hand through his hair. "I gave up everything for you. My job, that promotion they offered me in Newcastle. You're happy in Worthing: your job, Ellie, your friends..."

"I'm not. I've been pretending."

Pretending. He eyed her.

"And besides," she said, "you didn't give up anything. You love Worthing, and you hated Newcastle when you went for the interview."

"I did not!"

Rowena sighed. "I'm sorry, Donald. But I can't do this anymore."

He slumped down onto the bed, feeling the springs give under his weight. "You're making a mistake."

"Maybe. But it's my mistake to make."

Donald felt anger rise in his chest. "You selfish—"

Rowena flinched.

He stopped himself, taking a deep breath. "Who's the father?"

Her face creased in confusion. "What?"

"Ellie. The baby. Her father. Is she mine?"

Rowena's eyes widened. "How dare you!"

"Is she mine, Rowena?"

She shook her head, lowering herself to the bed and sitting at its end, her back to him. "Of course she is. This is..." She turned to glance at the notebook, now held tight in his hand. "This is since Ellie."

He tasted a sourness in his mouth. The crying from the bathroom had intensified. Rowena kept looking at the door, like she was torn about bringing Ellie out.

"How can I be sure?" he asked her.

"Because I say so." Rowena's voice trembled.

Donald stared at her, searching for any sign of doubt. "I don't believe you."

"That's your problem."

He turned away, his mind a blur.

He stood up. "I need some air."

Silence.

Donald grabbed his jacket – velvet, twenty pounds it had cost, and for what? – and headed for the door.

As he put his hand on the knob, he turned to her. "This isn't over."

She shook her head, not looking at him.

Bitch.

He slammed the door behind him, leaving his wife alone with the crying baby.

CHAPTER TWENTY-SIX

JUNE 2025

Meera rubbed her eyes, trying to shake off the grogginess. Suzi's cries echoed through the small house, pulling her from the remnants of a restless sleep. She picked up her phone to check the time and groaned.

Too early.

"Coming, Suzi," she muttered, swinging her legs out of bed.

Jill stirred beside her. "Your turn," she mumbled, barely awake.

"I know." Meera pulled on her dressing gown and slid out of the room.

In the next bedroom, Suzi sat upright in bed, clutching her stuffed rabbit. Her face was scrunched up, tears threatening. She pushed her arms upwards at Meera's entrance.

"Mummy."

"Hey, little one," Meera said softly, dragging on a smile. "Come here."

"Mummy."

Meera hoisted her daughter up on her hip, peppering her forehead with kisses that turned the little girl's sobs to giggles. Strictly speaking, they should all be getting another hour of sleep. But she knew if she forced it, it would just be an hour of torture.

"Let's get some brekkie, shall we?"

Suzi nodded, gulping in a loud sniff. Meera tickled her under the chin, prompting another giggle. Still she clutched the rabbit, Thumper. The thing was filthy and had started to smell, but there was no way Meera would risk putting it in the washing machine.

In the kitchen, she placed Suzi in her highchair and opened the cupboard, grabbing a box of Rice Krispies. Suzi's favourite. As she poured the cereal into a bowl, Suzi dropped her rabbit. It skidded across the floor, disappearing under the fridge.

"Thumper!"

Meera turned to see her daughter pointing at the fridge, and the leg sticking out from under it.

She sighed. "Great."

She set the bowl on the table and crouched down, peering under the fridge. The rabbit was stuck. She'd have to move the fridge.

"Hold on, Suzi."

With a grunt, Meera shifted the fridge, just enough to reach the toy. She grabbed it, but something else caught her eye. Mould. A dark patch spreading across the wall behind the fridge.

"Brilliant," she muttered, pushing the fridge back.

She handed the rabbit to Suzi, who squealed and clutched it to her chest. At least one of them was happy.

Jill appeared in the doorway, hair tousled. "Everything alright?"

Meera gestured to the fridge. "There's mould. Behind there."

Jill shrugged. "It's an old house, Meera. Just ignore it."

"Ignore it? Suzi's breathing that in."

Jill sighed. "We can't afford to fix everything, not right now."

Meera felt her frustration rising. "It's not about fixing everything. It's about making sure our daughter's safe."

Jill shook her head. "You're overreacting."

"Am I?" Meera snapped. "Or are you just not taking this seriously?"

Jill had chosen this house. Sure, it had looked like a joint decision at the time, but it was Jill whose eyes had lit up when they'd pulled up outside, Jill who'd fantasised about life in an antique. Meera would rather live somewhere modern and practical; she'd had plenty of experience of old buildings growing up. But Jill had grown up on an ugly modern estate in Swanage and had longed for a cottage of her own since she was fourteen.

Meera hadn't had the heart to deny her.

She'd spent the three years since they'd moved in regretting it.

Suzi looked between them, sensing the tension. She put the rabbit in front of her face. Meera took a deep breath, trying to calm herself.

"Look," Jill said, her tone softer. "I know there are problems. The plumbing, the wiring in the living room. But we can't do everything at once. We'll sort it, just... not today."

Meera nodded, though she didn't feel reassured. "Fine."

Jill moved closer, placing one hand on Meera's arm and the other on Suzi's. "We'll figure it out, okay?"

Meera wanted to believe her. But with everything else going on, it was hard to see how.

"Yeah," she said quietly. "OK."

Jill gave her a small smile and turned to Suzi. "How's my little girl this morning?"

Suzi beamed, dropping the rabbit to the floor. Meera watched them, feeling a pang of guilt. She hated arguing in front of Suzi. But she couldn't just ignore things either.

As Jill played with Suzi, Meera leaned against the counter, staring at the fridge. The mould was just one more thing to deal with. At least it was simpler than her situation at work.

But right now, she wasn't sure how much more she could handle.

CHAPTER TWENTY-SEVEN

ELLIE SHARP STOOD outside the imposing structure of Dorset Police HQ, her chest tight. She wished Sebastian could be here. But he'd had as much time off work as his boss would allow him, and was back in Norwich. She was on her own.

She took a deep breath and walked inside, her footsteps echoing in the spacious lobby. The building was modern, all glass and metal, and she felt small.

"Ellie Sharp?" A friendly-looking woman called from the reception desk.

"Yes."

"DI Scott and DC Legg are expecting you. This way, please."

Ellie nodded and approached the desk. The woman gave her a smile. "I'm Anastasia. Don't worry, they're both very friendly. You got the good ones."

Ellie frowned, wondering who the *bad* ones might be. Was she supposed to be reassured?

She followed the woman through the corridors, trying to steady her nerves. She was here to help. For her mum.

The woman led her into a meeting room. She remembered the

DI: a slightly overweight but stylishly dressed woman with neat blonde hair. Last time she'd been accompanied by another woman; this time it was a man, younger than the DI, with light brown skin and closely cut hair. The two of them were sat at a table, speaking in a low murmur as she walked in.

"DI Scott," she said.

"Ellie, thanks for coming in," said the DI, standing and extending a hand. "Please, call me Jill. This is Mike. DC Legg."

Ellie nodded and shook their hands in turn. "I remember. From your phone call."

"Can we get you a tea or coffee?"

"Um." Ellie looked between the two detectives as she sat down. They'd arranged the table so she wasn't opposite them but diagonally across. "Just water, please."

DI Scott gave her colleague a nod and he left the room.

Ellie straightened in her chair, clutching her bag. "I want to help. If I can."

Jill nodded. "We appreciate that. As you know, we've identified the body found at Upton Lake, with the help of the DNA sample you provided us with. It's definitely your mother, Rowena."

Ellie's throat constricted. She'd known from the phone call, but hearing it here was different. "Right."

The door opened and the man reappeared.

"Here," he said, placing a plastic beaker of water in front of her. She picked it up and gulped it down in one as he took the seat furthest from her.

Jill continued. "We need to piece together what happened to her. Her last movements. Anything you can tell us might help."

Ellie shook her head. "I was a baby. I don't remember anything."

"We understand," Mike said. "But you've been looking into her disappearance, haven't you?"

Ellie's stomach lurched. "I've... yes. I've always wanted to know what happened to her, ever since I was very young. I moved back here just in case, I suppose. I've looked up old news reports, tried to track down anyone who might have known her. There wasn't much. It's too long ago."

The detectives exchanged glances. Maybe with their resources, they'd be able to find more.

"But then," she continued, "Sebastian and I found the diary. Well, Sebastian did. She wrote letters in it, to a man called Peter. She was having an affair." She felt her face twitch. "You know that, though. We brought the diary in."

Jill leaned forward, nodding. There was a file on the table in front of her. The diary, maybe. Along with photos of her mum, from the lake.

Would Ellie be expected to look at those?

"Her diary could be important," Jill said. "Have you been able to find out who Peter was?"

"No. But we think he might've worked with her. She was an estate agent."

Jill exchanged a glance with Mike. "We'll go through the diary again, and we're already talking to the people who now work for your mum's former employer. They changed names, you know."

Ellie nodded. "Pritchard & Locke."

Mike raised an eyebrow, a smile playing at his lips. "So you have been investigating."

"Kind of. Is that OK?"

"Of course it is," said Jill. She reached out a hand on the table, as if she was about to take Ellie's hand in it. "Is there anything else you've found? Anything your father or stepmother might've mentioned?"

Ellie hesitated. "Dad never talked about Mum. And Verity... she didn't like me asking questions."

"Why's that?" Mike asked.

Ellie swallowed. "No reason."

Jill leaned in. "Did your father and stepmother meet while your mother was alive?"

Ellie frowned; surely they didn't think...

"No," she said. "He went on a cruise when I was four. Left me with my grandmother, she'd told him he needed to get away. He met Verity there. They came home and..." She felt her body slump. "They were married within months."

"You weren't close to your stepmum," Mike commented.

Ellie shot him a look. "That's not relevant. She didn't even meet Dad until—"

Jill had a hand out. "We didn't mean anything by that," she said. "But if Verity knew anything about Peter, that might be important. She had that notebook, didn't she? Maybe your father talked to her about it."

Ellie shook her head. "Verity never wanted to be reminded of Mum's existence. I reminded her of his first wife. She didn't like that."

Jill was writing in a pad. "We'll need to speak to your brother."

"Sebastian's in Norwich. He'll help if he can."

"Good. Anyone else you can think of? Any family friends, colleagues of your mother's?" She smiled. "Anyone you've uncovered?"

"There is Isobel. Izzy."

"From the Sandbanks?"

Ellie pursed her lips. So she wasn't as clever as she'd thought. "You know about her."

"Her name's on the police report, from when your mother went missing. She was on the baby-listening service, yes?"

"Yes."

"And there was an Ian Thompson, the duty manager."

Ellie shrugged. Isobel had mentioned the name, in a letter, but she'd never tracked him down.

"I've tried to find people who knew her. Other people. But it was so long ago."

"What about your father? Did he ever talk to you about your mum's disappearance?" Jill cocked her head. "I'm sorry, Ellie. I know this is hard."

Ellie hesitated, her fingers tracing the edge of her bag. "Dad... he didn't handle Mum's disappearance well."

Jill nodded, encouraging her to continue. "In what way?"

"He... he had a breakdown. I think. But it was the seventies. Men didn't admit to that kind of thing."

Mike leaned forward. "What did he do?"

Ellie swallowed. "He... he disappeared into his work. Left me with my grandmother a lot. That's where I was when he went on that cruise. Where he met Verity."

Jill put a hand on the file. "Did he ever talk about your mum after that?"

Ellie shook her head. "Never. It was like she didn't exist. Verity didn't help. She didn't want me asking questions."

"Did he ever mention Peter?"

"No. I don't think he knew. Not then."

Jill tapped her pen on the table. "But he found the letters."

"Yes. I suppose he must've known after that. But he never said anything."

"Do you think he'd suspected your mum was having an affair? Before that, I mean?"

Ellie shrugged. "I don't think so. He never talked about her. I've been thinking about it and I'm wondering if he was... ashamed."

Mike scribbled something in his notebook. "Ashamed of what?"

"Of not being able to keep her. Of her leaving him. I don't know." Ellie took a deep breath, trying to focus. "Verity... meeting her gave him a new lease of life. I was only small, but I know there was a change after that."

"How old were you when they got married?" Mike asked.

"Five. It was six months after he'd met her. Sebbie came along a few months after that." She shook her head. "Shotgun wedding. The most un-Verity thing that my stepmother ever did."

"It sounds like you weren't close," Jill said.

Ellie felt the hairs on the back of her arm prickle. "She didn't like me."

"Why's that?" Mike asked.

Ellie drew in a breath, thinking of all the nights she'd lain awake as a child, wondering what she'd done to deserve the coldness with which she was treated.

But she'd done nothing wrong. She was just the daughter of a woman whose memory could never be lived up to.

"It's like I said. I reminded her of Mum, I think. It's hard to walk in the footsteps of a woman who's dead."

"Did your father ever talk about your mother, after he met Verity?" Jill asked.

Ellie shook her head. "It was like Mum never existed."

Jill exchanged a glance with Mike. "Your father was suspected of being involved in your mother's disappearance, wasn't he?"

Ellie stiffened. "He was exonerated. There wasn't enough evidence." *No body, for one thing.*

"Do you think he was capable of hurting your mother?"

Ellie hesitated. "I don't know. He... he wasn't a warm man. But he loved her. I think."

Jill leaned back in her chair. "And you have no idea who Peter might be?"

"Sorry. I've tried to find out, but... it's like he vanished."

Mike scribbled in his notebook. "We'll find him."

Ellie nodded, hoping they would. For her mum's sake.

CHAPTER TWENTY-EIGHT

MIKE SAT AT THE TABLE, gazing at the notes in front of him. His eyes felt heavy, and he rubbed at them, trying to focus. The baby had been up all night again. Tina had left early, heading over to her mum's for some maternal support again.

Tina hadn't been like this with Louis. But it seemed that with two little ones to take care of, she was overwhelmed. Her mum Annie and sister Naomi lived an hour away in Lyme Regis, and he felt like she spent more time with them than with him these days.

Stop it, he told himself. She was only doing what she needed to, to cope. And it wouldn't be all that long before they switched, like they did last time; her at work and him at home. He'd heard rumours that the MCIT wasn't so easy to work in now. What would Tina make of DI Patterson?

"Mike?"

He blinked. "Uh? Oh, sorry, guv."

They'd taken to calling DI Scott 'guv', to differentiate her from the DCI, who was still boss. The boss hated being *ma'amed*, as she called it; he wondered how she'd feel if she was ever promoted.

The guv was at the front of the briefing room, ready to lead the discussion. Mike shook his head out; he needed to focus.

"Right, let's get started," she said, looking from him to Stanley and Katie. "There's a lot to go over."

Katie sat next to him, tapping her pen on her notepad. She looked like a meerkat, peering out at the world and ready to jump into action at any moment. Stanley was on the other side, arms folded, looking as tired as Mike felt.

"First, Ellie Sharp," the DI began. "Mike, d'you want to cover this one?"

"Oh. Oh, yes, of course." He opened his notepad. "She gave us Rowena's diary – her mum's. The notes to a bloke called Peter."

"We know that, Mike. What about the interview?"

"Sorry. Yeah. She didn't know much, really. Rowena disappeared when Ellie was a baby. She grew up with her dad and stepmum, Verity. She said they never talked about Rowena. It was like she didn't exist."

"Did she suspect her dad?" Katie asked, leaning forward.

Mike shrugged. "She didn't say it outright, but I reckon she wondered. Her dad was the last person to see Rowena. And there was clearly a shift in the family after Rowena died."

Katie frowned. "How would she know that? She wasn't even one year old."

"Well, that's... that's not the time I'm talking about. It was when she was a bit older, about four. Her dad met her stepmum on a cruise. Things changed after that. Her stepmum didn't like her, from the sounds of it."

"But she couldn't have had anything to do with Rowena's death?"

He shook his head. "They didn't meet until years after."

"What if they faked it?" Stanley suggested.

Mike looked at him. "Faked Rowena's disappearance?"

"Nah, not that. You can't fake a disappearance, can you? Faked their meeting. Donald knew all about Peter, he was having an affair with Verity, wanted Rowena out of the way. Killed her and pretended to meet his second wife years afterwards."

The guv was trying not to laugh. "You need to switch careers, Stanley. I'm sure they'd hire you to come up with daft ideas for crime dramas."

He flushed. "Just thinking aloud, guv."

She threw him a smile. "And thinking aloud is good. But I think your theory might be just a little far-fetched." She shook her head. "No, I think the key is finding this Peter."

Stanley nodded. "Maybe he killed Rowena. She dumped him and he couldn't take the idea of her being with Donald."

The guv was rolling her eyes. Katie sighed. Mike gave Stanley a nudge. "Maybe another far-fetched one, mate."

The DI turned to him. "It might not be. From what Rowena wrote in her diary, it was clearly a passionate relationship. Maybe something did happen between them?"

He raised an eyebrow. "She was killed by this Peter bloke?"

"At the very least, he might know something more about where she was on the night she died."

"Any idea who he is?" Stanley asked.

"I've been doing some digging," Katie said. "I spoke to Carys Pritchard at Pritchard & Locke and managed to get a list of staff from around that time. Rowena worked at the Worthing branch, but—"

"Why was there a Worthing branch?" Stanley asked. "It's not exactly round the corner."

She gave him a look. "Edward Locke, who owned the company, had a business partner called Victor Hitchin. He was based out of Worthing. The two of them operated their agencies as a partnership. Traded staff members, shared expertise, that kind of thing."

"But Worthing's a hundred miles away."

"Eighty-nine, to be precise. From the location of the old Locke & Co office in Canford Cliffs."

Stanley shrugged. "I still don't get it."

Katie sighed, glancing at the guv. "Rowena was a trainee at the time."

"No," corrected Mike, "she'd just finished her training."

"Right. She'd just qualified, if that was a thing in 1973. She was based at the Worthing office. Her opposite number in Poole was Geoffrey Locke, Edward Locke's son."

"The guy who then sold the business to Carys Pritchard," Mike said.

Katie nodded. "Yup. Anyway. Rowena and Geoffrey trained together, some of the time. They went to each other's offices. And—"

"So she came to Dorset a lot," said Stanley.

"Stanley, will you let me finish?" Katie looked like she might slap him at any moment.

"Sorry, mate."

A grunt. "So what I'm leading up to is that there was a man who worked at the Poole branch called Peter Didson."

Mike felt the room go still.

"Peter Didson?" the guv said.

Katie nodded, beaming.

"And where is he now?"

"I don't know that yet, guv, but I'm going to find out."

The DI smiled. "I bet you are. OK, keep looking into Peter Didson." She looked from Katie to Mike and Stanley. "You two got any major breakthroughs?"

"I was in the interview with you, guv," Mike said.

"Fair enough. Stanley?"

"I found Izzy Davison. She's living in a care home in Wimborne."

"We knew that."

"Yeah. But I've spoken to the manager. Turns out Izzy is fully compos mentis and can't wait to speak to us."

The guv was beaming. She clapped her hands.

"Good. So we have Peter Didson to speak to, as well as Geoffrey Locke. Katie—"

"On it, guv." Katie had her laptop open and was typing furiously.

"Good. So once we've located Geoffrey we can find out more from him about Peter, track down and make contact with Peter, too, and interview the ever-keen Izzy Davison."

"We've tracked down Geoffrey Locke, in Yeovil," Katie said. She read out an address.

"Good," said the DI. "Mike and Stanley, you go see Geoffrey. Katie, you're with me interviewing Izzy. I'll drive, so you can keep looking for Peter Didson en route."

"Guv." Katie's eyes were sparkling. Mike found her keenness irritating sometimes, but he couldn't deny she was good. She'd be his sarge before long.

He looked at Stanley. "Ready for a road trip, mate?"

"Ready as I'll ever be."

CHAPTER TWENTY-NINE

LESLEY LEANED back in her chair, staring at the screen.

Bloody Sadie Dawes.

The BBC iPlayer was open, a report playing from this morning's national breakfast news. It seemed that interest in this case had spread outside the county.

She sighed. Sadie had a Jackie Kendall-shaped bit between her teeth and wasn't letting it go. The report referred to Rowena being identified and gave a précis of her disappearance in 1973. But the focus of it was on Jackie Kendall, and the incompetence of the police in having failed to track her down, a year after she'd gone missing.

And, in particular, on how the police were now saying they had no interest in reopening the Jackie Kendall case.

Sadie had even managed to get an interview with Yiannis Kallias. He'd looked haggard, sitting in his living room, saying that the only way to find Jackie now was through his online campaign. Claiming he'd been let down and victimised.

None of that was true. But the truth wasn't important, not when it came to the media.

She picked up her phone. "It's the DCI. I need a word."

Two minutes later the door opened, and Hannah walked in, her expression neutral.

"Close the door," Lesley said.

Hannah did so, then sat down opposite Lesley. "You wanted to see me?"

Lesley placed a hand on the desk, trying not to show her annoyance. She'd summoned Hannah as soon as she'd seen the report; it wouldn't be long before Carpenter was summoning her.

"Sadie Dawes," she said. "Her report on breakfast news this morning. Did you see it?"

Hannah shook her head, her jaw tight. "I'm busy at that time of day. Driving into work."

Lesley grunted, holding the DI's gaze. "Did you have anything to do with it?"

Hannah's gaze flickered. "No. Why would I?"

"Because you've been pushing to reopen the Jackie Kendall case. And now the media's all over it."

Hannah shifted in her seat. "With respect, Ma'am—"

"I've told you about the *ma'aming*."

"Boss. With respect, boss, the press were all over the Jackie Kendall case from the moment that body was pulled out of the harbour."

"Rowena Sharp's body."

A nod. "Rowena's body. Yes."

"That's not what I'm asking you about, Hannah." Lesley jabbed at the screen of her laptop. "Are you behind this report about the police failing to find Jackie and victimising her partner?"

"No."

Lesley raised an eyebrow. "No?"

"No."

Lesley twisted the hand on the table into a fist. Hannah glanced down at it then back up into Lesley's eyes.

"I know you want this case reopened, Hannah. And I've been exceptionally accommodating in that regard. I've spoken to Car—"

"I know, boss. And I'm grateful for that. I promise you, we'll find something."

"Found anything yet?"

Hannah shrugged. "It's early days."

Lesley shifted her chair back, about to stand up.

"Yiannis Kallias," she said. "He's been talking to Sadie. Why do you think that is?"

Hannah shrugged. "He's frustrated. He thinks we didn't do enough to find Jackie."

"And do you agree with him?"

Hannah hesitated. "I think there are questions that haven't been answered."

Lesley tapped her fingers on the desk. "You've got less than a week, Hannah. To find something concrete. Otherwise, we're moving on."

Hannah nodded. "Understood."

Lesley leaned back. "And if I hear a peep that you've been blaming the original investigating team, or talking to people outside this unit—"

"I know, boss. You won't."

Lesley raised an eyebrow. "I should hope so. Have you uncovered any new evidence yet? The clock is ticking."

"We're working through the case files and evidence log from last summer, boss. There's a lot to go through. And..." she swallowed, then frowned, seeming to think better of what she was about to say.

Lesley had led the original investigation. It had been Lesley, with the backing of Superintendent Carpenter, who'd made the call to drop the case. There was simply no evidence of wrongdoing. Jackie Kendall had decided she wanted out of her life. Yiannis Kallias had done nothing wrong. That was all they'd been able to ascertain.

And then there was Carys Pritchard, who'd been like a bloody clam last summer and still wasn't giving much away. Was she scared? Had Jackie been threatened?

Maybe her disappearance wasn't a crime, but perhaps something leading to it was.

She stood up, sighing. "That's all, Hannah. Keep working on it, but don't let it affect your workload on other cases. And for god's sake, you'd better not end up making me look like an idiot."

CHAPTER THIRTY

STANLEY LEANED FORWARD in the passenger seat, fiddling with the entertainment system. "You mind if I hook this up to my phone, Mike?"

Mike nodded, glancing in the rear-view mirror. The traffic on the A35 was building up as they approached Dorchester, as ever. At least he'd be heading north and inland in a few minutes, and not continuing west with the crowds.

"No problem, mate," he said. "Just keep it low."

Stanley spent a few minutes tinkering with his phone before the voice of Sabrina Carpenter blasted from the speakers. Mike gave him a sidelong glance; he'd thought Stanley would be more into indie rock than teenage girl pop.

"So, what d'you reckon about DI Scott?" Stanley asked.

Mike raised an eyebrow, then looked back at the road. "She's alright. Seems to know what she's doing." This was the second case he'd worked with her; the first had been the body in Lyme Regis harbour, the Christmas just gone.

Stanley nodded. "Better than the sarge, you think?"

Mike considered. It felt odd trying to describe what the sarge had been like. He'd spent over ten years working with the man. "Different. DS Frampton was old school. Steady. DI Scott's more... flexible."

"Yeah, she's got a good vibe. Not like some I've worked with."

At last Dorchester was behind them. Mike put his foot down a little as they turned onto the A37, heading towards Yeovil. "You had some bad ones, then?"

Stanley shrugged. "Had a DI in CID. Started off all friendly, then turned out to be a right bastard. Never knew where you stood."

"DI Scott doesn't seem like that."

"Hope not. But you never know, do you?"

Mike narrowed his eyes. The traffic was slowing up ahead; an agricultural vehicle at the head of a line of cars. He sighed. "True. But she listens. That's a good sign."

"She does. And she's not afraid to get stuck in. Like the DCI."

Mike smiled. "*She's* one of a kind."

"Yeah, but the guv, the DI, she's got potential. Just hope she doesn't change."

Mike pressed the brake as he approached the rear of the jam. *Let's hope the tractor pulls over.* "We'll see. For now, let's focus on this Geoffrey Locke. Think he'll know anything useful?"

Stanley opened his notebook. "He was a trainee when Rowena was around. Might have known stuff about her, as a colleague."

"It was a long time ago. And he's in a care home now."

"You reckon he won't remember?" Stanley asked.

The traffic slowed almost to a standstill as the tractor pulled into a gap in the hedge, then started to move again. Mike shrugged his shoulders, trying to relieve some of the tension. He thought of Tina, at home in Sandford with the kids. Daisy had slept badly last night; would she be napping now? Would T have her feet up, watching daytime TV? Or would she be playing with Louis, or taking the two of them out for a change of scene?

Not long till he'd be there doing the daddy daycare act. He was looking forward to it.

Mike shrugged. "Let's hope he does. We need something solid."

Stanley put his notebook away. "You think this Peter Didson's involved?"

"Could be. Either way, he has to know something. Maybe she went to see him, the night she died. He was local."

"They let her husband off 'cos there was no body. Now there's a body."

Mike glanced at the satnav. It was looking like they'd make it to Yeovil before lunchtime, thank God. "He's dead, though. Can't try a dead man."

Stanley smirked. "Always the bloody husbands, though, isn't it?"

Mike chuckled. "Or the lovers."

Stanley grinned. "Or both."

Mike shook his head. "Let's just see what Locke's got to say."

Stanley settled back in his seat. "Yeah. Let's see."

CHAPTER THIRTY-ONE

JILL AND KATIE stood outside the Quay View Hotel. The sound of masts clinking in the breeze and seagulls squawking filled the air. Tourists strolled along Christchurch Quay, their chatter mingling with the distant hum of summer traffic.

"Nice spot," Katie said, looking up at the hotel. "Looks peaceful."

Jill nodded. She thought of her own home, and that patch of damp Meera had found behind the fridge this morning, then pushed it aside. *Perils of heritage buildings.*

"Let's hope Izzy Davison's in a talkative mood," she said. "You ready to lead this one?"

Katie nodded, with just a slight hesitation. "Yeah, I'm ready."

"Good. I'll step in if needed, but you take the lead."

Jill was keen to give her new team opportunities to develop their skills. She also wanted to see how they fared when given responsibility. Katie had proven herself to be keen and diligent so far, but how would that translate when she was up against a member of the public?

They entered the hotel and found themselves in a light, airy reception area. A tall woman stood behind the desk, her white hair neatly styled. She looked up, her expression a mix of curiosity and anticipation.

"Detectives," she said, coming around the desk. "I've been expecting you."

"Ms Davison," Katie began, "thanks for agreeing to speak with us. I'm DC Katie Young and this is—"

"Call me Izzy," Isobel interrupted. "It feels appropriate, given what..." Her smile dropped, then reappeared. "And of course, anything to help. I always hoped they'd find Rowena... just not like this." She smiled again. "Come into the dining room. I'll ask Veronica to make us coffees."

Jill watched as Katie walked ahead of her, Izzy by her side and a notebook in hand. They walked through into a large room with tables to one end and low sofas at the other. Isobel led them to a collection of easy chairs and spoke in low tones to a young woman with dark hair and a nervous look.

Katie perched on the edge of her chair. "You were working at the Sandbanks Hotel the night Rowena disappeared?"

"Yes, I was a junior receptionist back then. I was on the baby-listening service that night."

"Can you tell us what happened?"

Izzy nodded, her gaze distant. "It was a quiet night except for poor Ellie. The baby." She frowned. "Has she... Is she...?"

"She's living in Poole," Jill said. "She's helping us with our enquiries."

"Oh." Isobel looked perturbed. She looked back at Katie as if for reassurance.

"The baby?" Katie prompted.

"Oh. Yes. Well, she kept crying, on and off. I asked the duty manager, Ian Thompson, to check on her, and she went quiet for a while. But then it got to 6am and I couldn't take it anymore."

The young woman returned with a tray of drinks. Isobel grabbed hers and gulped at it.

"The baby was there," she continued. "But..."

"But?" Katie asked.

Isobel frowned. "The mother wasn't there. Rowena. No one was there, in fact. I went in and soothed the baby, then Mr Sharp appeared. I asked him where his wife was, but he just said he didn't know. Didn't seem bothered."

Jill cocked her head. "Did you find that odd?"

Izzy shrugged. "A bit. But it wasn't my place to question guests. I was more worried about the baby."

Katie continued. "Did you see Rowena at all the evening before?"

"She'd been in the bar earlier, but I didn't see her after that. She was... well, she seemed tense."

"Tense how?" Jill asked.

"I overheard something, a day earlier. She and Mr Sharp had been arguing. It wasn't the first time."

Katie looked at Jill, then back at Izzy. "Did you hear what the arguments were about?"

"No. Sorry. But they didn't seem to be having an awfully nice time. She went out, the evening before she disappeared. He stayed in the hotel, ate dinner on his own." She frowned. "I remember now, they were on full board. I thought she was mad, to waste a meal she'd paid for. One of the porters asked if he could have it, but Mr Thompson was having none of that."

"Did you notice anything else unusual the night you were on the baby-listening service?" Katie asked.

Izzy wrinkled her nose, thinking. "After I checked on the baby, I went back to reception. Mr Sharp came down later, asking if Rowena had returned. He'd changed. He seemed... agitated."

Katie nodded, writing in her notepad. Jill frowned. "Agitated how?" she prompted.

Izzy looked at her. "Like he was angry. But also worried. He kept pacing the lobby."

"And Rowena never returned?" Katie asked.

"No. By the next evening, she was still missing. The police were called eventually, and... well, you know the rest."

Jill exchanged a glance with Katie. Izzy's account matched what they knew, but the mention of arguments might mean that Donald knew about the affair with Peter.

Katie was scanning her notes. "You said that Mr Sharp ate alone, the night before Rowena disappeared."

"Yes. At least, I think it was that night." A pause. "Yes, it was. The conversation with the porter, I remember because it was a Saturday night and he didn't normally work then."

"I don't suppose you could put us in contact with the porter?"

"Dai? No, sorry. He died in a motorcycle accident, only three years later." Her shoulders slumped. "Poor man."

"Where did Rowena and Donald eat on the night she disappeared? Did Rowena go out?"

Izzy pursed her lips. "They didn't eat at all that night. In fact, it was odd, because they'd booked the baby-listening service, and most guests who did that were eating in the hotel restaurant. It meant they could relax, you know. Some of them went out, but most... Anyway, sorry. I'm waffling. They had a table booked but they didn't use it. I didn't see either of them in the hotel after I delivered the intercom device to their room, which would have been at 6pm or thereabouts."

Katie cocked her head. "Who was in the room, when you delivered it?"

"Oh, both of them. And the baby, of course. They... they didn't look happy. I wasn't sure if they'd been arguing, but I remember wanting to get out of there as quickly as possible."

Jill leaned forward. "You remember a lot of detail, from fifty-two years ago."

Isobel turned to her. "Do I? Yes, I suppose I do. It was a memorable time, Detective. I'd never experienced anything like that. The baby, and poor Rowena going missing, and now..." She let out a small noise, almost a squeak. "Do you think it was Mr Sharp? Do you think he killed her?"

Jill shook her head. "We don't think anything yet. We're just trying to piece together Rowena's last hours."

"Yes. Of course."

Katie looked at Jill, who gave her a nod. The DC stood up. "Thank you, Izzy," she said. "This is helpful."

Izzy sighed. "I always hoped she'd turn up alive. It's sad, really. She deserved better."

Jill stood. "We appreciate your cooperation. We might need to speak with you again."

"Anything I can do to help. I've thought about that night for years."

As they left the hotel, Jill felt a sense of progress, albeit slow. That was how it would be, on these very old cases.

"Good work, Katie," she said as they walked through the Priory gardens to reach the car park. "You handled that well."

Katie smiled, her eyes twinkling. "Thanks, guv. Izzy seemed genuine, didn't she?"

"She did. But we still need to find Peter Didson."

CHAPTER THIRTY-TWO

MIKE PARKED the car outside the care home. It was a small, unassuming building on a pleasant suburban street on the outskirts of Yeovil.

He looked at Stanley. "Got here at last."

Stanley nodded, finishing off a Snickers bar. "Two and a half hours. Can't you drive any quicker, mate?"

"Oi." Mike gave Stanley a mock punch. He liked working with Stan. He could be a bit odd sometimes, coming out with daft questions. But he was alright.

Inside, a nurse led them to Geoffrey Locke's room. The old man sat by the window, staring out at the garden. He turned as they entered, his eyes clouded but curious.

"Mr Locke," Mike began, "I'm Mike, this is Stanley. We're from Dorset Police. We'd like to ask you about your time working at Locke & Co."

Geoffrey blinked. "Locke & Co? I haven't heard that name in years."

Mike and Stanley exchanged glances. Given that Locke was Geoffrey's surname, this wasn't what they'd expected.

"You ran the company until a few years ago, is that right, Mr Locke?" Mike asked, trying not to shout. There was something about Geoffrey Locke that made him want to talk like he was with someone who didn't speak the same language.

A frown. "Did I? I don't remember that. I worked there, for my father. Are you confusing me with my father?"

Stanley took a seat next to Mr Locke. Mike waited as a woman in a brown uniform brought another chair in.

"He forgets things," she muttered to him. "Sharp as a whistle on anything before 1982, though."

"Thanks." He sat down and watched the woman leave the room, casting a smile and a raised eyebrow back at him. *Don't flirt back.*

Stanley leaned forward. "Can we ask you about 1973, Mr Sharp?"

"1973." His eyes brightened. "Good year. I met my Dilly that year, you know. January the sixth. Twelfth night." His mouth widened. "She doesn't know about Rowena, does she?"

Mike raised an eyebrow at Stanley. "Rowena?"

Geoffrey nodded vigorously. "That Rowena, she was a beauty. Long dark hair, thick and lustrous. I... I can't deny I had a bit of a thing for her." He looked up at Mike, his eyes wide. "Please don't tell Dilly."

Mike smiled. "Dilly doesn't know." He looked at Stanley. Had Rowena been having an affair with Geoffrey as well as Peter?

Stanley scratched his stubble. "Mr Locke, d' you mind telling me what your full name is?"

Geoffrey looked at him. "Geoffrey Edward Locke. The Edward is for my father. He runs the firm, you know. Ship-shape, he keeps it."

"No other names? Nicknames? No one ever calls you Peter?"

Geoffrey's cheeks turned red. "Don't tell him about Peter!"

"Sorry?" Mike asked.

Geoffrey clutched his arm. "Peter. Rowena's friend. She swore me to secrecy." His face crumpled. "Oh goodness, have I let the cat out of the bag?"

"You haven't done anything wrong, mate," Stanley said. "It's fine." He looked at Mike with an expression of slight panic.

Mike took a breath. "About Rowena..."

Geoffrey's face lit up. "Ah, Rowena. A breath of fresh air. Always full of life."

Mike watched the old man carefully. "What was she like to work with?"

"Fun," Geoffrey said, with a smile and a jerk on Mike's arm. "She'd come to the Poole office for her training. We'd grab fish and chips on the Quay during lunch. She loved it there."

"And when did she tell you about Peter?" Stanley asked.

Geoffrey's expression shifted. "She'd sneak off sometimes. I asked her if she had another job. Another job, of all things! Oh, I was so green."

"But you knew she was seeing this Peter bloke."

"Peter." A shadow crossed Geoffrey's face. "Yes. Peter. She loved him. Until... well, until she didn't."

"Do you remember the night she went missing?" Mike asked. The old man still hadn't released his arm.

Geoffrey jerked his head towards him, his breathing shallow. "No!"

"You don't remember?"

"No! Don't make me! That man. He killed her, he did." He shook Mike's arm.

"Who killed her?" Stanley asked, his voice low.

Geoffrey turned to him. "Her husband, of course. That jealous wretch of a husband of hers." He began to shake, tears forming in his eyes.

"Donald, it was," he shouted. "Donald did it!"

Mike held up a hand. "Mr Locke, calm down. What makes you say that?"

Geoffrey's voice was shaky. "He was... possessive. Didn't like her working with us. Didn't like her at all."

Stanley was scribbling notes. "Did Rowena mention feeling threatened by him?"

Geoffrey's gaze drifted. His body language slowed, the agitation gone. "She was scared. She wouldn't say it outright. Just... what's the word? Hints. Hints, that's it."

Mike exchanged another look with Stanley. "Did you ever meet Donald?"

Geoffrey nodded. "Once. He came to the office. Made a scene. Rowena was mortified."

Stanley leaned in. "What did he say?"

Geoffrey's eyes were distant. "He didn't like her working extra hours. Told her it was 'unbecoming'."

"And did you speak to him at all, after Rowena's disappearance?"

"No. Dear God man, why would I do that?"

Mike was beginning to regret the drive all the way over here. "Did you see her while she was at the Sandbanks Hotel?"

"No. I didn't even know she brought him there. Dreadful man. She should never have done it."

Mike looked at Stanley. The two of them shook their heads, a slow, identical movement.

"You need to leave." The nurse was in the doorway. "It's not fair to get him all upset like this."

Mike sighed. She was right. "Thanks for your time, Mr Locke," he said. "We're very sorry if we've upset you."

Geoffrey's eyes had regained their brightness. "Oh no, not at all. It's so lovely to talk about Rowena. Beautiful woman. Is she here? Has she come to visit?"

CHAPTER THIRTY-THREE

Meera parked outside Treetops Nursery, feeling a sense of relief. She'd managed to leave work early for once, even if it did mean she'd be going through case files after dinner. Suzi would be thrilled.

She stepped out of the car and looked up at the nursery. It was based in a converted Victorian house, surrounded by an elaborate garden edged with poplars that gave the place its name. A few parents were already gathered, chatting as they waited for their turn to pick up a child.

Meera joined them, nodding to a couple she recognised. "Hi, Zara. How's it going?"

Zara, a mum she'd spoken to a few times, smiled and jiggled a baby on her shoulder. "Hi, Meera. This one's just projectile vomited all over the car seat, but other than that, can't grumble. You're early today."

"Yeah, got lucky. How's Emily?"

"Full of energy, as always. I don't know where she gets it from."

Meera chuckled. "Tell me about it. Suzi's the same."

The door to the nursery opened, and two staff appeared, holding the hands of four children, Suzi among them. Her face lit up when she saw Meera.

"Mummy!"

Meera crouched down, arms open. "Hey, sweetheart."

Suzi ran to her, wrapping her arms around Meera's neck. "You're here!"

"Of course I am. Did you have a good day?"

Suzi nodded, her curls bouncing. "We painted! And I played with Emily and Max."

"Sounds fun."

One of the nursery staff approached, holding a clipboard. "Hi, Jill. Suzi's had a great day."

Meera's smile tightened. *Seriously? Confusing the Asian mum with the white mum?* "I'm Meera. Suzi's other mum."

The staff member blinked. "Oh, I'm sorry. I'll make a note."

"It's fine," Meera said, trying not to let it bother her. It wasn't the first time she'd had that *you don't look like a Jill* look.

She watched as Suzi threw hugs around her friends, saying goodbye. Meera loved doing this, being more involved now that Jill was back at work. It felt right.

Jill had done most of the early childcare, and Meera had always felt a bit sidelined. But now, with Suzi at nursery, things were different. She was enjoying it.

And she needed to stop complaining about work. About the DI. *Hannah.* Meera grimaced; how was she supposed to call a DI *Hannah?*

Stop it. She had a good life. A beautiful daughter, a wife she loved. *Focus on that.*

Suzi returned and grabbed Meera's hand. "Can we have pasta for dinner, Mummy?"

"Pasta it is. Let's get home."

As they walked to the car, Meera smiled down into her daughter's face. Whatever was going on at work, this was what mattered.

CHAPTER THIRTY-FOUR

JOHNNY SAT on the worn sofa in his dad's living room, looking around at the familiar clutter. Eric's house hadn't changed much since he'd retired in 2004 and moved to Poundbury. He'd left behind the home he'd once shared with Johnny's mum and the painful memories, something Johnny occasionally resented him for.

But here, nothing was changing. The same threadbare carpet, the same old photos on the mantelpiece. It felt like home, and that was the problem.

Eric settled into his wing-backed chair, the only piece of furniture that offered him any comfort these days. "You remember the Rowena Sharp case, don't you, lad?"

Johnny nodded. "I remember people talking about it. But I wasn't born in the seventies, Dad. Not by a long shot. I heard snippets, though. Mutterings."

"1973. I was just a young copper then. Sandbanks was a different place. Full of money, but not the kind you see now. More... shady."

Johnny leaned forward. *Even more shady than now, with people like the Kelvins owning waterfront mansions?*

"What d'you mean?" he asked.

Eric shifted, wincing slightly. "Oh, whispers, lad. Corruption. Organised crime. Some of us tried to look into it, but we were told to back off."

Johnny's dad had always been straight as a die. It must've been hard for him back then. "Did you work on the Rowena Sharp case?"

"Not properly. Bit of door-to-door, processing witness statements. But I had a couple of mates who were on the main team. Nasty business. That poor baby."

"What was the theory? They thought her husband did away with her, yeah?"

"Well, yes. They always think it's the husband, especially back then." Eric scratched his nose. "Thing is, Johnny lad, most times it *is* the husband."

Johnny nodded. "But he got off, right?"

A nod. "No evidence against the fella. No body either, that doesn't really help does it?" He chuckled. "Sorry. They've got a body now, though." He sighed. "Bet she's in a right state, poor woman."

Johnny sipped at his tea. He'd asked Mike about the case in a WhatsApp he'd tried to make as casual as possible. Mike hadn't revealed much.

The truth was, Johnny was intrigued. Being in the Met... well, it was OK. But he longed to be back here. Tramping all over beauty spots, fighting the wind and mud at crime scenes instead of spending all his time in lock-ups and dodgy housing estates.

He looked at his dad. "Did you have any theories? Did your mates?"

Eric chuckled, making his cup rattle against the saucer. Johnny was holding a mug, but his dad would always be a china cup man. It had been imbued into him by Mum.

"There was..." He gave Johnny a wary look. "Don't judge me on this, Johnny. It wasn't my idea."

"It was decades ago. Of course not."

"Good. There was a book on it. Everyone picked a suspect, or someone who'd known Rowena. Some of them were people we didn't even know existed. Like there was speculation that there was a bloke. Some fancy-man who she'd dumped and decided to do away with her." He frowned. "We were a right bunch of tossers, weren't we?"

"Different times, Dad."

"Still..." Eric shifted in his chair. "D'you want another one? I need to get that shopping away. Thanks for doing it, it's nice having you here to do that."

"My pleasure, Dad."

Much as he was fascinated by Rowena Sharp, there was something bigger on his mind. Something Eric had just given him an opening for.

"Dad," he said. "I've got something I wanted to talk to you about."

Eric cocked his head. "You have, have you? Is that why you're here, instead of on the end of a phone, like usual?"

"Er... yeah."

"Alice. She's pregnant again, isn't she?"

Johnny smiled. "No, Dad. Two's quite enough for us."

"And lovely kids they are too. But that flat of yours'll never fit another one."

No. *And hopefully we won't be in that flat for too much longer.* That was one of the things that Johnny hated about London; property prices so high that a two-bedroomed flat was supposed to be a family home.

He cleared his throat. "I want to come back, Dad."

Eric looked at him, surprised. "To Dorset?"

"Yeah. London's... it's not for me. Too expensive, too... everything. I miss it here."

Eric nodded slowly. "I wondered how long it'd take. You've got a family now. It's different."

"Yeah. And with Arthur Kelvin and his lot out of the picture, there's nothing keeping me away."

Eric gave him a sharp look. "You sure about that? You got mixed up in some dodgy stuff, Johnny."

"I know. But I didn't have a choice. They were threatening David."

Eric sighed. "I know. But you should've come to me."

Johnny shook his head. "And what would you have done? You were retired. And they had people everywhere."

Eric didn't reply. He just stared at the carpet, lost in thought.

"I spoke to Dennis," Johnny said. "Asked him if he could help with a transfer."

Eric looked up. "And?"

"He said he'd see what he could do. But he's retired, so..."

Eric nodded. "Well, if you want to come back, you should. Dorset needs good coppers. Always has."

Johnny smiled. "Thanks, Dad."

Eric leaned back in his chair, closing his eyes. "Just be careful, Johnny. The past has a way of catching up with you."

Johnny didn't reply. He knew his dad was right. But he also knew he couldn't stay in London much longer. Dorset was home, and he needed to find a way back.

CHAPTER THIRTY-FIVE

MAY 2024

Jackie Kendall stepped out of her car, smoothing down the trousers of her best work suit. The house in Canford Cliffs loomed before her, all glass and sharp angles. It was the kind of place that screamed money.

She glanced at her watch. The client was due in half an hour. Plenty of time to get the place ready. She had fresh flowers in the boot of her car, a bag of fruit on the passenger seat and some vases she'd bought from John Lewis in Branksome on the floor in the back. It had set her back a bit, but the commission on this place would be worth it.

The front door opened with a soft click. Inside, the air conditioning made the place cool, the scent of fresh paint still lingering. She'd need to open some windows. She wandered through the hallway, heels clicking on the polished floor.

The kitchen was a showstopper. Marble countertops, sleek appliances half of which she had no idea how you'd operate, and a view that stretched out to the sea. Jackie ran her fingers along the counter, imagining what it'd be like to cook here. Not that she cooked much.

She moved into the living room. Floor-to-ceiling windows framed the coastline, waves crashing against the cliffs below and distant holi- daymakers enjoying the sunshine further along the beach. You could see the whole sweep round to Bournemouth from here and even make out the Isle of Wight in the distance. She could see why people paid millions for a view like this.

Jackie shook her head. She'd have to sell a thousand houses like this, tens of thousands, to even think about owning a view like that.

She climbed the stairs, her hand trailing along the polished oak balustrade. The master bedroom was vast, with a balcony overlooking the water. She stepped outside and took in the sound of the sea, the breeze ruffling her hair.

"Not bad," she muttered to herself.

The en-suite was bigger than the ground floor of her entire house. She turned on the tap, watching the water cascade into the free- standing bath. Everything about this place was designed to impress.

She wandered back downstairs, checking her phone. Still time.

The study was tucked away at the back of the house. She pushed the door open, peering inside. A large desk dominated the room, with built-in shelves lining the walls.

Jackie hesitated. She wasn't supposed to go poking around. But curiosity got the better of her.

She stepped inside, running her hand over the desk. It was solid, expensive. She could picture some high-flying exec sitting here, making decisions that affected thousands of lives.

Her gaze drifted to the shelves. Books, mostly. A few awards. And a small safe, half-hidden behind a stack of files.

Jackie frowned. Why keep a safe in a house like this? Surely anyone who lived here would have a proper security system.

She turned away, heading back to the living room. *None of her business.* She was here to sell the place, not question the owner's choices.

She still had to check the garage. It was the only room the owners hadn't emptied. She'd never met them; Carys had told her she didn't want to. And it seemed they'd moved to another property before this place was sold.

Alright for some. But at least it meant the house was her dominion. She could control how it looked and what impression viewers received. Showing occupied houses was never easy. Showing luxury occupied houses was nigh-on impossible.

She frowned. Had she heard something?

Don't be daft. She rifled through the keys in her pocket, looking for the one leading to the garage. It was accessed in one of three ways: through the vast double doors at the front, via an outside door, or through the huge utility room leading off the kitchen.

The main garage doors would take longer to open than she had. And the outside door was too far away. She turned and made for the utility room.

Most of the locks in this place were remotely operated, using a system accessible via fingerprint or voice recognition. When she'd been given the portfolio, she'd had to provide her prints and a sample of her voice, so it could be trained to recognise her. She'd tried disguising her voice, seeing if she could trick the system, but it hadn't worked. This was no bog-standard Alexa.

The lock for the door that led to the lobby area joining house and garage was of the more old-fashioned variety. There was a keyhole, and an actual physical key.

She found the right key, inserted it.

"That's odd."

The key wasn't turning. She jiggled it, then checked the key ring.

Was she using the wrong one?

She tried the only one that looked similar, but that didn't work either. She returned to the original key, the one she knew was correct.

Jackie knew keys. They were her bread and butter. She'd make a bloody good prison guard.

She sighed and turned back into the house. She'd need to get a locksmith in, after going through the security procedure and getting the owner's approval of course. Meanwhile she could open up the garage from the outside.

She checked her watch: five minutes to go. She'd better get a move on.

CHAPTER THIRTY-SIX

LESLEY STOOD at the front of the briefing room, her gaze sweeping over the two assembled teams. The atmosphere was tense, a mix of anticipation and fatigue. The Rowena Sharp case was taking a toll on everyone, including the MCIT who weren't even investigating it.

Jill Scott was outlining the latest findings. "We've confirmed the body is Rowena Sharp. We've spoken to her former colleagues and her daughter. They've added nothing we didn't already know, but we have the diary. The focus now is on identifying this 'Peter' from that."

The door creaked open, and Katie Young slipped in, her face flushed with excitement. "Sorry I'm late," she whispered, taking a seat.

Jill gave her a nod then went to continue. "So," she began. "We've been trawling through census recor—"

"Sorry, boss." Katie had her hand up.

Lesley smiled, thinking of Tina, when she'd started. Always keen. But Katie took things to a whole new level.

"What is it, Katie?" she said, making Jill stop in her tracks.

Katie looked from the DI to Lesley, her eyes wide. "Sorry, boss. I didn't mean to..."

Lesley shook her head. "I can see from your face that you've got something you need to tell us. So tell us, then."

Katie licked her lips. She looked at Jill, who nodded.

"I've found him," Katie said, unable to contain her smile. "Peter. Peter Didson. He was an estate agent in Bournemouth."

Jill turned to face her. "How sure are you?"

Katie's breathing was coming in short bursts. "Pretty sure. I found some old trade magazines, from the seventies. Spoke to a mate at the Echo."

Jill looked surprised. "You didn't tell them what it was for?"

"Course not. Gill never asks any questions, anyway. We were at school together. So this Peter Didson, he worked at Hammond's estate agents in Boscombe, office on the high street, back before it was pedestrianised, yeah?"

Jill nodded, although Lesley suspected she had no more memory of traffic on Boscombe High Street than she did.

"So he was in the society pages of the Echo in May 1973. Attending some do for local members of the property trade."

"Since when did the Bournemouth Echo have society pages?" Stanley asked.

Mike turned to him. "It used to, ages ago. They dropped it in the noughties, I think. No one was interested."

"I bet."

"So," Lesley said, looking at Katie, "Peter was in the paper? Please tell me you have a photo."

She grinned. "I've got better than that."

Lesley realised she was holding a brown envelope. "You've got the photo in there?"

Another glance at Jill. Another nod. "I have, boss."

"Well, show us then."

Katie pulled a sheet of A4 paper out of the envelope and brandished it above her head. "You... Sorry. You won't be able to see it. Not all of you." She walked to the front and took the remote control for the whiteboard from Jill. "I've put it on the system."

Katie pressed a few buttons as everyone watched in silence. At last a newspaper cutting appeared on screen. At its centre was an image of a group of people. To one edge was a young man with dark hair and a round face, holding a glass of champagne.

"Peter Didson," Katie announced, pointing at him.

The other members of the group were middle-aged or elderly men.

All except one. The one who Peter Didson had his arm around.

"Is that who I think it is?" asked Jill.

"It is, guv." Katie was nodding so hard Lesley thought she might do herself an injury. "It's Rowena."

CHAPTER THIRTY-SEVEN

LESLEY STEPPED TOWARDS THE SCREEN, looking at the photo of Rowena Sharp and her lover. Both of them were smiling. He was half a step in front of her, looking at the camera, while she had her head turned slightly and was looking at him.

"Have you found out any more about him? Did he stay in the area?"

Katie nodded. "He did. Stayed with the same firm for twenty years after Rowena disappeared."

Lesley turned to her. "So he would have known about her disappearance. But he never came forward."

"Bastard," muttered Stanley. Lesley flinched but said nothing.

Jill was tapping her chin with a fingernail. "But now we know who he is, he can help us. Katie, where is Didson now?"

Katie's smile faded. "No idea. I can't find any record of him after the late nineties."

A murmur spread through the room. Lesley felt a familiar frustration, revealing itself as a tension in the muscles of her back.

Another dead end. Or was it?

"Alright," she said, regaining focus. "We need to confirm

Didson's connection to Rowena. Interview anyone who might have known about the affair. Colleagues, friends, family. Is that Boscombe estate agents still there?"

Jill nodded. "I'll get on it."

Lesley turned to the rest of the team. "What about Donald Sharp? Any developments?"

Mike Legg spoke up. "We interviewed Geoffrey Locke. He knew about Peter, but he wasn't very clear. And he accused Donald of killing Rowena."

Lesley frowned. "Accused? On what basis?"

"Locke's memory is... unreliable," Mike admitted. "But he mentioned a secret between Rowena and Peter. Something about Donald finding out."

"Did he have anything concrete to back up his accusation?"

Mike and Stanley exchanged glances. "Poor bloke was out of it," Stanley said. "Not sure he knew what he was talking about."

"No," added Mike, "he didn't have anything concrete."

Lesley tapped her fingers on the table. "We can't ignore it. But we need more than the ramblings of an old man."

Jill cleared her throat. "We also spoke to Isobel Davison, the hotel receptionist. She mentioned arguments between Rowena and Donald. Said he was agitated the night Rowena disappeared."

Lesley nodded. "Good. Keep digging. We need to build a clearer picture of that night."

Katie leaned forward. "What about Ellie? She might know more about her father's relationship with Rowena."

Jill shook her head. "Ellie's been cooperative, but she was a baby. She can't tell us anything more than she already has."

Lesley sighed. "Alright. Keep her informed, but tread carefully. It can't be easy for her."

The room fell silent as Lesley considered their next steps. The pieces were starting to come together, but they were far from a complete picture.

"Focus on Didson," she said finally. "Find anyone who knew

about their relationship. It might be related to her death. It might not."

"Is there any point," Mike asked, "with them all being dead?"

Katie tutted. Mike turned to her, arms held open in a don't judge me gesture.

Jill sighed. "He's got a point, boss. How does it work, if none of the potential suspects are alive anymore?"

"We don't know if Didson's dead. We don't know how Rowena died. And we don't know who killed her. So we can't assume the perpetrator is dead. Keep working on it." Lesley sighed. "Alright, let's wrap this up. Keep me updated on any developments."

CHAPTER THIRTY-EIGHT

THE COLD CASES team were already on their feet. Meera looked at DI Patterson, what were the MCIT expected to do?

Hannah wasn't going anywhere. She looked around at her team members, frowning at Nathan, who'd stood up. He sat down again.

"Er, boss..." Hannah began.

The DCI turned to her from a conversation she'd been having with Jill. She noticed the small huddle of the MCIT, seated at the front of the briefing room, and frowned.

"Yes?"

"I know it's not our full-time priority, but we do have some news on the Jackie Kendall case."

"Oh. Right. You do?" The DCI gestured at Jill, who tapped Mike and Katie on the back. Mike put a hand on Stanley's shoulder. The Cold Cases team, Jill, Mike, Katie and Stanley, turned as one and took their seats again. Mike and Stanley shared a look and Stanley shrugged.

"Thank you," Hannah said. "We've been able to glean some detail about Jackie's behaviour in the days running up to her death. Nathan?"

DS Strunk cleared his throat and flipped open his notebook. "I spoke to a Jheela Ashok."

"Jheel," said Stanley. DI Patterson looked at him, puzzled.

"Sorry," he said. "Just... Jheel's someone I've known for years. She gives me inside information on the property world in Poole and Bournemouth. It's amazing what you can find out about people moving around, shifting money from hand to hand, through the estate agents."

Hannah narrowed her eyes at him. "Why didn't you tell us you knew someone in the trade before?"

He looked at Jill. She leaned forward.

"Don't forget, Hannah," she said, "we were under the impression that the Jackie Kendall case was dropped." She glanced at the DCI, who didn't react.

Hannah was shaking her head. "You heard me get approval from the DCI to do some more investigation. We've been given a week—"

"Six days, now," interrupted the DCI.

Hannah flushed. "Six days to see if we can find anything that might give us reason to reopen the case. Nathan thinks he has something."

Jill looked back at her.

Stanley raised his hand. Meera bit her lip as the DCI rolled her eyes.

"Er," he said, "can I help at all?"

Jill turned to him. "No, Stanley. I need you on the Rowena Sharp case."

He shrugged. "Course, guv."

She turned back to Hannah. "So what was it that this Jheel Ashok told you?"

Hannah glanced at Nathan, who was flicking the sheets of his notepad back and forth. Meera was relieved she hadn't been involved in the interview with the estate agent; this was awkward enough as a bystander.

She just hoped Hannah wouldn't drag her into it.

"Right," he said. "So I spoke to her on the phone this morning." He looked at Stanley. "Very helpful, she was. Turns out she's known Jackie for years," another glance at Stanley, "and they used to meet for a drink every Wednesday night. Anyway, two Wednesdays before the last time Jackie's partner last saw her, she started acting weird."

"What kind of weird?" the DCI asked. She was at the front, leaning against a table with her arms folded across her chest.

He swallowed. "Jumpy. She made Jheel change the bar they visited, then did the same again the week after. In the middle of the evening, she made them move to a restaurant. Apparently, she'd never done that before." He flipped over a page. "And she spent the whole evening looking over her mate's shoulder. Made sure she was seated facing the door, and didn't take her eyes off it for a moment."

"Scared," said Hannah. She glanced at Meera, who nodded, unsure if she was supposed to contribute.

"Did she give any specifics?" asked the DCI. "Did Jackie tell her friend what she was scared of?"

"No," said Nathan, looking disappointed, "but Jheel did tell me it kicked in when she asked her about a house she was trying to sell. Fancy place in Canford Cliffs."

"Do we know the address of this fancy place?" the DCI asked.

"Yes," said Hannah. She gestured at Meera.

Meera flinched; she'd been so busy watching the dynamic between the three bosses that she'd forgotten she was expected to join in. "Erm," she said, and opened up her phone where she kept her notes. She read out the address.

"Has it sold, or is it still on the market?" Katie asked.

"Sold," Meera said.

"Who to?"

Meera looked down. "To an American couple, looking for a second home."

"Who was the original owner? The client?"

"A business. Dorchester Logistics."

"Shit," muttered Mike. The DCI was shaking her head.

"What?" Meera asked. "So you know it?"

"We do," said Mike. "It belongs to the Kelvins."

Meera frowned. "Arthur Kelvin? But he's dead."

Mike frowned, looking at Stanley. "Was Kelvin dead last July?"

"He was," said the DCI. "He died in February 2023."

"So it's not him," Meera muttered. "He can't have anything to do with Jackie disappearing."

Stanley, Mike and the DCI all turned to her, their expressions seeming to say *How can you be so naive?* She felt her stomach dip.

"What?" she said. "His family? But the nephews are either dead or in prison, and his wife..."

Dead, too. Being close to Arthur Kelvin often had that effect.

"There's Vera," said DS Strunk. "She'll have inherited all of her son's property."

"And added it to her own. And what she inherited from her late husband," the boss said.

Stanley whistled. "Lot of cash."

DS Strunk raised a finger. "And there's the Freemans, over in Devon."

"Who?" Meera asked. Hannah made a noise at the back of her throat.

The DCI turned to her. "You had much dealing with them?"

Hannah shook her head. "Not my remit. But they took over Kyle Kelvin's Devon operation, when you put him away. Haven't made a very good job of it, from what I've heard."

The DS nodded. "One of their key men was killed by another gang. After Jackie went missing, mind."

"Jesus," said the DCI. "Do we really need more of them?" She screwed up her face. "So there's a chance that the fact Jackie sold a house belonging to an organised crime gang had something to do with her disappearance. But—"

"Sorry, boss," DS Strunk said. "But she didn't."

"Sorry?"

"It wasn't her who sold it. The house was still on the market when she disappeared. It was Carys Pritchard who oversaw the sale."

"Is Carys Pritchard at risk?" Hannah asked.

The DCI shook her head. "If they wanted rid of her, they'd have done it by now." She chewed on a Bic biro she'd brought from her pocket. "OK, continue exploring. Find out what you can." She raised her eyebrows, looking at Hannah. "But for God's sake—"

Stanley cleared his throat and gave a pointed look towards the filing cabinets in the corner. On top of one was a metal tin; the old sarge's swear box.

"Really?" the DCI said. "For a *God*?"

"That's two of them," muttered Mike.

The DCI gave him a look. "I'll put something in later."

"He takes contactless," said Stanley.

The DCI laughed. "Can you imagine it? I'll sort it later, alright? But for now." She shook herself out and turned to Hannah. "Just be careful, alright? Make no mention of the Kelvins to anyone. But find out what you can about the transfer of that property. If Jackie worked on it, then something might have happened to her that led either directly or indirectly to her disappearance."

CHAPTER THIRTY-NINE

As they all filed out, Meera fell into step with Mike. She gave him a tight smile. "Alright?"

"Yeah." He yawned. "Sleep deprived, but you know how it is."

She smiled. "I certainly do." Suzi was getting better now; it was the biggest relief she'd ever experienced. "How's Tina?"

"Ah, you know. Can't wait to be back at work. We'll be switching places in six weeks."

"You looking forward to it?"

He wrinkled his nose. "Yeah. Yeah, I am."

She sniffed. They were in the corridor now, heading back to the two team rooms, which were side by side. Up ahead, Stanley was making a joke and Katie was groaning.

"All that stuff about the Kelvins," she said to Mike. "You think it's relevant?"

He sighed. "I tell you what, Meera, I thought we'd be shot of that lot now."

She chuckled. "They're like a chocolate stain on the best baby-grow, the one a grandparent bought as a present. Impossible to get rid of."

"They are that."

"Surely you're expecting to come across them again, in the cold cases team?"

"Huh? Well, being in cold cases doesn't change the fact that most of them are dead."

"Yeah, but they would have been even more of an influence a generation ago, wouldn't they? Vera Kelvin. What was her husband's name?"

"Gerard." Mike shuddered. "Died around the time I started in the MCIT, natural causes, supposedly."

"Impressive."

"Yeah. Not many of his type died in their beds."

They were at the door to her team room now, the only people in the corridor.

"Suzi giving you trouble at night too?" Mike asked as he put his hand on the handle to the Cold Cases room.

Meera shook her head. "No." She looked into the room behind him, through the glazed door. "What's Jill been saying?"

"Oh, nothing. Just... you look tired. That's all."

"Oh. No, I woke up early. We've... we've got a damp problem."

He nodded, looking as if he had no idea what that meant. "Expensive?"

"That's not the issue." She glanced through the door again. "You live in a modern house, don't you?"

He raised an eyebrow. "In Sandford. Mind you, I almost wrecked the place last year with my dodgy DIY." He laughed. "Get a professional in if you need anything doing, that's my advice."

She nodded in agreement. Hopefully somebody would be able to fix that damp.

"You've got an old place, haven't you?" he said. "The DI told me about it once, when we were driving to an interview. Sounds lovely."

"The DI?" How did Hannah know about her house?

"Your wife." He gestured behind him with his thumb, back into the room.

"Oh. Yeah, yeah, it's idyllic. You could say."

He gave her a grin. "Sounds perfect. Nice chatting, eh?" He turned and went through the door.

Meera stood in the corridor, her limbs heavy. Idyllic.

Was it? Or was it just a bloody pain in the arse?

CHAPTER FORTY

JILL WATCHED as Mike entered the team room, the last to return from the briefing. He'd been talking to Meera, lingering outside the door, occasionally glancing inside.

She leaned back in her chair, trying to ignore the twinge of curiosity. What were they discussing? Meera had worked with Mike in the MCIT before Jill had even joined the team, trying to reconstruct a murder in Tyneham. Messing about, it had sounded like at the time. They probably had stuff to catch up on.

So why did it bother her?

She shook her head, annoyed at herself. *You're better than this.*

"Right, everyone," she said, forcing her attention back to the team. "Let's get started."

Mike took his seat, glancing at her as he did so. Had Meera been talking to him about her?

Don't be ridiculous.

"Everything alright, Mike?" she asked, trying to sound casual.

"Huh?" Oh, yeah. He looked back at the door, realising. "I was bringing Meera up to speed on the Kelvins. She reckons we might come across them a fair bit, working on cold cases."

Jill felt the tension ease. She shrugged. "Maybe we will, maybe we won't." Truth was, she wasn't bothered by organised crime gangs. Any Kelvins she'd have cause to deal with would be either dead or very elderly by now.

He nodded. "Yeah."

Jill clapped her hands. Stanley and Katie were huddled over Stanley's desk, talking. Katie looked up at the sound, her eyes wide.

"Come on, everyone," Jill said. "Our mission for today is to find Didson. Anyone got any original ideas as to how we go about doing that?"

"There's credit card records from the time," said Katie, counting off on her fingers, "property records—"

"What about estate agents?" Mike asked. "Is there some kind of record of who acted on house sales? Like the land registry?"

Jill looked at Stanley. "Can you talk to this friend of yours, Jheel? Ask if she knows anything?"

He shook his head. "Already tried that, guv. Jheel's only been working in this area for six years. And in 1973 she was ten years off being born."

"But she might know someone who can help us," suggested Katie. "More senior members of her firm might have contacts. Memories even."

Jill nodded. "Good. Katie, I want you and Stanley to find out more about the Bournemouth and Poole estate agency scene in 1973 than it's healthy for anyone to know. Talk to Jheel again, use her connections. Keep following the links until we find someone who knew Peter Didson. If we can find him alive..."

"I know, guv," said Katie. "He could be—"

"He could be, he might not be. But he'll be able to shed more light on things."

Katie nodded. "Guv."

"Good. Mike, I want you to continue looking into the evidence from the time. Find out if there's anything we haven't seen yet. Check written records, clothing, anything that was taken. Can we take

DNA samples from anything Rowena left behind, or has too much time passed? Were prints taken from the hotel room? Anything you can find, however small it is."

"No problem, guv." Mike stood up, heading for the door.

"Where are you going?"

"Evidence store, guv."

"It's all on the system."

"All the stuff we've already looked at is, yes. But if there's anything we've missed, the only way to find it is by working through it all. Physically."

"You're right. Good. You go ahead and do that, let me know if you find anything."

"Will do." He continued to the door and out into the corridor.

Jill stood in the middle of the room, suddenly quiet. Stanley and Katie were at their screens trawling for links to Peter Didson. Mike was on his way downstairs.

They had no forensics, next to no pathology. This was impossible.

She felt cold creep up her spine. Was this how it would always be?

A case became cold, officially, after three years. She'd had visions of reopening cases from no more than ten years ago. Cases with proper evidence, and more that had come to light since, or else they wouldn't have been reopened.

Now, the only thing they had making them reopen the case was Rowena's body.

And the diary. *Don't forget the diary.*

She took a deep breath. This wasn't impossible. She could do it. She could show the DCI what she was capable of.

And she was going to start by going to the morgue.

CHAPTER FORTY-ONE

Dennis squinted at the ball on the tee, trying to decide if he needed new spectacles. He swung, the club slicing through the air, and the ball veered off to the right, landing somewhere in the rough.

He grunted.

"Not your best, Dennis," Fred called from behind him. Retired DS Fred Horborough, an old friend from local CID. They played together once a fortnight, when Dennis didn't make an excuse.

He hadn't made up his mind whether he actually liked golf. It was such a cliché: retire and spend the rest of your life with a nine-iron in your hand. But it got him out into the fresh air, this club in Wareham had reduced rates for retired police, and the buggy meant his knee had less to complain about, despite the distances covered. Fred had talked the manager into letting them use a buggy free of charge, on account of Dennis's injury being sustained in his police work. Dennis had found the whole conversation mortifying.

"Tell me about it," he muttered, trudging after the ball. The sun was out, but a breeze kept it from being too warm. Perfect weather, really. And the breeze was light, no excuse for his dreadful aim.

Fred joined him, his own ball landing neatly on the fairway. "You've got to relax, Dennis. You're too tense."

Dennis snorted. "I never was much of one for relaxing."

They walked on, Fred chatting about his latest DIY project. Dennis half-listened, nodding occasionally. He liked Fred, but sometimes the man could talk for England.

They reached Dennis's ball. He took a deep breath and swung again. This time, it went straight, landing just short of the green.

"Better," Fred said. "See? Relaxation."

Dennis shrugged off his irritation. "Perhaps."

They played on, Dennis gradually finding his rhythm. He still wasn't sure if he was enjoying himself, but it was better than sitting at home. Pam couldn't give him her attention every hour of every day, and as she'd said to him this morning, he needed as much light exercise as he could handle.

As they headed back towards the clubhouse, Dennis heard voices. A group of men were walking a little way ahead, their conversation carrying on the breeze.

"... Rowena Sharp," one of them said. "Tragic, really. Such a beautiful woman."

Dennis's ears pricked up. *Rowena Sharp.* The case Lesley had asked him about.

"Did you know her?" another man asked.

"Mm-hmm," the first man replied. "I knew her."

Dennis slowed his pace, straining to hear more.

"Don't talk nonsense," a third voice said. "You're just looking for attention."

Dennis looked at the man, the one who claimed to have known Rowena. He was older than Dennis, in his seventies at least, but ageing had treated him more kindly than it had Dennis. He could imagine the man being the type who'd have enjoyed attention from women, in his youth.

Maybe one of those women had been Rowena Sharp. It wasn't impossible.

Fred was looking at him, hands on hips. "Everything alright, Dennis?"

"Fine," Dennis said. "Just... thinking."

They reached the clubhouse. Dennis watched the group of men head into the bar. He turned to Fred.

"Fancy a drink?"

Fred raised an eyebrow. "You buying?"

"Er... Why not?"

In the bar, the men were already seated at a table in the corner. Otherwise, the space was empty. It was only 11:30; the place would be full within the hour. Non-members were allowed in here, and it was popular with retirees who preferred sitting and eating lunch over getting out there and playing golf.

He nudged Fred towards a table two along from the group of men.

"What's going on, Dennis?" Fred asked as they sat down. "We normally sit over there, by the window."

"I fancy a change."

"You? You never *fancied a change* in all your life. What are you up to?" Fred looked past Dennis at the men, then gave a knowing smile. He winked at Dennis, who grimaced.

"Just... humour me, Fred."

Fred shrugged. "Very well. But you're still buying."

Dennis ordered their drinks, keeping an ear on the conversation at the other table. The man who'd mentioned Rowena was talking again.

"... such a shame," he was saying. "She didn't deserve what happened."

Dennis leaned back in his chair to get closer, pretending to be interested in Fred's latest story about his garden. He caught snippets of the conversation.

"... always thought she was too good for him..."

"... Peter, you didn't even know her..."

"... I did, I'm telling you..."

Dennis sipped his drink, his mind racing. *Peter.* That was the name Lesley had mentioned.

Fred was looking at him expectantly. Dennis realised he'd missed a question.

"Sorry, Fred. What was that?"

"I was asking if your begonias had turned out as well as you expected this year. I know you put a lot of work into preparing the ground."

Dennis frowned. *Begonias?* "Yes. Oh, yes, they're lovely." He pulled on a smile. "All that preparation paid off."

The waitress arrived with their drinks; ginger beer for Dennis, a pint of bitter shandy for Fred, whose experience arresting drunk drivers back in the day had led to him forming the firm opinion that this didn't count.

Fred took a long gulp of his drink, then wiped his lips. He eyed Dennis. "So are you going to tell me what's going on?"

Dennis considered lying, then shook his head. "Just... something I'm working on. Unofficially."

Fred chuckled. "Still playing detective, eh?"

"Old habits." Dennis smiled. "Old habits."

He listened as the conversation at the other table moved on to other topics. But he'd heard enough. *Peter.* He kept glancing over at the man, making a mental note of his features.

Could he find someone with access to the membership list, track down the man's address? Maybe rope Fred in to help?

No. That would be unethical. He'd pass on what he'd heard to the DCI and let her deal with it.

Fred finished his drink. "Another?"

Dennis shook his head. "I should be getting back. Thanks for the game, Fred."

Fred stood up. "Anytime, Dennis. And next time, try to relax a bit more."

Dennis managed a smile. "I'll try."

He watched his friend as he stood up and shrugged on his jacket, his senses tingling.

He'd overheard something important. Something that might even be evidence.

It was the most exciting thing that had happened to him since the day he'd got himself this leg injury.

CHAPTER FORTY-TWO

JILL ENTERED THE MORGUE, the sterile smell hitting her immediately. She spotted Dr Gareth Bamford, the pathologist, near the back, examining a set of notes.

"Gareth," she called out, her voice echoing slightly.

He looked up, smiling. "DI Scott. Good to see you."

"Thanks for this, I know it's short notice. You've finished the post-mortem?"

He nodded. "This morning. I was surprised you didn't send anyone."

She pushed back mild embarrassment. "Apologies for that. Would it have made a difference?"

"To be honest, not really. Most of the useful information will come from the tests we're running on the contents of her lungs and stomach. And Dr Moreau's report, of course."

"Dr Moreau?"

"Forensic anthropologist. I spoke to...?"

Of course. "The DCI told me. Sorry." She really needed to find a way to get more sleep. This being back at work was taking its toll.

"You want to see her? She looks quite different, now we've cleaned her up."

"Please."

He nodded, gesturing for her to follow. "This way."

They walked through a set of double doors to a long, narrow space lined with drawers, and a table in one corner with a computer on it. Gareth checked the records, then went to one of the drawers. He pulled it out to reveal Rowena's body, covered by a sheet.

Jill steeled herself. She'd seen plenty of bodies before, but this one had been in the water for decades.

The pathologist pulled back the sheet, his movements gentle and respectful. "Here she is."

Jill leaned in, careful not to touch anything. The body was skeletal, with little flesh remaining. What was left was darkened, almost black. Rowena was smaller now, without all that mud stuck to her.

"Not much to go on," she said.

"Unfortunately not," Gareth replied. "The mud has kept her preserved for longer than might otherwise be the case, and we'll know more about that when we've run a full analysis on its contents. But yes... it's not easy to look at."

Jill swallowed. There was a sharp taste in her mouth, and not just from the smell of formaldehyde which permeated the space. "Did you find anything useful during the PM?"

"Very little in the way of physical evidence. No wounds that might have led to death, although with a body this old...." He gestured down at the body.

She nodded. Poor woman. How had she got into the water? Pushed in alive, dumped there after death, or just an unfortunate accident?

"I don't suppose you can tell if she drowned?"

"Not after this length of time, no. But there's surprising amounts we can deduce. It just takes time." He straightened up and pushed the drawer back in its slot. "This isn't something we deal with all that regularly."

"No. Will you be able to tell how long she's been in the water?"

"With this degree of damage, it's difficult. Like I say, we're running tests on the mud we took from inside her body, comparing it to the deposits on the outside. The mud in her lungs may date back from the time of death. Once we've analysed its chemical constituents, things will hopefully be clearer."

Jill felt a shiver run across her skin. Mud, that had remained in this woman's system for over forty years...

Focus. "Chemical constituents," she said. "What kind of thing are we talking about here?"

"Pollutants, mostly. We can trace when certain pollutants were prevalent in the area. We've got someone from the Environment Agency helping us out, and the National Rivers Authority that came before them. It might give us a rough timeline."

"That's something, at least."

Bamford nodded. "And there's the forensic anthropologist. Doctor Carla Moreau. She's got experience with bodies that have been in water for extended periods."

"Moreau," Jill repeated. "I've heard of her."

"She's good. She'll be able to tell us more about the state of the bones. Any signs of trauma, that sort of thing."

Jill looked at the door hiding the remains of Rowena Sharp. "Do you think there's a chance we'll find out how she died?"

Gareth shrugged. "It's possible. But we'll need to wait for Dr Moreau's analysis."

"Right. Thanks."

He gestured towards the door and she fell into step beside him, trying to ignore the fact that the cold in here made her want to curl up inside one of those drawers and go to sleep.

"I'll keep you updated."

"Appreciate it."

Rowena Sharp had been missing for decades. Now they had her body, but even with modern science, it had been fifty-two years. Would they ever discover what had happened to her?

CHAPTER FORTY-THREE

JOHNNY PUSHED the wheelchair along the supermarket aisle, glancing down at his dad. Eric's face was set, determined. He'd refused to do his shopping online, despite Johnny's attempts to persuade him.

"Don't trust it," Eric muttered. "I like to see what I'm buying."

Johnny sighed. "It's easier, Dad. You don't have to leave the house."

Eric shook his head. "I like getting out. And I don't want someone else picking my apples."

Johnny steered them towards the fruit section. He'd never pictured himself doing this, having to parent his own dad. Eric had seemed like a force of nature when he was growing up, like a tree that would never be felled.

"You need to take it easy, Dad. Your health's not getting any better."

"I'm fine. Just need to keep moving."

Johnny knew better than to argue. Eric was stubborn, always had been. But he worried. The old man needed him, and he wasn't any use a hundred and fifty miles away in London.

They stopped by the apples. Eric inspected each one, taking his time. Johnny shifted his weight, impatient.

"You heard anything about your transfer application?" Eric asked, not looking up.

Johnny's shoulders slumped. "Not yet. Sent in the application, but it's been radio silence."

"Give it time."

"I don't have time, Dad. I need to get back. London's... it's too much."

Eric placed a couple of apples in the basket on his lap. "You miss Alice."

Johnny nodded. "And the kids. It's not right, us being apart."

"You don't need to stay over here, you know. I'll be fine on my own."

Johnny clenched his jaw. "I want to help."

Eric grunted as he put an apple into a bag. "Like I say, you don't need to. I've got meals on wheels, and the district nurse comes in—"

"That's not the same, Dad, and you know it. And besides, London's just too expensive, with two kids. Did I tell you how much childcare costs?"

Eric smiled. "There you go. It's not just because of me. But..."

"But what, Dad?" Johnny was beginning to wish he'd gone back to London. Every conversation seemed to go round in circles, and sleeping in his old bed made him feel like he was twelve.

"But what, Dad?"

"Maybe it's for the best." Eric pointed towards the bananas.

Johnny turned the wheelchair, frowning. "What d'you mean?"

Eric shrugged. "Just... Dorset's not all that different from London, you know. You have this rose-tinted image of it. And the Met. Well, the Met may get a bad press, but..."

Eric grabbed a bunch of bananas. Johnny sighed. "They're working on that, Dad."

"That's not what I mean."

"What do you mean?"

"Take me to the aisle for tea and coffee, will you? We're almost out of Gold Blend."

Johnny sighed and scanned the ceiling for a sign of the correct aisle. The Tesco on the edge of Dorchester was huge and confusing. But, as Eric repeatedly reminded him, it was easier to navigate by wheelchair than the smaller, friendlier shops in town.

Johnny turned the wheelchair into the aisle for tea and coffee. "It's home," he said. "Whatever you say about Dorset, London isn't the same."

Eric didn't reply, instead focusing on reading the labels on three different types of coffee. They all looked the same to Johnny.

What was with his dad comparing Dorset Police to the Met? What wasn't he saying?

Eric had always been cryptic, especially about his time in the force. Johnny knew better than to push him.

As they moved to the next aisle, Johnny's mind drifted back to London. The cramped flat, the noise, the constant pressure. He hated it. He wanted to bring his family back to Dorset, where they belonged.

"Dennis said he'd help," he said, more to himself than to Eric.

"Frampton's a good man. He'll do what he can."

"The DCI's the problem. She doesn't trust me."

"Can you blame her?"

Johnny flinched. "I didn't have a choice, Dad." He lowered his voice. "Arthur Kelvin had me over a barrel."

Eric sighed. "I know, son. But you should've talked to me, instead of letting them do that to you."

Johnny clenched his jaw. "I thought I was protecting you. And David."

Johnny's brother David was living in Bristol now. He was clean, and well away from all this. Or so Johnny hoped.

Eric reached up to pat Johnny's arm. "I know. But you can't let the past eat you up."

Johnny nodded, pushing the wheelchair towards the checkout.

He hoped Dennis could convince the DCI. He needed this transfer. For his family. For himself.

As they queued, Eric spoke again. "You ever think about leaving the force?"

Johnny blinked. "What?"

"You've got skills, Johnny. You could do something else."

Johnny frowned. "This is all I know, Dad. And I want to make things right."

Eric didn't reply. Johnny wondered if his dad had ever felt the same. Had he wanted to leave the force? He'd been a uniformed sergeant for forty years and retired at sixty-five, carriage clock and all. Johnny had always assumed he was devoted to the job.

Had he been wrong?

They paid for the shopping and headed back to the car. Johnny helped Eric into the passenger seat, folding the wheelchair and stowing it in the boot.

As he drove back to the house, Johnny considered his situation. He needed to get back to Dorset. He needed to prove himself. Not just to the DCI, but to his dad. And to himself.

Eric stared out of the window, silent. Johnny wondered what he was thinking. What he'd never told them about his time in the force.

"Thanks for the help, son," Eric said as they pulled up outside the house. Despite being new, on the inside Eric had made it look exactly like the house he'd lived in with Johnny's mum for forty years.

Johnny nodded. "It's my pleasure, Dad."

Eric grunted and heaved himself out of the car and into the house on crutches, his movements slow and painful.

Johnny felt his limbs grow heavy. He should be here, helping his dad. Not stuck in London.

CHAPTER FORTY-FOUR

JILL GRIPPED THE STEERING WHEEL, her mind on the meeting with
Dr Bamford. The drive from Poole Hospital to Winfrith was familiar,
the route passing Upton Lake where Rowena's body had been found.

She glanced at the clock and smiled. She'd be home in time to see
Suzi before bed. Maybe even give her a bath, if Meera hadn't already
done it. Meera had applied for part-time hours now that Jill was back
to working full time. Hopefully, the fact that the Jackie Kendall case
was going nowhere would help with that.

Her phone buzzed and she tapped the hands-free.

"DI Scott."

"Guv, it's Mike."

Jill nodded. She'd worried about Mike when he'd been assigned
to her team, wishing she'd got his wife instead. But he seemed to have
stepped out from Tina's shadow and was proving to be a valuable
member of the team. She was even wondering if she might suggest he
take the sergeant's exam. With three DCs on the team, there was a
gap waiting to be filled.

But that was something for another day. "What have you got for
me, Mike?" she asked.

"Are you still with the pathologist?"

"Just left. There isn't much new, they're still running tests on the mud. They've brought in a forensic anthropologist, hopefully she'll be able to fill in some gaps. Tell me you've got something helpful for me."

"I've been going through the evidence store from 1973. It's not in great shape, but there's a diary. Donald Sharp's."

Jill raised an eyebrow. "Another diary?"

"Yeah. Proper one this time, not just a notebook. It describes an argument with Rowena on the night she disappeared. Not much detail, though."

"Interesting. Anything else?"

"Later entries show he felt guilt. There's one after the funeral. He writes about feeling responsible."

Jill frowned. "Responsible for what? Anything specific?"

"Sorry, guv. Doesn't say. But there's more. I found a pocket at the back of the diary. It had a handwritten receipt."

"A receipt?"

"For petrol. Dated the night Rowena disappeared. From a garage in Worthing."

Jill's grip tightened on the wheel. "Worthing? That's miles from Sandbanks."

"Exactly. Why would he be there?"

She frowned. "That's where Rowena and Donald were living, wasn't it? At the time she disappeared. It's where the estate agents she worked at was based."

"You're right. Do you want me to drive over there, see if I can find the petrol station?"

"Do some googling first. Anyone working there in 1973 won't be there now, even if the place is still open."

"No. You're right. Sorry guv, I got a bit—"

"It's OK, Mike. You're following your instincts. But no. I think we might need to track down anyone who might have seen him in

Worthing that night, but not from the petrol station. Maybe he went home, a neighbour..."

"It was fifty years ago, guv."

She felt her body droop. "You're right. How can we possibly expect anyone to remember?"

"Yeah."

She was approaching Wareham now, about to take the turn for the bypass. "I'll be with you in a few minutes," she said. "Keep looking through that diary. In particular, see if you can find any sign that Donald was looking for Peter. If my wife disappeared after I'd discovered she was having an affair, that's the first thing I'd do."

A pause, then, "Yeah, me too."

Jill smiled, imagining Mike thinking of Tina in the same way she was thinking of Meera. Things weren't great between her and Meera right now – the bloody house, as usual – but there was no way either of them would consider having an affair.

Rowena Sharp, it seemed, had been different. So what sort of man did that make Donald Sharp? And, more pressingly, what sort of man did it make Peter Didson?

CHAPTER FORTY-FIVE

JILL STRODE INTO HQ, her mind on what Mike had told her. She hurried to the top of the stairs and turned towards her team room, anxious to discover whether he'd found more in the evidence store.

Stanley was outside the door, shifting from foot to foot.

"Stanley? Everything OK?" She gave an uneasy laugh. "Is this an ambush?"

His cheeks reddened. "Sorry, guv. Can I... can I have a word?"

She sighed. "Of course. Let's go to my office."

They turned away from the team room and went to Jill's office. Inside, she closed the door and leaned against her desk. "What's up?"

Stanley wouldn't meet her eye. "It's a bit... sensitive."

She frowned. Stanley was the outspoken one of the cold cases team, the one who never hesitated to voice what was on his mind, no matter how ridiculous. It could be an asset when you needed answers to daft questions.

But now, he looked like he wished the carpet would swallow him up.

"Stanley? You've dragged me into my office. You were waiting for me when I got in. There's clearly something up."

"Yeah."

"Are you going to tell me what it is?"

She looked at him. Maybe he was resigning. Or requesting a transfer. He had to confess something awful. He'd been involved in the deaths of police officers while she was away looking after Suzi.

Don't be ridiculous.

Stanley had investigated those cases. No way was he dodgy.

He cleared his throat. "While you were out, DS Strunk came to see me."

"Nathan? Why?"

"He asked me to help with the Jackie Kendall investigation."

Jill slid into her chair, gesturing for Stanley to take the other one. He did, his movements awkward. Suddenly he seemed taller and more gangly than before.

"Help how?" she asked.

"He wanted me to call Jheel, the estate agent. I've known her for years. Do some digging into the properties Jackie was selling."

"What did you say?"

"I told him I'd have to pass it by you first."

She nodded. "Good. That was the right thing to do."

Stanley continued, his words tumbling out. "I thought our case was active, and the Jackie Kendall case wasn't supposed to be taking up police resources. We've got a body, and there's no reason why Nathan couldn't speak to Jheel again. But he's a DS, so I felt uneasy."

Jill raised a hand. "It's OK, Stanley. You're full-time on the Rowena Sharp case. Nathan's perfectly capable of calling your estate agent contact." She sighed. "Look, we're two teams, but we're intertwined, right? You used to be in the MCIT, so did Mike."

"Er... yeah."

"So we will work together. We have briefings together, from time to time. We share resources, when it helps."

"Should I have...?"

"No. The Jackie Kendall case isn't active. The MCIT isn't

supposed to be using significant amounts of their own resources, let alone ours." She stood up. "You did the right thing, Stanley."

He pushed his legs out to stretch in front of him. "Thanks, guv. That's a relief."

She smiled. "Is that everything? I don't suppose you've tracked down Peter Didson yet?"

He shook his head. "Sorry."

"No. Well, keep plugging away. That's our top priority. And the MCIT can't pull us away from it."

"No, guv." He stood and went to the door.

"If this kind of thing happens again, speak to me," she said. "Any cross-team working should be done through me and DI Patterson."

Stanley looked relieved. "Yeah."

"Get back to work, Stan. We've got enough on our plate."

After he'd left, she stared at the door for a few moments. Did she need to raise this? Was it important?

She sighed and opened the door, walking past her team room to Hannah's office. The layout had been designed so each of them could be right next to their teams: office, team room, office, team room. But Hannah had taken the wrong office and was at the far end from her team, putting Jill and the Cold Cases team in the middle. It worked for her; she liked to be close by, would have preferred to be in with them.

But the distance seemed to suit Hannah. *Each to their own.*

As she passed the Cold Cases team room, the door opened and Mike emerged. "Guv?"

"Sorry, Mike. Just need to deal with something quickly, and then I'll be right in."

He nodded, looking disappointed. "OK. Right." He looked in the direction she'd been walking then went back into the team room.

Jill blew out a breath. *This shouldn't be so hard.* She straightened her shoulders and knocked on Hannah's door.

"Come."

Jill opened the door, slipped in, and closed it behind her.

Hannah was at her desk, working in silence. She looked up, perturbed, as Jill stood opposite her.

"Hannah, have you got a minute?"

"If you can make it quick," Hannah replied, looking back at her screen.

Jill took a breath. "Stanley just came to see me. He mentioned Nathan had asked him to help with the Jackie Kendall case. Wanted him to call an estate agent."

Hannah's expression didn't change, and she didn't look away from her screen. "And?"

"If you need someone from my team, just let me know. I'll do my best to help."

Hannah leaned back in her chair, her gaze on Jill now. She licked her lips and raised an eyebrow. "Your Stanley wouldn't have been much help anyway. Nathan's already made the calls. He's established which properties Jackie was selling and who they belonged to. He and Meera will be out first thing in the morning, knocking on some doors."

Jill felt her stomach clench. "Visiting the Kelvins?"

"What little of them is left, yes. Mainly associates. You want me to fill you in on the full detail, or do you trust me to run my team as I see fit?"

"I trust you. Of course."

Hannah looked at her. "You just said it, Jill. You have your team, and I have mine. You allocate your resources the way you see fit, and I'll do the same."

Jill tried to push down the dread. Meera could handle herself. "Very well," she said, standing up.

Hannah raised an eyebrow. "Really? Is that it?"

Jill hesitated.

Hannah continued. "Half these teams are married to each other, the other half used to work together, and they're all in and out of each other's pockets like a dodgy twenty-pound note. I don't see why we can't informally share resources as and when we need to."

Jill placed her palms on the desk and leaned over. Hannah flinched.

"I have no problem with sharing resources," Jill said. "But a DS approaching a DC with a request, especially on a case that isn't even supposed to be active, when we've got a high-profile case in the—"

Hannah snorted. "You think Rowena is more high profile than Jackie?"

Jill clutched the edge of the desk. "We have a body in the Rowena Sharp case. For all we know, Jackie just decided to move away from the area."

"And you know that because you're more familiar with the case than I am, I suppose?"

"No. Of course not—"

"Or maybe your wife's been filling you in."

Jill pushed her weight off the desk and stood up straight. "Nathan asking Stanley for his help. It could be seen as an abuse of authority."

Hannah laughed. "Is this about where Nathan used to work?"

"No," Jill replied. "I wasn't involved in the Dugdale or Angus cases, so—"

"Yes, but people talk," Hannah said. Her phone rang, and she gave Jill a pointed look. "I need to take this." She glanced from Jill to the door and back again.

Jill turned and left, wishing she hadn't knocked on Hannah's door in the first place.

CHAPTER FORTY-SIX

Mike looked up as the DI entered the team room. He was at a table that had been dragged in to hold the contents of the evidence store from when Rowena Sharp had originally disappeared. He'd spent the afternoon working through it all and was now sitting back in a chair, staring at all the evidence bags, wondering how many hands they'd worked their way through over the years, and if anything could have gone missing during that time.

He imagined procedures weren't as tight in the seventies.

What was he missing?

"Alright, guv," he said, gesturing towards it all. "Here's your evidence store."

She pulled up a chair and sat next to him. "That plus what we have from her body."

"There's just the body itself, surely? No belongings would still have been on her."

"You're right. Nothing on her at all. We only knew who she was from the DNA match from Ellie."

He nodded, staring again at the bags.

The DI leaned back in her chair. "So, what've we got?"

Mike opened a folder. "There's the diary, court records from the failed prosecution of Donald Sharp, documents from the Sandbanks Hotel, and files from Rowena's work in Worthing."

"You gone through more of the diary?"

"Yup. From 1973, and one from 1974. He stopped writing in that one when the court case ended."

She nodded. "Anything about Peter Didson?"

"Nothing. Not a mention."

The guv frowned. "So he didn't know about the affair. He'd vent in his diary."

Mike shrugged. "The diary changes, day after Rowena disappeared."

"Twenty-first of July, right?"

"That's the last day anyone saw her. The day they had the argument. From the 22nd, it becomes less of a diary, more of a legal record. Notes from interviews, names of officers and legal staff he encountered. More of an attempt to record anything he might use in his case or in a formal complaint than a personal account."

"And he did that right from the day she was reported missing?"

He nodded. "Looks dodgy, doesn't it?"

"Well dodgy, mate." Stanley was at his own desk, writing up notes from earlier, and listening in, it seemed.

The DI wrinkled her nose. "But Donald went to Worthing when Rowena was away from the hotel room, according to that fuel receipt."

"Handwritten," Mike said. "Could have been faked."

"Wasn't everything handwritten in those days?"

She was right. "S'pose so."

"And there's nothing in there about Peter Didson. No attempt to track him down, make contact with him?"

"Nothing. Either he didn't follow up on what Rowena wrote, or he didn't discover her diary until later."

She tapped her chin with her fingernails. The guv always had perfectly manicured nails. He wondered how she did it, with Suzi so young. If Tina tried that, Louis would either try and paint the walls with her nail varnish or grab her nails assuming they were sweets.

But then, Louis was eighteen months younger than Suzi.

"OK," she said. "I think Donald was hiding something, something he didn't put in this diary."

He nodded.

She tapped those nails on the desk. "We need to know more about Rowena's state of mind before she went missing. Any contacts in Worthing who might shed some light?"

"I can start looking online, see if any of them are still alive."

"Good. If you find anyone, head over there and speak to them. We need to understand what was going on in her life."

Mike made a note. "And I can speak to Ellie and Sebastian again. They might remember something now."

He could imagine the two of them discussing the diary, and the fact that Rowena's body had been found. Churning over memories. Maybe uncovering some they'd forgotten about.

"Do that," the guv said. "We need to know what they know about Peter and their father's attitude towards him."

Stanley walked over to them. He glanced at the files on the table. "Anything new from the evidence store?"

Mike shook his head. "Nothing about Peter. Pretty much nothing about Donald."

Stanley grunted. "Figures."

The DI stood up, glancing at the evidence bags. "Not easy, these old cases, eh?" She raised an eyebrow, smiling at him and Stanley.

Mike chuckled. "Almost as old as your house, guv."

Her eyes narrowed. "What?"

He shifted in his seat. "Er, nothing."

"Mike," she said, her tone sharpening. "What've you heard about my house?"

He licked his lips and swallowed. "Just... Meera was telling me about some problems you've been having with damp. Sounds tricky."

The guv's posture stiffened. She stared at him for a moment, then something passed across her face and she visibly calmed herself.

"Sorry," she said. "But my home life isn't something we should be discussing at work. Keep me updated on Worthing."

"Yes, guv," Mike replied, as the DI left the team room.

When the door was safely closed, Stanley whistled. "What was all that about?"

Mike shook his head. "No idea, mate. No idea."

CHAPTER FORTY-SEVEN

LESLEY DECIDED to check on her two DIs before heading home. Elsa was celebrating a big new client, and there'd be Champagne and a Chinese takeaway for dinner. She was looking forward to it.

She made her way to the corridor below hers, where the MCIT and Cold Cases offices were. She knocked on Hannah's door.

"Got a minute?"

Hannah looked up from her desk, her expression neutral. "Sure."

Lesley gestured towards Jill's office with a tilt of her head. "Come with me."

Hannah stood up, looking uneasy, as Lesley turned and walked towards Jill's office. She knocked and opened the door. Hannah loitered behind her, scratching her cheek.

"Evening, Jill," Lesley said. "I just wanted to get the two of you together for a quick update."

Jill looked up from her computer. She smiled, then spotted Hannah behind Lesley, and her face hardened. "Of course, boss."

Lesley gestured for Hannah to sit, but she remained standing. Lesley took the seat opposite Jill's desk. If Hannah wanted to stand, then that was her lookout.

"Come in further," Lesley said. Hannah was hovering by the door. The DI shifted around the room until she was leaning against the wall by Lesley's chair.

Lesley frowned but said nothing. She was learning that Hannah didn't always behave in ways you expected.

She turned to Jill. The desk had a line of photos on it, facing diagonally so that Jill could see them, and so could anyone entering the room: Jill and Meera's wedding day, Jill in a hospital gown holding a scrunched-up Suzi, Jill, Meera and Suzi playing in the snow. Lesley wondered if she should do the same for her own desk.

No. Not when your wife's a criminal lawyer and your daughter's an eighteen-year-old who would rather spend an afternoon playing golf with Dennis than pose for a family photo.

"Let's start with you, Jill," she said. "Any progress with Rowena?"

Hannah made a disgruntled noise. Lesley gave her a sidelong glance but said nothing.

Jill cleared her throat. "We've got a full name for the Peter in the diary: Peter Didson. But we haven't tracked him down yet. That's our top priority. We're also planning on speaking to Ellie and Sebastian again."

Lesley nodded. "What about the evidence from the original case?"

"We've got Donald's diary, and a receipt from the night Rowena disappeared which appears to show him being in Worthing." Jill checked her notes. "But none of it's conclusive. The diary's odd. A whole list of technical and legal details about the case. No personal feelings."

Lesley frowned. "You think that's suspicious?"

Jill shrugged. "Could be his way of coping."

Hannah gave the wall she was leaning on a little thump. "We've had a breakthrough on the Jackie Kendall case."

Jill gave her an irritated look, then arranged her face into a look of calm.

Lesley raised an eyebrow. "Go on, Hannah."

Hannah pushed her shoulders back, shifting her weight so she was no longer leaning against the wall. "We know Jackie started behaving differently after she took on a property owned by the Kelvins."

"I already know that," Lesley said.

Hannah met her gaze. "Yes, but we now know who's running Kelvin operations in Dorset."

Lesley felt a twinge of unease. "Who?"

"Vera Kelvin."

Lesley frowned. Surely that was impossible. The late Arthur Kelvin had inherited oversight of the family firm, both above-board and not, when his father, Gerard, died. His two nephews were out of the picture: one dead, one in prison. But there had to be someone else further down the tree.

"Vera's in her eighties," she pointed out.

Hannah shrugged. "From what I've heard, that wouldn't mean much to a woman like Vera Kelvin."

She had a point. "Maybe. So, are you planning on speaking to her?"

Hannah shook her head. "We know that wouldn't work. So we're pulling together a list of her associates."

Lesley felt a familiar dread. "Such as?"

Hannah glanced at Jill, then looked back at Lesley. She'd slumped back now to lean against the wall.

Stop looking so... so casual. This was nothing to be casual about.

"The Kelvin family's solicitors," Hannah said. "They would have been involved in any property sale."

Jill looked at Lesley. "Isn't your...?"

Lesley nodded. "Yes. My wife Elsa Short used to be a partner in the firm that looks after the Kelvins' legal affairs. But she left almost two years ago." She turned to Hannah. "I doubt she'll be able to help you."

Hannah looked back at her, saying nothing.

Lesley hesitated. If the team thought talking to Elsa would give them a lead, she couldn't stop them.

She sighed. "Just tell me, before you speak to any of these people, yes? I have history with the Kelvins, and so do a number of members of the team. We need to tread carefully."

"Of course, boss," Hannah said.

Lesley stood up. "Good. Anyway. I have a celebratory meal to get home to. And you both..." She looked at Hannah, realising she knew nothing about the woman's private life. "... I'm sure you have places to be. Have a good evening, and keep me informed."

She left the office, noting that Hannah waited five seconds, then moved to her own office. She sighed. It was normal for DIs to work together, to compare notes. To slag off the boss, from time to time. That was almost expected.

But this pair...

She shook her head. *Teething problems. They'll get used to each other.* As she was leaving the building and making for her car, her phone buzzed: Dennis.

She answered the call, puzzled. Dennis never called her unless it was to change the time for their monthly meeting. And she'd only seen him the day before.

"Evening, Dennis. Everything alright?"

"Could be, boss... Lesley. I've got something for you. Might be nothing, but..."

She used her free hand to click the car open with the key fob and slid into the driver's seat. Bluetooth kicked in and she placed her phone on the charging pad in the centre console. "Go on."

Dennis sounded out of breath. She hoped he wasn't overdoing it. "I overheard a conversation at the golf club," he said. "Some chaps talking about Rowena Sharp. One of them was called Peter. Could this be your Peter Didson?"

She'd been about to reverse out of the parking space but stopped herself. "Could be. Did you catch a surname?"

"Sorry, just Peter. I haven't seen him there before, nor the other chaps. But then, I'm only a new member myself."

"How often do you go to the golf club, Dennis?"

"Not as often as I should. But..."

"Yes?"

"But I can become more of a regular if it would help."

Lesley smiled. *Typical Dennis.* Would the man ever retire?

She felt a lump rise in her throat: *just like his old friend, Tim Mackie.* He'd continued sniffing around cases after his retirement. And look what it had done for him.

"Think you can find out where he lives?"

"I can try. But can't you do it officially?"

"We'd need a warrant to get the membership list. I'm not sure you overhearing a name is enough for that."

"Of course." He paused. "There's a visitor's book. I've seen it."

"Of course." She didn't stop to ask how he would manufacture an excuse to read through that; he could work that out himself. "Good work, Dennis. Thanks. I'll get someone in Jill's team to follow up with you."

"Glad to help. Send Mike over, eh?"

She smiled. "I'll see what I can do."

"Thanks. And..."

"Yes?"

Silence.

"Dennis? Don't tell me your golf buddies have thrown up another piece of evidence."

"No. It's... I saw..."

She narrowed her eyes. "Who did you see?"

"No one. Not now."

Lesley stared at the phone. *Not now.* Typical Dennis, to be cryptic like this. She thought back to the time he'd taken off work with depression, when the investigation into DCI Mackie's murder had been reopened. His arrest, and subsequent release without charge.

"You sure you don't have something you need to get off your chest?"

"No. Not my place."

Lesley sighed. "OK."

"You need me to help with anything else? With the case?"

Her smile broadened. Was visiting him every month a good idea? Was she just making it harder for him to accept retirement?

But she enjoyed their tea parties. And she valued his advice and relative detachment.

"Not for now," she said. "But keep your ears open, will you?"

"I always do."

She ended the call, feeling a flicker of hope. She ducked her head to look up out of the windscreen of her car, towards Jill's office.

The light was off. Jill had a young family, and it was getting late. Lesley would tell her in the morning. For now, she had a celebration to enjoy.

CHAPTER FORTY-EIGHT

Meera opened her mouth and widened her eyes at Suzi as she heard Jill's key in the lock.

"Mama's home!"

Suzi laughed, clapping her hands. "Mama!" She ran out of the kitchen to the tiny hallway. Meera heard an 'oof' followed by the sound of Jill placing kisses all over their daughter's face, something she liked to do when she got in from work.

She smiled, waiting for the two of them to enter the kitchen.

As they did, she felt her smile drop. Jill's posture was stiff. She was talking in an upbeat voice to Suzi but wouldn't look at Meera.

Meera stood up. Maybe she'd had a tough day at work. "Hi, gorgeous. How was your day?"

Jill gave her a blank look, then turned back to Suzi. "How's my little Su-su? Is she the funniest little girl in the whole world?" She lifted the front of Suzi's t-shirt and blew a raspberry on her tummy, causing Suzi to collapse into giggles.

"Jill?" Meera said.

"Here." Jill held Suzi out and put her in Meera's arms. "I need to get changed." She tickled under Suzi's chin. "See you in a minute, funny girl."

Suzi giggled again. Meera held her, watching her wife leave the kitchen without so much as a smile or a kiss for her.

What the hell's going on?

Ten minutes later, Jill was downstairs again and setting the table while Suzi waited in her highchair, chattering about her day at nursery. Jill kept looking at the toddler, reacting to her stories and exclaiming in all the right places. But she still hadn't spoken to Meera.

"Jill, love. Is everything OK?"

Jill looked at her. She slammed a fork down on the table, making Meera jolt.

"Careful, Mama," Suzi said, giggling.

Jill forced a smile. "Sorry, sweetheart."

Meera frowned. "Are you alright?"

"Fine," Jill replied, not looking up from the table.

They sat down to eat. Suzi was in high spirits, telling a story about a friend's toy dinosaur. Meera tried to engage, but Jill had descended into silence.

"Mummy, can we have ice cream?" Suzi asked when they'd finished their fish fingers and chips.

"Maybe," Meera said, glancing at Jill. "If Mama's up for it."

Jill gave a tight nod. "Sure."

After three bowls of ice cream, eaten in near-silence, Meera took Suzi up for her bath. Jill stayed downstairs, tidying up. Meera could hear the clatter of dishes being stacked with more force than normal.

Once Suzi was in bed, Meera found Jill in the living room, staring at her phone. She closed the door and sat down next to her wife, worried.

"Jill, what's happened?"

Jill looked up, her expression guarded. "Nothing."

"Please, that's not true. I'm worried about you." Meera swallowed. "You've been off all evening."

Jill sighed, setting her phone down. She looked into Meera's face for the first time since entering the house two hours earlier. "Mike mentioned something today. About our house."

Meera tensed. "Is that all?" She laughed. "I thought someone had died."

Jill's look was harsh. "*Is that all?* Let me tell you what Mike said. He said our home – the home we're bringing our daughter up in – is a dump. And that you've been complaining about it."

Meera shrank back. "I might've mentioned the mould."

"Might've?"

"Alright, I did. But it's not like I was slagging off our home."

Jill stood up. "Why does a junior member of my team know more about our domestic situation than I do?"

Meera felt her jaw tense. "Junior? He's the same rank as me."

"That's not the point, Meera."

"Isn't it? You think I'm beneath you, don't you?"

Jill's expression softened. She brought a hand up to her face and rested her cheek in her palm. "That's not what I meant."

"Then what *did* you mean?"

Jill rubbed her face, smearing mascara across her forehead. "I just... I don't like the idea of you discussing our private life with my team."

Meera forced herself to sit down again. This time, she was further along the sofa from Jill. "I wasn't *discussing* it. It came up in conversation."

Jill shook her head. "It shouldn't have."

Meera clenched a fist. "I'm sorry if I embarrassed you, but we've got a little one to think about. That mould's not safe."

"I know that," Jill snapped. "But we can't fix everything at once."

Meera took a deep breath. "I'm only trying to do what's best for Suzi."

"So am I."

Jill stood up just as Meera did the same. They stared at each other awkwardly for a moment then both looked at the floor.

Jill stepped to one side, making for the door without making physical contact. "I'm going to bed."

"Jill, we should—"

"I'm tired. Just let me sleep, yes?"

Meera watched her go, her chest tight. She listened as Jill's feet ascended the stairs. It wasn't even 8pm; Suzi had been in bed no more than half an hour.

Was Jill really that tired?

If she needs time to herself, that's fine. She's not the only one.

She reached for the TV remote, determined to stay down here until she knew her wife was safely asleep.

CHAPTER FORTY-NINE

LESLEY PARKED her car outside HQ, looking up at the new building. Its modern design was a far cry from the old office, still being slowly dismantled. Running two teams was a challenge she hadn't got used to yet, but at least she didn't have that drafty office with its vast windows facing out over the car park anymore.

She headed inside, nodding at a few familiar faces. The atmosphere was subdued, as always, but the new building had its perks. It felt more professional, more fitting for the work they did.

Her phone buzzed. Carpenter wanted to see her. She sighed and made her way to his office.

"Lesley," he said, looking up from his desk. Sitting on his desk was a Danish pastry on a plate, and a cup of what looked like espresso. She wondered if she'd be offered anything. "Come in."

She stepped inside, closing the door behind her. "Sir."

He gestured for her to sit on one of the four easy chairs near the window. There was no sign of coffee on the low table between them.

"I've been reviewing your teams," he said.

She looked back at him, her skin prickling. Was someone about to get moved on? Was there something she didn't know about?

"Sir," she said. "The teams are still bedding in. I'm sure—"

He waved a hand in dismissal. "It's not that, although I have heard rumours of conflict between your two DIs. I do hope it's the kind of healthy competition that can help two teams work harder, rather than the kind that ends up on the front pages of the *Echo*."

"It's all under control, Sir."

"Good. But with Tina Abbott on maternity leave, you're short-staffed."

She nodded. "We're managing. And she'll be back soon. I—"

"At which point her husband will bugger off on his leave."

Lesley swallowed. "I have a plan in place for sharing resources between the teams when Mike's leave starts. I'm sure—"

"Lesley, I want to help you. I think you could use an extra team member."

"Oh." She slumped back in her chair. She didn't want him thinking she couldn't cope, but in today's resource-poor police force, no DCI with two brain cells to rub together would refuse extra staff. "Who?"

"DC Johnny Chiles. He's asked for a transfer back to Dorset."

Lesley stiffened. "Johnny?" She closed her eyes for a moment, thinking back to the last time she and Carpenter had discussed the DC. How much had she told him?

Carpenter was smiling. "I've been speaking with your old side-kick, Dennis Frampton."

"Dennis? Why?"

"Don't worry, Lesley. He's not trying to undermine you. We just... well, we have the occasional chat. We're members of the same golf club, you see."

Lesley pursed her lips. *These men and their bloody golf.* She'd be half-tempted to take it up herself if the idea didn't want to make her throw herself off Hengistbury Head.

"Anyway. Dennis told me that Johnny has applied for a transfer. I checked the system and it turns out it's been processing for a few weeks."

"These things take time." Lesley's brain was whirring, trying to remember who else knew about the blackmail Johnny had been subjected to by the Kelvins. Was it just her and Dennis?

But now, Arthur Kelvin was dead, and his nephews out of the picture. She'd had no hint that Vera Kelvin had been involved – she'd never stoop so low as to concern herself with a lowly DC. And besides, Lesley wasn't entirely convinced that Vera had come out of retirement. Why grind the organ when you have monkeys to do it for you?

"Johnny's move to the Met was a sensible move for him, Sir. I'm sure—"

"It seems he's not entirely happy there."

How the hell would Carpenter know how happy Johnny was?

Dennis. Of course. Lesley sighed.

"You think he should come back."

"I do. He has relevant experience, both with the geography and the personnel. He was an accomplished detective, according to his record. And you need more people."

She couldn't deny that. And if she told Carpenter why she didn't want Johnny back, she'd have to admit that she'd lied to him four years ago, when she'd told him Johnny was requesting a transfer to London.

Four years. Had it really been that long?

Carpenter stood up. "I know you have concerns. But you need more officers. And his experience can't be denied."

She stood to face him. "Very well, Sir."

"Good. I'll leave it to you to let him know."

Lesley felt her stomach dip. Johnny, back in the team. She couldn't stop it, but she'd be keeping a bloody close eye on him.

CHAPTER FIFTY

JILL STOOD at the front of the Cold Cases team room, watching her team settle in. Mike looked tired, as usual. Stanley was sipping a Coke, his usual breakfast Snickers nowhere in sight. Katie was on her screen, making use of every second before the briefing began.

Jill cleared her throat. Katie pushed her chair away from her screen and Stanley swallowed the last of the Coke, crumpling the can and throwing it in the recycling bin to the side of the room. He grinned as it landed inside.

"Right," she began. "I've been speaking to the DCI. We've got some intelligence on Peter Didson. Potential intelligence, anyway."

"They've found him?" Katie asked, leaning forward straight-backed.

Jill shook her head. "We don't know that yet. The DCI had a call from a retired member of the MCIT, Dennis Frampton."

Mike chuckled. "Might have known the sarge wouldn't take retirement seriously."

Jill gave him a look. "Dennis is now enjoying his retirement, it seems, and he's joined a golf club. He overheard a conversation there, about Rowena. One of the men involved in this conversation seems to know her. And his name was Peter."

Stanley leaned back. "Good for the sarge. That's brilliant."

Jill put up a hand. "We don't know for sure if it's the same Peter. And Dennis has no idea if the man he overheard is a member of the club, or where he lives."

Mike snorted. "He'll find a way of working that out."

Jill looked at him, one eyebrow raised. "That's what he told the DCI."

Mike smiled. "See?"

Katie was on her screen again, typing. "Wareham golf club," she said. "Near Sandford. You can probably see it from your back window, Mike."

"No such luck." Mike turned to her. "Have you seen how small the gardens are on my estate?"

She began to laugh, then dropped her gaze to the table. "Sorry, guv."

Jill frowned; did Katie think she was some sort of tyrant?

Katie was back on her screen. "So there are parts of the club that non-members are allowed to access. Where did DS Frampton say this conversation took place?"

"I'm not sure," Jill told her. "It might have been the bar, I imagine."

Katie nodded. "There's a 'Bar and Kitchen'," she said, doing air quotes. "Open to the public." She looked up. "Who does that? Goes to a golf club bar when there are perfectly good pubs?"

"Members' wives," Stanley told her. "Pensioners. That'll be what it's for."

Katie pulled a face.

"Either way," Jill said, "Dennis is working on identifying who the Peter that he overheard is. I'm sure he'll ask some of his fellow members, see if—"

"He'll check the visitors' register," Stanley said. "They keep a book, in the smaller clubs. People have to sign in."

"But surely that's computerised," Katie said.

"You'd think so, wouldn't you? But this is golf clubs."

She shrugged.

"OK," Jill said. "Mike, Dennis has asked for you to follow up with him. I'll leave you to determine how you do that. Katie and Stanley, I need you to go to Ellie Sharp's flat. See if the last few days have given her the opportunity to remember anything new."

"Righto, guv," Stanley said. Mike stood up and pulled his jacket off the chair behind him.

Jill raised her voice to be heard over the scraping of chairs. "I'll speak to the DCI about Worthing and Norwich. I'm not confident there's anything useful for us in Worthing, and we don't know if Sebastian Sharp will be of any more help. But they're the backups, in case we don't get anywhere with this Peter."

The team ignored her; they were already halfway out the door.

She sighed. *Oh well, at least they're keen.*

CHAPTER FIFTY-ONE

DI ZOE FINCH stepped out of her car and looked up at Workington Police Station. The building was unremarkable as ever, flat, grey-rendered walls and the ubiquitous stone-framed windows she was getting used to seeing on just about every building in western Cumbria.

She walked through the entrance, nodding at a couple of uniformed officers she recognised. Her stomach was fluttering but she maintained an outward calm. She'd had enough false starts and dashed hopes when it came to tracking down the woman she hoped she'd just got a lead on. It didn't pay to get too excited.

Inside, the duty sergeant, PS Coombs was at his desk, typing away. He looked up as she approached.

"DI Finch. What can I do for you?"

She placed a palm on his desk, trying to ignore the fact that it was sweating. "I heard you had a walk-in earlier. A woman asking about protection?"

The sergeant wrinkled his nose. "Yeah, she was in a right state. Didn't stay long."

Damn. Hopefully she hadn't gone far. Zoe leaned on the counter. "Did she tell you why she needed protection?"

He sucked through his teeth then looked around. "Why don't you come through?"

She followed the sergeant, clenching and unclenching a fist. Was it Olivia Bagsby who'd come in here? It had to be, surely. Olivia was back in Cumbria now. And the sergeant wouldn't have needed to talk to her in private for anyone else.

When they were inside an interview room and the door was closed, she put her hands on her hips. "She asked for protection, you said. Did she say why she needed it?"

"Something about something she'd seen. She wouldn't say much, she was garbling. But I got the impression she'd witnessed a crime and was scared she'd be on some sort of hit list."

Olivia. It had to be. "Did she... did she give a name?"

Zoe held her breath. If Olivia had any sense, she'd give a false name. Zoe hadn't told her that she suspected the organised crime boss Myron Carter had allies within Cumbria Police, but an intelligent woman like Olivia Bagsby would have worked it out for herself. And now Olivia had met up with David Randle, she'd know all there was to know about corrupt police.

"Said her name was Jackie. Wouldn't give a surname, though."

Zoe tensed. "Jackie?" That meant nothing. "What did she look like?"

"Tall woman, blonde hair, but you could see the roots. Grey-brown. Clothes looked like they'd been smart once, but now... well, they were a bit worse for wear."

Zoe nodded. Olivia hadn't been blonde, and she hadn't been all that tall, not the one time Zoe had met her. But memory could be deceptive. "What did she say?"

"Not much. Just kept asking about protection. Said she needed to be safe. Then she bolted before I could get any more out of her."

Zoe rubbed her forehead. "Did she leave anything? A number, an address?"

"Nothing. Just... Hang on."

He led her out of the room and back to the front desk, where he tapped on his computer keyboard. "I thought she might have given a surname too, but I wasn't sure if it was her surname or someone else's."

"Go on."

He sniffed. "Kelvin."

"Kelvin?"

"Yeah. Mean anything?"

Zoe felt her body droop. She'd heard the name Kelvin, alright. But it had nothing to do with Olivia Bagsby.

"Thanks, PS Coombs. You've been very helpful."

"I'll let you know if she comes back."

"Thanks. I'm sure you will."

She left the police station, dragging her feet.

So it wasn't Olivia Bagsby.

But the name. *Kelvin.*

She shook her head, pulling out her phone as she climbed into her green Mini. This might not be the breakthrough she'd been hoping for in her own pursuit of organised crime in Cumbria, but she had a pretty good idea her old Lesley would want to hear about it.

CHAPTER FIFTY-TWO

MIKE PULLED into the car park at Wareham Golf Club, taking in the neat rows of cars and the well-kept grounds. The place had a certain charm, even if golf wasn't his thing. But it would be a long time before Louis and Daisy allowed Mike to get half an hour to himself for anything, let alone a full round of golf.

He spotted the sarge outside the clubhouse, giving him a little wave. The former DS looked relaxed, but Mike knew better than to assume that meant he was taking it easy.

"Mike," Dennis greeted him as he approached. "Good to see you."

"Sarge. Thanks for meeting me." Mike took the sarge's outstretched hand and shook it.

Dennis held onto his hand, giving him a look. Mike laughed, uneasy. "Dennis. I can't get used to it."

The sarge dropped his hand. "You will. Just like I am."

Mike raised an eyebrow; the sarge bringing him here in pursuit of a lead didn't exactly feel like accepting retirement.

"Thanks for helping us with this," he said as they entered the clubhouse.

"Not at all. Any excuse to get out of the house." Dennis led him into a spacious restaurant where he walked to a table by the window. His trademark tweed jacket was already hung over the back of the chair. Mike smiled. *Some things never change.*

Mike sat down, looking around. The view was impressive, with the course stretching out into the distance, framed by trees. A few golfers were out, taking advantage of the clear weather.

"Nice spot," he said.

"It is. Helps me clear my head."

A waitress appeared, and Mike ordered a coffee. Dennis gestured to the menu. "You eaten? The sandwiches here aren't bad."

"I'm fine, thanks Sa... Dennis." Mike shifted in his seat. Nice as it was to see the sarge again, this wasn't a social call.

"Can I have a Belgian bun please, Sapphie," Dennis said. Mike raised an eyebrow. He'd never seen Dennis this at ease.

After a moment's silence while they gazed out at the green, Mike leaned back in his chair. "So, you mentioned you'd overheard something? Relating to the Rowena Sharp case?"

Dennis looked over towards the bar where the young woman was making their drinks. He nodded. "I was here the other day, playing a round with Fred. We were in the bar afterwards, and I couldn't help but overhear a group of blokes talking."

Mike smiled. *Couldn't help but overhear.* Dennis would always be a copper, retirement or not.

"What were they talking about?"

"Rowena Sharp."

Mike straightened. "Go on."

"They were talking about her disappearance. One of them used another one's name. Peter."

Mike licked his lips. "Peter Didson?"

Dennis nodded. "I had no way of knowing. But..." He glanced over at the bar again, lowering his voice. "They keep the visitor's book out on the reception desk. Not digitised yet, fortunately. I managed to distract Clara on reception and swiped it, just temporarily of course. Took a few photos."

Mike couldn't hide his amusement. "You nicked it?"

Irritation crossed Dennis's face. "Borrowed. It was back on that desk within five minutes. Anyway, I didn't take the time to look at any names while I had it, but I checked once I had the photos loaded on my phone."

Mike frowned, wondering what Dennis meant by *loaded on my phone*. "And?"

"I checked the names from the day I was here with Fred. One of them was Peter Didson."

Mike felt warmth spread through his chest. *At last.* "You're sure?"

"Positive. I might be retired, but I haven't lost my touch."

The waitress returned with Dennis's bun and two coffees.

"Since when did you drink coffee?" Mike asked.

"It keeps me sharp. Only before lunchtime, though, or I don't sleep."

Mike wondered what it was like to contemplate a full night's sleep, caffeine or no. "So I don't suppose your visitors' book requires people to add their address?"

"Unfortunately not. But it does include a space for your home-town. Optional, of course, but he wrote in it."

Mike was about to sip his coffee, but stopped with it halfway to his mouth. "And?"

"It seems your Peter Didson is local. Well, local-ish. Lives in Osmington, just outside Weymouth."

CHAPTER FIFTY-THREE

LESLEY SAT AT HER DESK, savouring the quiet, broken only by the muffled hum of vehicles coming and going beneath her window. She'd been given an office that looked out over the gated area where squad cars were housed, and liked to watch them coming and going; there was something hypnotic about it.

She sipped her coffee – a Colombian blend, she'd had a machine installed in her new office – and stared at her notes on Rowena Sharp and Jackie Kendall. The cases were tangled, each thread pulling in different directions. Was the estate agency link relevant? Or was it pure coincidence, and the only connection between the two cases was actually her?

Her phone buzzed. She picked it up: Zoe Finch.

"Zoe," she answered, leaning back in her chair. "How's things in Cumbria?"

"Oh, the usual. Chilly, bleak, beautiful."

Lesley gazed out of the window. It was over thirty degrees here, the sun blazing in a sky so blue it was almost white. She couldn't imagine anywhere in England being chilly in late June.

"You don't normally call at this time of day," she said.

"This isn't a social call."

Lesley straightened in her chair, almost knocking over her cup. "Oh?"

"We had a walk-in yesterday. Workington nick. I thought it was Olivia Bagsby."

"You've still not found her?"

Lesley had helped Zoe in her hunt for the elusive Olivia. To no avail, it seemed.

"No, and it wasn't her this time either. But it was someone I think you might be after."

Lesley frowned. "Who?"

"She gave her name as Jackie. She mentioned the Kelvins. I did a quick search on current cases in Dorset and came across Jackie Kendall. Is she still missing?"

"She went missing almost a year ago. You've got her now?"

"Sorry. She buggered off again. But I wanted to let you know, she's here."

"And she's alive." Lesley tapped her biro against the desk, feeling a mix of relief and frustration. "What has she said about the Kelvins?"

"That's the thing, I don't know. She walked into the station, spoke to the duty sergeant, and then left. He told me she mentioned the name Kelvin and said she was called Jackie. But that's all I've got."

"You think she might come back?"

"I've got no idea. Sorry I can't be more help."

"Well, you've confirmed for me that we're not running a murder inquiry anymore, so that's helpful."

"Why did she leave Dorset?"

"No one knows, not even her partner. But she was acting strangely after taking on the sale of a property which belonged to the Kelvins, or one of their businesses. She's an estate agent. Was." Lesley frowned. "I don't suppose she could be working for a firm up there?"

"Not by the way she was dressed."

"Hmm."

"So the Kelvins are still active? I thought you'd got rid of them."

Lesley sighed. "It seems not. Look, I'm going to have to send someone up to Cumbria. See if we can track Jackie down. If she reappears, tell me immediately, yes?"

"Of course. It'll be good to see you."

Lesley smiled. "Oh, I'm driving a desk these days. I don't think it'll be me."

"Still..."

Lesley gazed out of the window. Watching the cars coming and going was one thing, overseeing whatever was going on between her two DIs another. But this was becoming an inter-force operation. It needed a senior officer.

"I'll be in touch, Zoe. Thanks for letting me know."

CHAPTER FIFTY-FOUR

Jill parked the car outside Peter Didson's house, a modest bungalow on the edge of Osmington. It had taken them half an hour to drive just nine miles, holiday traffic heavy on the A352. Parked in the driveway was a blue Toyota that looked like it hadn't been washed in years. The garden was overgrown, weeds creeping over the path leading to the front door.

Mike wrinkled his nose. "Doesn't look like he's expecting visitors."

"Let's see what he has to say," Jill replied, stepping out of the car.

They approached the door, and Jill knocked firmly. After a moment, it opened, revealing a man in his seventies. He looked them up and down, suspicion etched on his face.

"Mr Didson?" Jill asked.

"That's me. What do you want?"

She gave him a smile she hoped was reassuring. "I'm DI Jill Scott, and this is DC Mike Legg. We're from Dorset Police." She looked past him to see if there was anyone else in the house, but there was no sign of another person. "We'd like to ask you a few questions about Rowena Sharp."

His expression shifted, a flicker of something – recognition, maybe – crossing his features. "Rowena Sharp? Is that the woman whose body you found in Poole Harbour?" He frowned, shaking his head. "Nasty business."

Jill felt Mike tense beside her. She twisted her hand in his direction: *leave it.*

"We have reason to believe you knew her. That you might have been in contact with her around the time she disappeared."

Didson looked past her into the street, then turned to look along the way they'd come. He looked back at Jill and held her gaze for a long moment. She watched as he took her in.

You bastard. He was trying to judge whether he could lie.

She sighed. *I can wait it out.*

At last his features settled into what looked like resignation. "I knew her, yes. Come in."

He stood back and gestured for them to pass him, then closed the door behind him. Inside, the house was cluttered but clean. Peter led them to a small living room, waving for them to sit on the worn sofa. He remained on his feet, standing stiffly by the door like he might bolt at any moment.

Jill looked up at him. "Take a seat, please, Mr Didson."

"I have back pain." He rubbed his back. "Better off standing, if you don't mind."

She exchanged a glance with Mike, who shifted forward in his seat. Didson was forty years older than him, at least. If he tried to run, he wasn't getting far.

Jill looked up at Peter. "Can you tell us how you knew Rowena?"

"It was a long time ago."

"1973."

He shook his head. "1972, that's when we met. We... we were colleagues, of a sort. She worked for an estate agent in Worthing, I was at Hammond's in Boscombe. We met on a training course run by Locke & Co. The firms had an arrangement, sharing resources, training each other's new recruits. That was me and Rowena. She'd come over to Poole, I'd go over there. We learned the job together."

"And you became friends?"

"I know what you're getting at."

She raised her eyebrows, saying nothing.

"I was in a relationship with Rowena. I loved her."

"Did you know she was married? That she had a baby girl?"

He frowned. "That's hardly a crime. Yes, yes I knew about Donald and Ellie. But she was miserable. She was going to leave him. We had plans. Move to London, where no one would know us. It was the early seventies, Detective. Donald would have had no interest in seeking out his baby daughter. We could have started again." He sighed.

"But you didn't," Mike said.

Peter let out a short laugh. "July 1973. She was in Dorset for a family holiday, although really I thought it was an excuse to spend time with me." He looked from Jill to Mike. "She'd quit by that point, you see. No excuse to see each other."

This was news to Jill; no one had said anything about Rowena quitting the firm. Had she lied to Didson about it?

"She was staying at the Sandbanks Hotel," Jill said.

He shrugged. "She didn't tell me where she was staying. Didn't trust me not to go there and confront her. Or have it out with Donald. Cold fish that he was."

"Why would you confront her?" Mike asked.

"Because she dumped me. Told me it was over. She didn't want to wreck her baby's life, as she put it. My theory was that Donald had found out and threatened her in some way."

"Was he violent towards her?" Jill asked.

"No. Oh no, he wasn't capable of that. Violence requires emotion, you see. But she told me that I had to let her go. That I shouldn't try and trace her." He slumped back against the door, which shifted under his weight. He put a hand out behind him to catch his balance.

"Did you?" Mike asked.

"Did I what?"

"Try and make contact with her."

Didson narrowed his eyes. "I know what you think of me. Having an affair with a married woman, and one with a baby, too. But it wasn't like that. I loved Rowena. I respected her. I... I wouldn't want to put her at risk. So I moved away."

"You moved?" Jill asked.

He nodded. "It was a Saturday, when she told me it was over. On the Monday morning I resigned. I had holiday owing me so I didn't even have to work my notice. I got on a train to Bristol and never looked back."

"Not London?" Mike said.

Peter's face dropped. "No. That would have been too..." He shuddered.

Jill looked at him. "What date was it? The night she told you it was over?"

He frowned. "The twenty-first of July. A date that will always be etched in my mind. I never married, Detective. Never had children. It was like my life ended that night. And now... now you've found her body. Was she in the water for long?"

Mike coughed. "You don't know?"

Peter looked at him. "Don't know what?"

Jill stood up. "Mr Didson, Rowena's body has been in the harbour for a very, very long time. We haven't ascertained the exact timings yet, but we believe it was decades."

He paled. "Decades?"

"She went missing on the night of the twenty-first of July, 1973. After she spoke to you."

His eyes widened. "No."

Jill glanced at Mike. She looked back at Didson. "So you're telling us you didn't know."

"Know what?"

"We believe that Rowena died that night. The night you say she dumped you. You were the last person to see her alive."

He grabbed hold of the door handle. Mike took a step forward, but Jill frowned to stop him.

Peter looked up at them. "She's been dead for fifty years?"

"Fifty-two," said Mike.

Peter swallowed. He gave out a hoarse sound, like a strangled sob. "My God." He looked up at them. "I had no idea."

CHAPTER FIFTY-FIVE

KATIE SAT in the passenger seat, staring out at the Dorset countryside as it blurred past. Stanley was driving, which irritated her. He was just that bit too slow for her liking.

"You alright, Katie?" Stanley cocked his head. "You've been quiet."

"I'm fine." She shifted in her seat, not happy that he'd noticed. "Just impatient to get on with it."

He smirked, turning back to the road. Did he know what she'd been thinking?

"Here we are." Stanley was parking by the side of the road, a few doors up from Ellie Sharp's flat. *At last.*

Katie pushed open the passenger door and was outside Ellie's building in moments. She tried to resist looking at her watch as she waited for Stanley to lock the car and join her.

"She's not going anywhere, you know," he said as he joined her at the front door.

She shrugged. "Maybe she is."

Stanley shook his head and pressed the buzzer. Katie had already done it before he arrived but she wasn't about to tell him.

The door buzzed and she pushed it open. Stanley followed her up the stairs. Ellie's door was already open. Was that wise, given that she was associated with a murder inquiry? She hadn't asked who was at the door before buzzing them up.

Focus, Katie told herself. This was what she did; noticed too much, commented on too much. She needed to filter out the stuff that wasn't important.

Ellie Sharp was in the doorway. She smiled as she recognised them.

"Oh, hello," she said. "Come in. Please."

Inside, Sebastian was sitting on the sofa. He gave them a nod. Katie exchanged a look with Stanley: *that saves a trip.*

Ellie hovered by the door. "Can I get you anything? Tea, coffee?"

Katie wrinkled her nose, making Ellie's smile drop. Stanley cleared his throat and Katie adopted a more neutral expression. This place didn't smell great, though. Stale takeaway curry?

"Tea for me, please," said Stanley. "The strongest coffee you can make for Katie here." He smiled, and Ellie smiled back. Katie stiffened. So he'd been paying attention.

She blew out a slow breath, trying to regain her composure. She looked at Sebastian, who was still on the sofa, flicking through screens on his phone. He yawned.

"Here you are." Ellie placed two mugs on the coffee table and went away to bring in two more; one for herself, one for Sebastian. She sat on the sofa next to her brother and gestured for the two detectives to sit as well.

Katie cast around, then chose an upright chair near the window. It gave her a good vantage point. Stanley took an armchair that looked vintage.

"So," Stanley began, as Katie gulped her coffee then winced at the heat. "We wanted to update you on the case. We've managed to trace Peter. From the letters."

"You have?" Ellie looked wary. Katie wondered if she'd ever really wanted to find her mother's former lover.

Stanley nodded. "He's local. Lives in Osmington. That's just this side—"

"... of Weymouth. I know it. Near the White Horse."

"That's the one."

"Shit," muttered Sebastian. He put a hand on his sister's knee. "You OK, Els?"

She swallowed. "Yeah." She looked at Katie. "Can I meet him?"

Katie felt her face stiffen. "Er... I don't think that would be appropriate. Not while—"

"No. You're right. If he killed her, then talking to me would just compromise your investigation, wouldn't it?"

Katie narrowed her eyes. The last time she'd seen Ellie, the woman had been distraught. Where did this matter-of-factness come from?

"Our colleagues have gone to see him," Stanley said. "They'll be asking him about his relationship with your mother. About his movements in the days around her disappearance."

Ellie looked at him. "Her murder, you mean."

Katie held out a hand. "I don't think..."

What was it she didn't think? Did she not think Rowena was murdered? Did she not think Peter had done it? She wasn't sure.

She gulped down a slurp of coffee and almost spilt it.

Stanley gave her a look. Stanley had never looked at her like that. It was normally her giving him the *what are you doing, you idiot?* look.

Was she difficult to work with?

She tensed her jaw. *Stop it. Let him lead. Observe.*

"Is there anything else you've remembered?" Stanley asked Ellie. "Anything that's come to mind since you last spoke to the police? It doesn't matter how small it is and—"

"Actually, yes. I've found something." Ellie glanced at Sebastian, then stood up.

She disappeared, returning with an envelope. "It's a sympathy card. From Peter Didson, to my dad."

Katie took a pair of gloves from her pocket and reached out for the card, careful not to touch it. "A sympathy card?"

"Yeah. They held a memorial service for Mum a year after she disappeared. After the court case against Dad ended. He'd accepted she was probably dead by then."

"You don't remember it?" Stanley asked.

Ellie shook her head. "I was a toddler. Not allowed to go. My auntie Maureen told me about it, years later."

Katie slipped the card into an evidence bag. "Thanks, Ellie. This could be important."

"Anything else?" Stanley asked.

Ellie shook her head. She looked at Sebastian, who followed suit.

"No," he said. "It was all years before I was born. And the aunt was Ellie's on her mum's side, she died in the nineties. My family weren't involved in the service."

Damn. That would be someone to follow up with, if she'd still been alive.

"Only our dad attended." Ellie's voice sounded strained. "None of his family."

Stanley cocked his head. "Do you know why not?"

She shook her head. "They... well, they weren't kind to him, after the court case. He was exonerated under the law, but not in the eyes of my grandmother. They never spoke again."

Katie nodded, wondering what it must be like to grow up without a family. Her mother dead, and her father's family estranged. *Poor woman.* No wonder she looked wrung out.

"Thanks for your time," Stanley said. "And for this." He gestured at the evidence bag Katie was holding. She nodded, afraid of yawning again if she spoke.

They left the flat, heading back to the car. Katie slid into the passenger seat, holding the evidence bag.

"You sure you're alright?" he asked. "You were weird in there."

She leaned back. "Sorry, Stan. I'm just... did you believe her?"

"About what?"

"The card? It suddenly turning up like that. And when we told her we'd found Peter, did you see her face?"

He indicated to pull out of the parking space. "What about it?"

"Her expression changed, just for a moment. So briefly that it was like she was trying to hide it."

"You sure?"

She nodded. "She looked... excited."

Stanley grunted. "But a sympathy card," he said. "What kind of bloke sends that to the husband of a woman he had an affair with?"

Katie wrinkled her nose. "Not to mention a woman who he might have been the last person to see."

"Yeah."

She stared out of the window. The two of them drove in silence, reaching County Gates Gyratory before she broke the silence.

"A man with a guilty conscience, maybe."

Stanley leaned back. "Or someone who wanted to rub it in."

She nodded. "Either way, it tells us something about him. I think."

She lapsed into silence again, a thought occurring to her as they crawled through the rush-hour traffic alongside the Tesco on Poole Road. She should have told him to take Lindsay Road instead, it was more convoluted but quicker.

"How did he know?" she said.

Stanley was focused on the road, trying to keep up with every slight movement in the traffic. "Huh?"

She straightened in her seat. "Who told him?"

"Peter?"

She nodded. "He clearly knew Rowena was dead, or he wouldn't have sent the card."

"There was a court case."

"That's true. But how did he know about the memorial service? There's no way Donald would have told him."

Stanley looked at her. "You're right. How would he have known?"

Katie allowed herself to disappear into her thoughts, lulled by the movement of the car as they left the traffic behind on the A35.

"We need to find out who told him," she said. "It can only be someone connected to her. And that person might know something."

CHAPTER FIFTY-SIX

LESLEY SAT ON THE SOFA, a half-empty glass of wine in hand. The living room was becoming even more homely. Elsa had bought yet more cushions, and Lesley had to admit they added warmth. And then there was the added bonus of balling them up behind her back when it was aching from too long spent sitting at a desk.

Elsa sat beside her, flipping through case files on her laptop. They'd enjoyed the leftovers of last night's Chinese takeaway, and the air of quiet celebration was lingering.

"You're quiet tonight," Elsa said, stroking her hand with a forefinger.

Lesley took a sip of wine. "Just thinking."

"About?"

"Johnny Chiles."

Elsa put the laptop to one side. "What about him?"

"He's coming back to Dorset Police."

Elsa's finger stopped moving. "What? But he went to the Met, didn't he? I thought..."

Lesley sighed. "You thought right. He went to the Met because Arthur Kelvin was blackmailing him. He'd forced Johnny's brother to act as a drugs pusher because he was in hock to the man. Yes. I know it sounds awful, and I know I should have told Carpenter at the time; but—"

"But he was vulnerable. You wanted to protect him."

Lesley nodded. She placed her glass on the table. "Johnny's not a bad man, Els. He's not corrupt. He just got very, very unlucky."

"Isn't that what everyone says, when they've done something terrible?"

Lesley looked at her. She was right. Elsa would have had a hundred clients telling her they'd just had a run of bad luck. She'd known of bent coppers who'd made the same excuse.

Was Johnny really any different?

"I thought you didn't want him back," Elsa said, her voice gentle, like she was trying to calm a bear.

"I didn't. I don't." Lesley shook her head. "Carpenter's decided it's happening. And I haven't exactly been honest with him."

"You didn't tell him?"

"I didn't."

"Who knows?"

"Dennis. Just Dennis. Johnny spoke to him, asked him to intervene, help him secure a transfer back. It seems he spoke to Carpenter."

"Dennis did?" Elsa looked incredulous. "Surely that's overstepping the mark."

Lesley scratched her forehead. "It's just Dennis, Els. He's loyal. He wants to help Johnny. The two of them... well, they go back a bloody long way. Worked together for years before I appeared here."

"That doesn't matter, though. Surely?"

"I don't know. Dennis has retired now, so if Johnny comes back..."

"Yes?"

"It means I'm the only person who knows what he did." She turned to her wife. "Have I made a huge mistake?"

Elsa's expression softened. "Why didn't you tell Carpenter, at the time?"

"Because it would've ruined Johnny's career. And Dennis... he vouched for him. Said Johnny was a good officer, just caught in a bad situation."

"You trusted Dennis's judgement?"

Lesley nodded. "I did. I still do. But I'm not sure I can trust Johnny."

Elsa leaned back. "So..." She raised her arms and placed her hands behind her head. "You have two choices."

Lesley nodded. "Come clean or do nothing."

Elsa looked at her. "Or you can tell Johnny he needs to come clean."

"That amounts to the same thing as me telling Carpenter. I'm not going to let Johnny – Dennis, even – take the fall for this without me getting at least some of the shit."

Elsa rotated her head, stretching out her neck muscles. "What difference will it make, if you tell Carpenter?"

"Johnny's career will be over. Possibly mine too."

"Dennis's pension?"

Lesley felt a chill grip her chest. "I don't know." Shit. She couldn't do that to Dennis. She shook her head. "I can't tell him."

Elsa nodded. "I'm the last person to advise you on this, after the things I did at my old firm."

Lesley considered. Elsa had been a partner at Nevin, Cross and Short, Arthur Kelvin's solicitors. She'd represented him in his legal businesses and his not-so-legal ones. But she'd found a way out. She'd managed to slide away from the firm without putting herself at risk.

This was different. No one's life was at risk here.

"It's not the same," Lesley said. "I know how scared you were, back then."

Elsa stroked her face. "I know how it feels, though. Professional death, or the threat of it, can feel like real death."

Lesley swallowed. Was she right?

"So you think I should let Johnny come back, despite my misgivings?"

A shrug. "It's that, or risk yourself and Dennis. But only you can decide. You have to go with your conscience."

"Thanks."

Elsa pulled Lesley in for a hug. "I'm not being much help, I know."

No, you're not. But Lesley wasn't about to say that out loud.

CHAPTER FIFTY-SEVEN

ELLIE SAT at the kitchen table, her fingers tracing the photo of the sympathy card on her phone. She'd given the card itself to those detectives, and the notebook with those letters, and now the photos were all she had left of her mother.

Not to mention...

Peter. Her mother's lover. They'd met before she was born, in the summer of 1972.

Ellie had been born in March 1973.

Which meant...

Sebastian was standing with his back to her, frying sausages for their tea. He looked round. "You alright, Ellie?"

She shook her head. "I was only a baby when Mum went missing." She jabbed at her phone. "She'd met Peter Didson the summer before. What if...?"

He put the spatula down. "What if what, Els?"

She licked her lips, the skin of her face feeling tight. "What if Peter Didson is my father, Sebbie?"

Sebastian leaned against the counter. He scoffed. "Don't be daft, El."

"Mum was having an affair with him. From the summer before I was born, up to the summer after." She looked into her brother's eyes. "I was born in March, which meant I was conceived in June the previous year." She frowned. "It would fit."

Sebastian turned to switch the hob off, then sat down beside her. He grabbed her hands and held them in his own. "Ellie, you're a Sharp. You've always been a Sharp."

She looked at him. "Maybe I'm not."

He sighed. "Look. Even if that bloke's sperm made you, it doesn't make him your dad. Our dad was the one who brought you up. He was the one who—"

"He never looked at me the same, Sebastian."

"Sebastian? Since when did you start calling me that?" He laughed. "Oh no, Els. Now you've decided I might not be your brother by blood, don't go getting all formal on me."

She forced a smile. "I need to speak to him."

He shook his head. "That's daft. Look, Els, this guy is irrelevant. Genes or no, our dad is your dad. Was. Donald."

She looked at him. Had he never noticed? "Verity hated me. Maybe she knew."

'Knew what?"

"That I was the cuckoo in the nest. An impostor."

"What? Don't be daft." He grabbed her shoulders and pulled her towards him, giving her a hug she didn't return. "Stop thinking like this, Els. This is your family. Me. Our various weird aunts and uncles. It's been your family for over fifty years. Surely you don't—"

"I want to see him." She pulled out of his grip. Suddenly she felt old.

To reach the age of fifty-two, and only then learn who your father is.

"I don't think that's a good idea," Sebastian said.

She looked at him. "Where was it they said he lived?"

"I don't think..."

"Osmington. That was it, wasn't it? It's not a big place." She stood up. "I'll finish the sausages. You're good on Google. Find him for me. Please?"

He slumped back in his chair.

"Sebbie, if you don't help me with this, I'll do it on my own. Do you want me to go and find the man who was the last to see my mother alive alone?"

"No."

"Thank you." She turned her back on him and started stirring the sausages, aware she was manipulating him. But she had to learn the truth.

After a few moments, the sausages were done. She grabbed some bread from the bread bin, ignoring the fact it was going stale, and sliced the sausages in half lengthways to make sandwiches.

She plonked two plates down on the table. "Here. Have you found him yet?"

"Yes." Sebastian sounded resigned.

"Good. Let's eat these, then head over there."

"I think it can wait unti—"

She looked up. "He ran once, Sebbie. Let's not wait for him to run again."

CHAPTER FIFTY-EIGHT

MIKE SAT ON THE SOFA, cradling a mug of lukewarm tea. The house was quiet, save for the occasional creak from upstairs. Tina was up there, responding to a call from Louis about ten minutes ago. He was going through a phase where he kept changing his mind about which soft toys he wanted in bed with him; sometimes it could take half an hour to get it right. Mike was convinced it was a delaying tactic to put bedtime back.

The door opened and closed softly. Tina appeared in the doorway, her expression tired but relieved.

"Kids settled?" he asked.

"Yeah, we plumped for three squish mallows and Mr Bear in the end."

"Good old Mr Bear." Mr Bear was a toy Annie had bought for Daisy while Tina had been pregnant, but that Louis had taken a shine to. His little sister would never know that the beloved Mr Bear, with his missing ear, had originally been intended for her.

Tina dropped onto the sofa next to him. "Not watching TV?"

"It's all crap at this time of night. And I didn't want to disturb you."

She glanced towards the ceiling. "Don't worry. Daisy has her white noise, it drowns anything out. And Louis is in his lovely new bedroom." She rubbed Mike's leg. "Well done on getting that finished."

"Took me long enough."

"It did, but you got it done in the end." She smirked. "Not without a few mishaps, mind."

Mike tensed. After the fiasco that had been splitting their bedroom in half to provide space for Daisy, he was never doing DIY again.

She leaned back, rubbing her temples. "How's the case going?"

Mike took a sip of his tea. "OK. Not sure about the two teams, though."

She raised an eyebrow. "That DS Strunk's an odd one. He was mates with Collingwood, did you know?"

"Yeah. But he's on the level, T. Seems OK. Bit more up to date than DS Frampton, too."

"That wouldn't be hard. Anyway, you haven't got to work with him. You're effectively the DS in your team, what with you having DI Scott and a bunch of DCs."

"I'm just one of the grunts."

She turned to him, her brow furrowed. "You're not a grunt, Mike. You're more experienced than Stanley or Katie, and Jill knows it. I've seen how she relies on you."

"Really?" He wasn't sure he'd witnessed that.

Tina nodded. She leaned forward and picked up the remote, idly flicking through Netflix. "How's the case going, anyway? Any closer to working out what happened to Rowena?"

"Possibly. We interviewed Peter Didson today."

Tina's eyes narrowed. "The estate agent? The one who was involved with her?"

"Yeah. He claims he didn't know she was dead until the reports came out."

Tina coughed. "Really? And you believe him?"

Mike shrugged. "He seemed genuine. Said he moved away after she dumped him. Lived in Bristol for a bit, got married, then came back here eventually."

"Convenient," Tina muttered. "Have you considered he might be lying?"

Mike thought of Didson's reaction when they'd arrived at his doorstep. It had seemed genuine enough. "Well, yeah. But why would he come back here if he had something to hide?"

"Maybe he thinks it's the last place anyone would look. Hide in plain sight, and all that. Or maybe he felt some kind of compunction to come back here now that Rowena's been found."

Mike shook his head. "He's been back here for a few years. Long before she turned up."

Tina sniffed. "Still. Sounds off to me."

Mike looked at his wife. Why didn't he have her instincts? "It's possible. But if he didn't know she was dead, he couldn't have killed her. And I watched his face when we told him the news. He... he seemed shocked."

"Could just be that he's a very good actor," Tina pointed out. "Or maybe he had someone else do it."

Mike rubbed his temples. It wasn't that kind of crime. Or at least, he didn't think it was. "We'll be checking his story. Katie and Stan have gone to see Ellie Sharp; maybe she'll remember him."

"She was what, four months old?"

He felt his body deflate. "Yeah." Ellie wouldn't remember a thing.

Tina finally settled on a programme: *Squid Game*. "You OK watching this?"

"It's a bit gruesome."

"Too much, with you dealing with a fifty-year-old corpse?"

"No." He swallowed. "No. Stick it on. It'll distract me."

After ten minutes of gratuitous violence, Tina turned to him. "Ellie might know something about her dad. You told me that Geoffrey Locke accused Donald Sharp of killing Rowena."

Mike shook his head. "He wasn't exactly coherent; dementia, I assume. I wouldn't give what he said too much weight."

She pursed her lips. "What about her notebook, the letters? Any mention of Donald?"

Mike shook his head. "Not directly. But it does suggest Rowena was planning to leave him."

Tina sighed. "That could be a motive for Donald."

Mike shook his head. "We've got a receipt from the original evidence store. Donald went to Worthing that night. The baby-listening service said he was out from 11 pm to 6 am. It would have taken him—"

"Two hours each way."

"Longer. There was no M27 in those days."

She sniffed. "True. But why did he go to Worthing?"

Mike shrugged. "That's where they lived. Maybe after the argument, he decided to go home."

"Then changed his mind." Tina paused the TV and turned to him. Mike smiled, remembering how she'd been when she was on maternity leave with Louis. She'd dragged him into Wareham and started questioning people in the Chipperies about a piece of evidence that had been left with Arthur Kelvin's body.

Arthur Kelvin.

He inhaled. "I was talking to Meera earlier. They reckon the Kelvins might be involved in the Jackie Kendall case."

"I thought that wasn't being reopened."

"They've still got a few more days to find something that'll justify it being reopened."

"And a link to the Kelvins would certainly do that. But they're off the scene now, aren't they? That Birmingham gang have been moving into their territory."

"They weren't big enough. Looks like Vera's firing up the Kelvin operations again. Or at least, buying and selling property."

"Which isn't the same thing."

Mike looked at his wife. "The Kelvins don't do anything without there being something dodgy going on."

"Even selling a house. So was Jackie their estate agent?"

"Looks like it."

Tina blew out her cheeks. "If she knew something..."

"Yeah." Mike placed his hands between his thighs. Poor woman.

"Let's just hope she simply decided she wanted a change of scene," Tina said.

"Yeah. Or that if it was because of the Kelvins, they don't find her."

CHAPTER FIFTY-NINE

MAY 1972

Rowena Sharp stepped into the Locke & Co office in Poole, smoothing down her shirt dress. The fabric clung to her, a brown and orange floral pattern that she knew suited her. She'd dressed to impress, even if it was just a training course.

The open-plan office, nothing like the offices she'd worked in before, buzzed with activity. Phones rang, and voices murmured in low tones. The air smelled of fresh coffee and the faint tang of cigarette smoke. The side wall was papered in a bold, psychedelic palette, with geometric patterns that were bang up to date.

At the rear was a group of low chairs, each upholstered in an olive velvet that reminded her of the chairs she'd been coveting for her own house. In one of them was a young man, around her age. He was tall, with dark hair framing a round face. His skin was smooth, unlike most of the men around her.

She took in his blue suit with wide lapels and flared trousers. She smiled, pleased she'd made an effort if this was what people in this office dressed like.

He stood up, smiling at her. His eyes were large and dark and his expression intense. She swallowed.

"You must be Rowena. Rowena Lansbury?"

She almost corrected him, then remembered she'd chosen to use her maiden name when she joined the firm. It was what all the modern women were doing.

"Yes, that's me."

"Peter Didson." He extended a hand. "I'm in training, too."

She shook his hand, noting the firm grip. "Nice to meet you."

He looked her up and down, not bothering to hide it. She found herself torn between wanting to cover herself up and wanting to expose herself to his stare.

Donald never looked at her like that.

"Shall we?" He gestured towards a group that was gathering in a side room separated from them by a glass partition. The room had large pot plants in each corner, the terracotta neatly matching the colour of the walls.

They joined the others, and Rowena listened as the course leader introduced himself. She barely registered his name, too aware of Peter sitting beside her.

"So, where are you based?" Peter asked, leaning in slightly.

"Worthing. What about you?"

"Sandbanks, I found myself a studio a couple of streets back from the sea. Bit of a commute to the office in Boscombe, but worth it for the location."

She nodded. "I've heard it's beautiful."

He looked into her eyes. "You should visit sometime."

She smiled, aware that her mouth was dry. "Maybe I will."

The course leader turned on an overhead projector and started going over the agenda for the day, but Rowena couldn't concentrate. She couldn't shake off Peter's presence, the way he occasionally glanced at her.

"Have you been with Locke & Co long?" he asked during a break.

She shook her head. "Hitchin & Son. They're a partner to Locke & Co. Based in Worthing. Four months. You?"

He nodded, his eyes not leaving hers. "Just over two. I was in London before. Needed a change of pace."

"London's a bit much, isn't it?"

He laughed. "You could say that. And you? How do you find Worthing?"

"It's... quiet."

"Not a fan of quiet?"

"Not really."

He grinned. "Then you'll like Bournemouth. I'll take you to Le Cardinal sometime."

"What's that?"

"Only the hottest nightclub in town. You'll love it."

She found herself grinning. She would be on this course for three days, staying in a guest house near the pier. "I might have to take you up on that."

The course leader cleared his throat, and Rowena forced herself to focus. But her mind kept drifting back to Peter. The way he looked at her. The way she knew she shouldn't look back.

As the day drew to a close, Peter caught up with her as she gathered her things.

"Heading back to Worthing tonight?"

She shook her head. "I'm here for the next three days."

He raised an eyebrow. "Really? Where are you staying?"

"The Ocean View. In..."

She stopped herself. Telling a strange man where she was staying probably wasn't ladylike.

But then, nor was the way her blood was rising to her face.

"In Boscombe," he said. "That's where they always put people up." A pause. "Near my office."

She licked her lips, feeling awkward. "Anyway, it's been lovely to meet you. I really should head over there now."

He nodded. "Do you have a lift?"

"Sorry?"

"Have they booked you a taxi, or do you need a ride?"

Rowena felt her stomach clench. "They've... yes... they've made all the arrangements. Thanks."

He narrowed his eyes at her. "Where is it, then?"

"Sorry?"

"Your cab?"

They were standing in the road outside Locke & Co. There were no cars driving their way and only a few parked, two of which were delivery vans.

"I'm sure it'll be along soon," she said.

"I'd be happy to offer you a lift."

"Thank you. You're very kind."

He shrugged. "Well, it's your shout. Good to meet you." He put out his hand.

Reluctantly, she shook it. He tipped his forehead and then turned away from her.

Rowena watched him walk away. He stopped at a mustard Ford Capri about two hundred yards away.

She'd never been driven in a Capri. Donald had a Princess, dull old thing.

"Err!" she called, just as he opened the driver's door and bent down to get inside. He stopped and looked back at her. She felt her stomach lurch.

She waved.

"Sorry!"

He closed the door, walking back towards her. "Are you alright?"

"Yes." She was out of breath, despite not having taken a step. "Can I ask for that lift, after all?"

CHAPTER SIXTY

JUNE 2025

LESLEY CLUTCHED her phone as she stared out of the window towards the car park, a sense of relief washing over her.

"Zoe, that's brilliant. Thank you."

"You'd better get up here quick, though," Zoe replied. "If she wants to disappear again, I'm not sure I can stop her."

Lesley checked her watch. "Give me half an hour, then I'll have a time. But you can expect me later this afternoon."

"Looking forward to it."

"And thanks again. I don't know how you managed it, but I'm proud of you."

"Only doing my job."

Not entirely true, Lesley thought. It wasn't Zoe's job to help Dorset Police when they weren't getting results themselves.

But it hadn't been the fault of anyone in Dorset that Jackie Kendall had run off to Cumbria, and perhaps it was only the personal connection that meant she was within their grasp now.

She plunged her phone into her pocket and hurried to the door, making for Carpenter's office on the top floor. He was at the top, she was one floor below, and her teams were another floor below that. At least it got her step count up.

She knocked on his office door and entered without waiting for a response. She knew he was in; his car had arrived in the car park while she'd been on the phone. He looked up from his desk, eyebrows raised.

"Sir, we've tracked Jackie Kendall down. Properly, this time."

His eyes widened. "Where?"

"Workington. Cumbria. She came back to the police station. Seems she's run out of money and was getting desperate. DI Finch has spoken to her about witness protection, but—"

"She can't make promises like that on our behalf."

"No." Lesley approached the desk and put a hand on it. "Jackie's asked us not to do anything official. She won't be questioned unless it's informal. She's also asked that we don't add anything to our case files about her appearance." She shook her head. "She's scared, Sir."

"I'm sure she is. But, Lesley—"

"Jackie was representing the Kelvin family, or one of their firms at least, in a property sale. I believe she read, heard or witnessed something that put her in danger. She can help us."

He screwed his eyes tightly shut then opened them again. "Bloody hell, Lesley. I thought I was shot of the Kelvins."

She shrugged. "It seems Vera Kelvin has taken up the reins."

"Vera? She's... how old is she now?"

"Seventy-four, Sir. Young enough to—"

"Young enough to give us trouble, and if my recollection of her is anything to go by, she'll still be doing so when she gets her telegram from the King." He frowned. "Do known criminals get telegrams?"

"No idea. Sir, I need your authorisation to take an officer to Cumbria. We need to—"

"You need to not promise anything concrete to Jackie Kendall."

"With respect, if we don't—"

"You haven't even spoken to her yet. Yes, go up there. Take your whole team, for all I care. But for God's sake, I want to be fully briefed before I can authorise anything like witness protection."

Lesley gripped the desk tighter. "Sir. Of course."

He waved a hand. "Well go on then. I suspect you want to get on the motorway." He winced. "Don't envy you. The M5 and M6 in June."

"We'll be fine, Sir. It's still early."

It was 8:15am. She could only hope Hannah was already in.

CHAPTER SIXTY-ONE

JILL STOOD at the front of the briefing room, waiting for the team to settle. Mike, Stanley, and Katie took their seats, each displaying their own brand of morning energy – or lack of it.

"Right," Jill began. "Rowena Sharp. We've got some new angles to consider."

She looked out the window as a commotion caught her eye. DCI Clarke and Hannah were heading towards the DCI's car, all but running. She frowned, then turned back to her team.

"Peter Didson," she continued. "We've confirmed his identity and current whereabouts. But he claims he didn't know Rowena had died."

Stanley leaned forward. "And we know now that Donald went to Worthing, so he didn't kill her."

"We have that receipt," Jill nodded. "It's not perfect, given that it's handwritten. But—"

Katie was shifting in her seat, lifting her right shoulder like she wanted to put her hand up.

"Katie?" Jill asked. "You look agitated."

"Sorry, guv. But you just said Peter said he didn't know Rowena had died."

Jill nodded. "That's what he told us."

She raised an eyebrow at Stanley, who nodded. "He was shocked, guv. Seemed pretty genuine."

Katie was shaking her head. "That doesn't fit." She glanced at Mike, who was nodding along. "He sent Donald a condolence card. When they had a memorial service, a year after—"

"What kind of sick shit sends the husband of his dead mistress a condolence card?" said Stanley.

"Have you got it?" Jill asked Katie.

Katie nodded. "It's in evidence. I've put a photo on the system." She stood, reaching for the remote control for the whiteboard, and pressed a few buttons.

With deepest sympathy, the message on the front said. Katie flicked to the next photo, of the interior. It was addressed to Donald Sharp and signed by Peter.

"It doesn't say which Peter," said Mike. "Could be anyone."

"Uh-uh." Katie chewed her tongue, tapping on the control and screwing up her face as she looked for something. A moment later she nodded, a look of triumph on her face.

"Hang on." She brought up the case file, where there were scanned documents from the legal firm. Contracts, agreements, all from around the time of Rowena's death.

She opened one and found a signature at the bottom.

"Peter," she said. "The signature from the sympathy card, and this one from his work. Same loop on the 'e', see?"

Jill stepped closer to look. Katie had the two photos side by side: a contract with a client to sell their house with Locke & Co, and the sympathy card.

Sure enough, there was a flourish on the 'e' that looked distinctive. And the capital 'P' was significantly larger than the rest of the text, in both images.

"That's him, alright," Stanley said.

Jill nodded. "It is." She looked at Mike. "Mike, what exactly did Peter Didson say to us when we told him about Rowena's death?"

"Hang on." He opened his notebook. "When I told him Rowena died in 1973, he said, 'She's been dead for fifty years?'. I replied in the affirmative and he then said, 'My God. I had no idea.'"

He looked up. "Not much room for manoeuvre there."

Jill nodded. "So he's—"

"He's lying, guv," Mike interrupted. "I... I've been thinking about it, and I know I was convinced at the time, but now I think about it, it felt off when we were talking to him. His reaction. It was too much. Fifty-two years after someone you knew for a year dies, and you react like that?"

Katie and Stanley exchanged glances.

"Do we need to go back and talk to him, guv?" Mike said.

Jill licked her lips. She thought of the DCI, running out of the building with Hannah.

What was going on?

"We do," she said. "And this time, I think we need to speak to him under caution."

CHAPTER SIXTY-TWO

SUTTON SCOTNEY WASN'T a service station Lesley often used. It felt like the nineties had never ended, and the Costa wasn't great. But her car was running low on fuel, and there was no way she was waiting for the next stop at Oxford Services, which was even worse.

She leaned against the car, watching Hannah stride towards the service station. The journey to Cumbria was long, and once she'd briefed Hannah on the call from Zoe, they'd barely spoken in the hour and a half they'd been on the road. Lesley needed caffeine, and she imagined she wasn't the only one.

Her phone buzzed: Jill.

"Boss, where are you? I saw you and Hannah running out of the building. I was in a briefing with my team, and I saw you speeding out, and I got worried. Is everything—"

"Slow down, Jill. We're following up a lead in the Jackie Kendall case."

"I thought that was closed."

"Jackie's turned up. In Cumbria. So it's open again. Hannah and I are on our way to interview her."

"That'll take hours."

Lesley sighed. "Another seven, I should imagine. But needs must. You sound agitated. What's up?"

Jill's voice steadied. "Sorry, boss. We've got a lead on Peter Didson. He sent a condolence card to Donald Sharp. The signature matches his handwriting."

"And?"

"We also spoke to Didson yesterday, and he claimed he didn't know Rowena was dead until recently."

"But he sent a condolence card, so—"

"He's lying to us, boss." Jill's voice was speeding up again. "We've spoken to him once, and I have to admit he seemed slippery."

'Slippery isn't enough to accuse a man of murder, Jill."

"I know. And I'm not saying he did it. But he knows something, I'm sure of it. I want to interview him under caution, boss."

Lesley considered. Peter Didson was the only lead they had on Rowena's death. If he proved a dead end, they'd have to close the case. Fifty-two years was just too long.

"Very well," she said. "But don't grasp at straws, just because pickings are slim."

"No, boss. I'll keep you informed."

"Thanks."

Lesley hung up as Hannah emerged from the service station, carrying two coffees. Lesley took hers gratefully, wishing she'd asked for a second one for the journey.

Hannah eyed her. "Something going on?"

Lesley pushed back her irritation. Hannah had a way of asking questions that seemed designed to get people's backs up.

But then, everyone was different. And it probably worked with witnesses. *Go easy on the woman. Give her a chance.*

"Jill's team has a lead on Didson," she said. "They're bringing him in for questioning."

Hannah brushed a stray hair from her face, not meeting Lesley's gaze. "Under caution?"

"Mm-hmm. Jill's handling it."

They got back in the car, Hannah taking the wheel this time. As they pulled onto the A34, Lesley studied her.

"Everything alright between you and Jill?"

Hannah kept her eyes on the road. "Of course, boss."

"Only, you seem a little tense around each other."

Hannah's jaw tightened. She shook her head, then forced a stiff smile. "Don't know what you mean. Everything's fine."

Lesley wasn't convinced. "I need my DIs working together, Hannah. Both of you. Whatever it is, whether it's rivalry between the teams or something else, sort it out, OK?"

Hannah's focus on the road was unwavering. "Of course, boss."

Lesley sipped her coffee, shifting her gaze to the road ahead. The team dynamics were fragile. She needed them focused.

"Let's get to Cumbria," she muttered. "We've got work to do."

CHAPTER SIXTY-THREE

JILL PARKED outside Peter Didson's house, a modest bungalow on the edge of Osmington. The street was quiet, with only the distant hum of traffic from the A353.

"Not much going on here," Mike said, glancing around. There were no cars parked on the road, but the same blue Toyota they'd seen last time was in the driveway.

Jill nodded. "Let's see if he's in."

They approached the front door, and Jill pressed the doorbell. They waited, listening for signs of movement inside.

Nothing.

She rang again, then knocked firmly. "Mr Didson? It's DI Scott and DC Legg from Dorset Police."

Still no response.

Mike shifted between his feet. "Maybe he's out."

"His car's here," Jill pointed out, nodding towards the Toyota.

Mike leaned closer to the door, listening. "Can't hear anything."

Jill stepped back, scanning the windows. The curtains were drawn. "Let's check round the back."

They walked around the side of the house, peering over a side fence into the overgrown, poorly-tended garden. No sign of life.

"Looks like he's not in," Mike said.

Jill frowned. There was a chance he could have left on foot, gone to the local shops maybe. But Osmington wasn't exactly a metropolis; most things had to be done by car around here. And Peter Didson, if he was as bright as she suspected, would have worked out that they'd want to speak to him again.

"Let's try the front again," she said.

Back at the door, Mike crouched down, peering through the letterbox. "Hang on."

Jill frowned. "What is it?"

"There's something... ah, shit."

"What?"

"There's someone on the floor."

Jill tensed. "Can you see who it is?"

"Can't tell. Looks like a man."

Jill straightened. "We need to get in there."

Mike nodded. "I'll call it in."

As Mike phoned in for uniformed backup, Jill tried the door handle. Locked.

She stepped back, assessing the door. "We can't wait. If he's in trouble..."

Mike ended the call. "They're on their way, but it'll be a few minutes."

Jill nodded. "Right. Let's do this."

Together, they braced themselves against the door. With a coordinated push, it gave way, swinging open with a loud crack.

They stepped inside. The hallway was dim, the only light coming from a doorway to one side. At the far end, lying on the floor between hallway and kitchen, was a form that looked like a man.

Jill moved forward, her senses on high alert. "Mr Didson?"

The figure didn't move.

Mike stepped past her.

"Careful," she said, spotting blood on the doorframe behind what could only have been Didson. "This could be a crime scene."

"He might need help."

"Of course." She nodded and Mike dropped to the ground, turning the person so they could see the face.

It was Didson. His face was pale, his body unmoving.

"He's dead," Mike whispered.

"Yeah." Jill felt nausea rise in her chest. He looked like he'd been dead a while.

Mike moved into the kitchen, stepping over Didson's body.

"Careful, Mike. Don't contaminate the crime scene."

He glanced back. "If he's been attacked, they might still be here."

Jill stayed in the hallway, looking at the bloodstains on the doorframe. There were what looked like fingerprints in them. "What do you see?"

"There's a knife," Mike called out. "On the floor, by the back door."

Jill moved forward, careful where she placed her feet. She joined Mike in the kitchen, noting the knife's position. It was covered in blood.

"Looks like it was dropped," Mike said.

Jill nodded. "We need to get out of here. Quickly. We can't risk contaminating anything more."

Mike stepped back, his face pale. "Right."

Jill led the way back to the front door. "Call Forensics. We need them here now."

CHAPTER SIXTY-FOUR

LESLEY GRIPPED THE STEERING WHEEL, eyes fixed on the road ahead. The M42 looped around Birmingham, a familiar route that reminded her of the years she'd spent in Force CID covering the West Midlands. Hannah sat beside her, silent, scrolling through her phone.

Lesley's phone buzzed. She checked the screen: Jill.

"Jill," she answered, "have you spoken to Didson?" Hannah looked up, placing her phone on her lap and listening in.

Jill's voice was flat. "I went to his house with Mike. He's dead, boss."

Lesley tightened her grip. "What happened?"

"Mike and I knocked on his door. No answer. Mike saw him through the letterbox, so we had to force entry. We found him in the kitchen. Blood everywhere. Looks like a stabbing, there's a knife here."

"Have you called Forensics?"

"On their way. I've secured the scene."

"Good. Make sure it stays that way. No one goes in or out until they arrive."

"Understood."

Lesley glanced at Hannah, who was staring out the window. "We're on our way to Cumbria. I'll need updates."

"I'll keep you posted, boss."

"Right. And Jill, make sure your team follows protocol. I don't want any mistakes."

"Of course. We... we would have disturbed some things when we came in."

"Understandable. He might have been alive."

"Yeah." Lesley could hear relief in Jill's voice. "I've logged everything, and I'll compile a full report."

"I'm sure you will."

"Gail's just arrived," Jill continued. "She's got one of her team."

Lesley allowed herself a small smile. "Is it the ridiculously tall one?"

"Yeah." Jill sounded bemused.

"He's good," Lesley said. "Tell Gail exactly what happened when you went into the property. It'll be fine. When did you last speak to Ellie Sharp?"

"Yesterday. Katie and Stanley went to see her."

"Good. You need to find her. She's got a motive."

"I know. She might have thought Peter killed her mum."

"Is that what you think?"

"We have no working hypothesis. Right now we're more focused on Peter's death."

"That's not cold," Hannah interrupted. "You need to speak to Nathan, get the MCIT involved."

Lesley waved a hand. "No. This is connected to a live case that Jill's team are running. Jill, stick with it."

Hannah grunted.

"Will do, boss," Jill said. "Katie and Stanley are already on their way to Ellie's flat."

"Keep me updated, Jill. I want to know everything."

"No problem."

Lesley ended the call and frowned at Hannah. "Why did you do that?"

Hannah twisted her lips. "Peter Didson has just been killed. It's not a cold case. My team have more experience w—"

"But Jill's team know the people involved. They'll have material that might be relevant. And as far as experience is concerned, it's not like they've all been stuck doing cold cases forever. I understand your reasoning, Hannah. But this is my call, and I say it's Jill's case."

Hannah nodded, her jaw tight.

"If we need extra resource from your team, I'll let you know."

Hannah frowned. She took a few shallow breaths, then nodded. "Of course, boss."

CHAPTER SIXTY-FIVE

JILL STOOD in her protective suit on the threshold of Peter Didson's house, watching as Gail Hansford and her colleague Gavin hauled their kit inside. Mike was on the phone, pacing near the driveway.

"Katie, we're at Didson's now," Mike said, rubbing his forehead. "You with Ellie yet?"

Jill turned her attention to Gail, who was surveying the doorframe that they'd torn apart when she and Mike had gained access.

"This is in a bad way," Gail said.

Jill felt herself tense. "DC Legg saw him through the letterbox. There was a chance we could help him, so—"

Gail put a hand up to stop her. "You don't have to explain yourself to me. Nor Mike. I'm only sorry you didn't get to him in time." She glanced towards the kitchen. "I'm no pathologist, but I reckon you were a good few hours too late. There's blood everywhere, he wouldn't have lasted long."

Jill nodded, and moved to one side for Gavin to pass, carrying equipment. He towered over everyone, his presence in the house somehow inappropriate. And all that blood made everything seem smaller and more claustrophobic.

Jill followed them inside. The kitchen was still, the air heavy with the metallic scent of blood. Peter Didson's body lay near the door, the knife at the opposite end of the room. Bloodstains leading from the body to the knife looked like skid marks; it had been thrown, or cast aside.

But by whom?

Gail knelt beside the back door, examining the knife without touching it. "It's got to be the murder weapon," she said, her voice steady. "We'll need to process it for prints and DNA."

Jill nodded. "There's a lot to work through here."

Gail moved to the walls, inspecting for any signs of struggle. "Blood spatter's consistent with a single blow." She looked at Jill. "Normally that means a crime of passion, as they used to say. The killer didn't stop to think." She frowned. "But we'll need to confirm."

Gavin was setting up his camera, documenting the scene. "Gail," he called out, pointing towards the front door. "There's a Ring doorbell."

Jill's eyebrows lifted. "We're in luck," she said, looking at Gail.

Gail gave a small smile. "Let's hope it was working."

Mike was in the doorway to the house, not stepping inside. "Katie and Stan are on their way to Ellie's," he called. "Shouldn't be long."

"Good," Jill replied. "Let's hope she's there."

Mike nodded, looking at the walls. "You think she could've done this?"

Jill sighed. Ellie was a woman in her early fifties, slightly built. She didn't seem strong enough. But the woman had been emotional each time Jill had met her, and emotion could lend a strength that otherwise might not be there. "We can't rule her out. Not yet."

Gail stood, dusting off her hands. "Gav, can you get started on the doorbell footage? See if it caught anything useful."

"On it," Gav said. He moved into the living room, ducking under the doorframe. He searched the room and pulled out a router from behind the TV.

"Let's see if we can get into that doorbell," he muttered, setting up his laptop.

Jill watched from the doorway. "You can access it from here?"

Gavin nodded. "If the Wi-Fi's still active, I should be able to. Just need to find the right network."

He tapped away, his fingers moving over the keys. Jill glanced back towards the kitchen, where Gail was still examining the body.

"How's it looking in there?" she called. She felt useless. Uniform were already doing door-to-door. Maybe she should get out there and assist.

"Blood spatter's telling a story," Gail replied. "But you need to let me piece it together."

Leave me to do my job, in other words. Jill turned her attention back to Gavin.

"Any luck?"

He grinned. "Got it. Let's see what this doorbell's recorded."

Jill moved closer as Gavin pulled up the footage. The screen showed the front driveway and the blue Toyota, the view from the doorbell camera. He sped through recordings of movement outside – two deliveries, a van passing – until he came to one showing two people standing at the door.

"D'you recognise them?" he asked.

Jill's eyes narrowed. "That's Ellie Sharp."

Gavin looked at her. "And the other one?"

Jill swallowed. "Her brother, Sebastian."

They watched as Ellie turned to Sebastian, pointing to a car parked at the end of the driveway. The two of them spoke for a moment – shouted, it looked like – and then Sebastian walked to the car and got in. Ellie disappeared from view, probably going into the house.

He flicked to the next recording. Ellie, leaving the house. She approached the car. Sebastian got out of it and she paused to speak to him, her movements agitated. Then she gesticulated at him and they both got into the car before driving off.

"Jill," he said. "She's..." He pointed at Ellie's figure onscreen. The image wasn't clear, but there were unmistakable signs of blood on her clothes.

"Shit," Jill muttered.

She pulled out her phone, dialling Katie.

No answer. She tried Stanley next. Still nothing.

Shit.

"Mike!" she called, stepping towards the front door.

He appeared in the doorway. "What's up, guv?"

"Where were Katie and Stanley when you last spoke to them?"

He shrugged. "About five minutes from Ellie's flat. Why?"

Jill's heart sank. "Oh, hell," she muttered. "We might have a problem. Call it in, I need Uniform over there on the hurry-up." She pulled in a shaky breath.

"What do I tell them, guv?"

"Tell them there's a risk of violence."

"From Ellie?"

She nodded, gesturing towards Gavin's laptop. "We've got Ellie on Peter's doorbell camera, covered in blood. Katie and Stanley... They could be in danger."

CHAPTER SIXTY-SIX

ALMOST THERE.

Lesley parked the car at Lancaster Services and climbed out of the driver's door, stretching out her leg muscles and groaning. Six hours they'd spent behind the wheel, between the two of them, and the hardest bit was still to come. Rural roads, and dark descending.

Her phone rang just as Hannah emerged from the passenger side.

"You go on ahead," she told the DI. "I'll get this."

"You want me to get you a coffee?"

Lesley shook her head. "I'll need something more substantial. I'll follow you in." She hadn't eaten since a bowl of muesli at breakfast, not counting the three Twixes she'd found in the glove locker, and she was bloody starving.

She waved Hannah on as she answered the call.

"Gareth. I hope you've got something big for me."

"Pretty big," the pathologist replied.

"Good. Because I'm having the day from hell."

"That bad?"

She wrinkled her nose. "You don't need to know about my worries. Tell me what you're calling about."

"I've got news about Rowena Sharp."

Lesley put a hand on the roof of the car. At last. "Yes?"

"Carla has been able to examine some of the soft tissue in her throat. We've also conducted an analysis of the mud in that part of Poole Harbour, and of the broad movements of the water in the fifty years since she died."

"Sounds like a mammoth undertaking."

"It is, but we do know one thing for sure, at least."

"Which is?" Lesley clenched her fist and rapped it on the car roof. Let this be good.

"Cause of death."

"I'm not in the mood for suspense, Doctor. What was it?"

"Drowning. Rowena Sharp drowned, and the evidence is looking like she drowned in Poole Harbour."

Lesley blew out a long breath. "When?"

"Sorry?"

"How long ago? Did she drown in 1973, or did she live another twenty years and then drown later in life?"

"The decomposition, and the condition of the teeth. Plus there's the contents of her stomach..."

"Which point to what?"

"There's traces of a red food dye in her stomach. Amaranth. It was withdrawn in the seventies because of safety concerns."

"So she died in the seventies."

"I can't pinpoint any closer than that, but—"

"Thanks, Gareth. You've been helpful."

CHAPTER SIXTY-SEVEN

STANLEY PARKED the car outside Ellie Sharp's building. There was no sign of Ellie or her brother. He looked at Katie.

"Ready?"

She nodded, her eyes flashing. "Let's see what they've got to say."

They headed up the stairs, ignoring the lift. The corridor was brightly lit, smelling of cleaning fluid. Stanley knocked on the door.

No answer.

He knocked again, louder this time. "Ellie? It's DC Brown and DC Young from Dorset Police. Stanley and Katie. We spoke yesterday."

Still nothing.

He exchanged a look with Katie. "Try the handle."

She did. The door swung open and she gave him a look of triumph.

Inside, the hallway was empty, all the doors closed. The living room was the first on the left, he remembered.

He opened it to find Sebastian Sharp sitting on the sofa, leaning forward, his head in his hands.

"Sebastian? Everything OK?"

No response, just trembling. Stanley couldn't see the man's face, but it looked like he was crying.

"Stanley." Katie nudged his arm. He looked up and in the direction she was pointing.

A pile of clothes sat beyond the solitary armchair. Shirt, jeans, a sweater. All covered in blood.

Shit.

He looked back at Sebastian. The man was fully clothed, some blood smears on his sleeve but otherwise clean. He stepped forward.

"Sebastian? Is Ellie here?"

Sebastian continued crying.

"Stan!"

He turned at the sound of Katie's voice.

"What?"

She was in the hallway. The bedroom door was open, as was the kitchen. There was no one inside either of them.

Katie put a hand against the remaining door. Stanley raised an eyebrow.

"Locked," she said. "I can hear her in there."

He nodded.

"You go and get those clothes," Katie said. "Before Sebastian does something with them. They're evidence. I'll..." She cocked her head towards the locked door, which he figured must be the bathroom.

"Right." Stanley hurried into the living room to find Sebastian sitting in silence now, the tears dry. He stared into space, his eyes wide.

Stanley pulled gloves from his pocket and scooped the clothes into an evidence bag from his shoulder bag.

"Sebastian," he said, as he scoured the living room for any more evidence, "you OK?"

Sebastian turned his head towards him. He frowned, shook his head, then brought his hands up to his face.

Stanley was stepping towards him when he heard a noise from

the hallway. He went out to see Katie standing by the bathroom door, speaking softly.

"Ellie, can you hear me? It's DC Young. Katie. Me and Stanley. We're here to help."

A muffled voice came from inside. "Go away."

"I'm sorry, Ellie, but you know we can't do that." She turned to see Stanley standing in the doorway to the living room. Her gaze went down to the evidence bag and she winced before turning back to the bathroom door.

"Ellie, we need to know you're safe," Katie said. "Can you open the door?"

Stanley took a few steps towards her, half an eye on the room he'd left.

"Lock the outside door," Katie said. "Just in case."

"Right."

A key was hanging in the lock. Stanley turned it, careful not to make contact, then placed it in another evidence bag. He went back to Katie, outside the bathroom.

"Ellie?" Katie said. "I can't talk to you through a door."

Silence. Then, a shaky breath. "I didn't know. I didn't know about him."

"About who, Ellie?" Katie asked, her voice steady and her gaze on Stanley.

"Peter. My father. They never told me."

Stanley took a few steps back to check the living room. Sebastian was still on the sofa, motionless.

Should he go back in there, try to get the man to talk? *No.* If Ellie burst out of that door, Katie might need backup.

"Ellie, we can help you," Katie said. "Can you open the door, please?"

More silence. Stanley could hear his own breathing in the quiet.

"Ellie, we're not going anywhere," Katie said. "We need to know you're OK."

A click. The door opened a crack, and Ellie Sharp's face appeared, pale and tear-streaked.

Stanley stepped back, giving her space. Katie stayed where she was, her expression calm. Ellie kept the door in front of her, only one side of her face visible.

"Ellie, let's sit down and talk," Katie said. "Can you come out?"

Ellie nodded, her gaze darting to the living room. "Is he...?"

"Sebastian's fine," Stanley said. "He's upset, but he's still here."

Ellie looked at Stanley, then at Katie. "I didn't know," she whispered. "I didn't know what he'd done."

Stanley bit his lip. "What did he do, Ellie?"

Ellie shook her head, tears spilling. "I didn't know. I didn't know."

Katie took a tiny step forward. "Let's sit down, yeah? We need to understand what's happened."

Stanley heard a noise and looked behind him, then turned back to Ellie. "Sebastian's here."

Katie nodded. "Ellie, your brother's here. Will you at least talk to him?"

The bathroom door opened. Ellie stood there, wearing only a bra and a pair of leggings. Blood smeared her arms and stomach.

She stared at Sebastian, who was a few steps behind Stanley.

"You're not my brother at all," she said, her voice shaking. "Don't you see? That's why our dad – Donald – resented me. That's why Verity hated me. They knew. They knew. That bastard Peter knew, and he never came to find me."

"No one resented you, Els. I don't know what you're talking about."

She threw her head up and let out a shriek. "You never saw it! Your sainted mother, she hated me. She knew I wasn't her stepdaughter, let alone her daughter, and she hated every minute that I was alive and in her house."

Sebastian stepped forward again, brushing past Stanley. "I don't care, Els. I'm your brother. Dad was your dad. He brought you up. Surely—"

She shook her head. "He killed her, Sebbie." The fury in her eyes disappeared, replaced by sorrow. "Peter. My fucking birth father. He killed my mum."

Sebastian frowned. "What?"

"He told me. He told me what happened. He went swimming with her after she told him it was over. That was when she died. He killed her, Sebbie. I've spent my whole life looking for her, hoping she was somewhere out there. But he killed her."

CHAPTER SIXTY-EIGHT

JULY 1973

ROWENA HAD no idea where Donald had gone. After he'd finished shouting at her, he left the hotel room, slamming doors like there was no one listening.

Now she was outside, staring at the sea. Ellie was safe; the baby-listening service had been hired for the evening before any of this had happened. The plan had been to go out for dinner with Donald, then slip off at some point, feigning a headache. She knew Donald well enough to predict that he wouldn't follow her back to the room. He was tired of her headaches. Tired of her, probably.

The plan hadn't gone the way it should.

She sighed and looked at her watch, a beautiful Timex Donald had bought her for their wedding. It was one of a few pieces of jewellery she could wear openly; most of the ones she owned were from Peter.

7:30pm. She'd arranged to meet Peter on a jetty at eight.

She brushed the sand off her skirt and walked around the side of the hotel, glancing upwards, wondering if Ellie was OK. *I'll be back in an hour, my sweet.*

She crossed the road leading to the harbour, only having to wait for one car to pass. In less than ten minutes, she was on the jetty that Peter had described.

He was there already. Peter always arrived early; he knew her timekeeping was never as accurate as she'd like.

She swallowed, not wanting him to see her crying. The argument with Donald had left her drained. She couldn't go on like this, but she wasn't sure if she should do what Donald wanted, or just leave him.

She put her forefinger and thumb into her mouth and let out a shrill whistle. Peter turned and smiled.

She walked up to him, not caring if anyone saw, and let him fold her in an embrace. It felt good. His body was warm, his hands soft.

Unlike Donald. Donald was too skinny. Too cold.

But Donald was her husband. Ellie's father.

Peter bent to kiss her. She gave herself up to it, knowing now it would be one of the last. Without realising it, she'd made her decision.

She owed this to Ellie.

She pulled away. "I need to talk to you."

He smiled. his hands on her arms. "Talk away."

She shook her head. "Not like that. This is serious."

His smile dropped. "Not this again." He sounded exasperated.

"I know you don't like it," she told him. "But you knew I was married when you met me. You knew I was married when you took me to bed, that first evening. I thought you were expecting something fleeting, something that wouldn't last more than a few days."

He cocked his head. "Is that how shallow you think I am? You have my baby, and you still think I don't want to be with you?"

She shook her head. "Ellie isn't your baby."

He tightened his grip on her arms. "Yes," he said. "She is. You know that the very idea that she could be Donald's is ridiculous."

Rowena pulled back. "You haven't met her. You haven't seen her nose, or the way her forehead wrinkles when she smiles." She closed her eyes. "She's Donald's. She looks like, she acts like him. I'm sorry."

He squared his shoulders, his gaze hardening.

"I know she's not Donald's," he said, "because you weren't sleeping with him last summer. You were sleeping with me."

She looked down at the ground. "I was," she said. "I mean, I did. Just a couple of times." She looked up at him. "If I hadn't slept with him, he'd have suspected."

He squeezed her arm. She yanked it away.

"You're hurting me."

"You're hurting *me*," he told her. "You're lying to me."

She looked at him, suddenly realising that she couldn't end this. Not honestly, at least.

She forced a smile. "Let's not argue."

He took a few breaths, his gaze hard on her face. "You started it," he said.

Really? Was he going to be this childish?

She forced the smile to stay in place. "Come on." She gave him a wink. "Let's swim."

She was wearing a bikini under her dress, a brand-new pink floral number she'd bought from C&A. She knew she looked good in it. She slipped off the dress and ran to the water.

Was it deep here? She wasn't sure.

Better be careful.

Instead of jumping off the jetty, she sat on its end and lowered her legs in. She'd been right to be careful; her toes were brushing the bottom of the harbour.

She slid in and waded out to where it was deeper. She swam a few strokes, the water soothing her nerves. She turned towards Peter and waved.

"Come on," she cried. "It's lovely in here."

He stared at her for a moment then stripped off to his Y-fronts. She looked around, worried someone might see. But there was nobody in sight.

She turned and swam further out. The water was cool, just what she needed.

"Hey!"

She felt a splash on the back of her neck. She turned to see Peter right behind her. *How did he get here so quickly?*

She forced a smile. "This is bliss."

It would be more blissful alone.

He returned the smile, his eyes sparkling. "That bikini suits you."

She felt her face heat up. Suddenly, she didn't want him to touch her.

She turned and swam away from him, wondering if there was somewhere she could hide. Could she steal one of those boats and take it over to an island in the middle of the harbour? If she did, what would she do next?

Ridiculous, she told herself. Steal a boat? *You're being ridiculous.*

"Rowena, darling!"

She turned to find him right behind her again. Why was he such a strong swimmer?

He put his hand on her shoulder and pulled her towards him. She felt her limbs freeze but let him kiss her.

The last time.

But he wasn't letting her go.

"Peter," she said. "Please. I'd rather just swim."

He shifted his weight, reaching his hand under the water. After a moment it emerged holding his underwear. He gave her a grin.

"Skinny dipping?"

She stared at him. "No," she said. "Don't be ridiculous."

He reached out and grabbed the strap of her bikini. She shrieked. "Peter, stop it!"

He laughed. The bikini was a halterneck, just a bow holding it in place. He had it undone in an instant, and she was topless.

She watched as he slung her bikini top across the surface of the water. It landed somewhere in the darkness.

She turned to him. "I wish you hadn't done that."

He laughed. "It's only me, darling. It's not like we haven't seen each other like this before." He reached out and pulled her towards him, fondling her breasts. She swallowed down bile in her throat.

She kicked out hard, her foot making contact with his chest.

He grunted. "Stop that."

She stared at him for a moment, then blinked and turned to swim away from him, her heart racing. She'd never felt scared of him before, but he was acting... strange.

She'd made it a few strokes when she felt something against her foot. A hand?

She cried out. But the hand had hold of her ankle.

She kicked out, yelling and splashing as much as she could, hoping someone might see. But she already knew there was no one around.

She turned to face him, hoping she could convince him to let her go.

"Peter!" she spluttered, the water suddenly cold. "Stop it! You're scaring me." She took a breath and swallowed what felt like her entire body's weight in water.

She cast about. How far from the shore were they?

"Stop fighting me," he said. "It's just me."

She closed her eyes, focusing on her breathing. *It's OK. It's just Peter.*

"Please, darling," she said, relieved that he'd let go of her foot. He was moving around her, his arms sculling in the water. She cast about, searching for the most direct way back to shore.

She felt his hand gripping her arm. She tensed.

"Come here," he said, his voice hard.

She didn't want to *come here*. She wanted to get back to land. She wanted her daughter.

"Peter, let's go in. I'm getting cramp. We can—"

His grip tightened and she went down, the water eclipsing her words. *We can talk on land*, she thought. *Please.*

She pushed against his hand with her free arm and brought herself up so she could breathe in again. Dots were forming in front of her eyes, her vision blurring.

"Peter," she gasped. "Please."

Peter's mouth was next to her ear. She tensed, feeling his breath on her skin. *Help.*

"He can't have you," he said. "You're mine."

She opened her mouth to speak but she had no breath. She gasped in what air she could. "Pet—"

"You can't leave me," he said.

She felt the grip tighten. Movement against her legs; he was wrapping his legs around her thighs.

Help.

She tried to push up, tried to kick out. But he had her firm.

Please stop.

She turned to look at him, hoping he'd see the fear in her eyes. But his face was full of anger.

She gasped, losing her balance as he pulled her closer towards him. Her head went under the water again.

She lashed out, struggling to push against his legs. But she didn't know which way was up, which way was down.

Her arms flailed. Further into the water or further up, she didn't know.

"Peter," she cried, but her voice was muffled. She was underwater, and as she opened her mouth to shout, she took in water.

Dirty harbour water. It made her gag. She spat, then pulled in a breath without meaning to, filling her lungs with yet more water.

The last thing she heard was Peter shouting her name.

CHAPTER SIXTY-NINE

JUNE 2025

Lesley wasn't quite ready for the sleek modern building that DI Zoe Finch worked in these days.

The Hub was just as new as the new Dorset Police HQ, but far more incongruous, in its hilltop setting a few miles outside White-haven. Lesley sat in an interview room, Jackie Kendall opposite her. The woman seemed smaller than the photos Hannah had shown Lesley from the estate agent's website. Older.

Not surprising, given what she'd been through.

Next to her was Zoe, whose presence Jackie had specially requested. Hannah was in the next room, watching via video feed. Lesley hoped she wouldn't throw a hissy fit about being excluded.

Lesley threw what she hoped was a reassuring smile across the table. "Thanks for waiting for us to get here," she said. "I know it took a while."

"Eight hours and twelve minutes," Jackie replied, looking back at her. She pushed a stray clump of hair from her face.

Lesley frowned; surely it hadn't taken that long? But then, from the time Zoe had told her they were coming...

"Jackie talked to me this morning," Zoe said. "You told me you're worried about going back to Dorset, aren't you?" She looked at Jackie with a cock of the head.

Lesley was enjoying seeing Zoe in action. The last time they'd worked together had been after the bomb attack on New Street Station. How long ago was that, three, four years? It felt like longer.

During those years Zoe had developed a confidence she hadn't had in Birmingham. Too busy being intimidated by David bloody Randle, her old Superintendent.

"I can't go back," Jackie said. "I'm not sure I should even be speaking to you."

Lesley nodded. "You made the right decision. We can help you. If someone's threatening you, we can put them behind bars. They can't harm you."

Jackie shook her head. "We all know it's not as simple as that."

Lesley leaned forward. "Why not?"

"People like... people like the ones who're after me. They have friends." She glanced at Zoe. "They've probably got associates up here. Maybe even officers planted at this station."

Zoe opened her mouth, then closed it again. Lesley wondered what she wasn't saying. Surely she hadn't found herself in the midst of police corruption again?

"No one saw you enter this building," Zoe said. "No one will see you leave. We do this kind of thing all the time. Witnesses are often scared."

"Am I free to leave, whenever I want?"

Zoe nodded. "You are."

Jackie looked at Lesley. "Well?"

Lesley repeated the nod. "Yes, Jackie. You've done nothing wrong and we have no reason to detain you." She sighed. "We don't even know what it is you need to tell us."

Jackie frowned. "I'm not sure I'm going to tell you anything."

Lesley exchanged a glance with Zoe, who shrugged. She leaned forward.

"Jackie," she said. "We've spoken to Yiannis, and—"

"Yiannis." Jackie's posture slumped. "How is he?"

"He's fine. He misses you. He's been running an internet campaign to find you."

A smile. "I saw that. He's all over social media."

"We can help you get back to him."

Jackie looked horrified. "No way. I can't... they know where I live."

"My colleagues told me you were broken into last year. Your house. Is that related to the reason you don't want to go back there?"

A nod. Jackie sniffed and wiped her nose on the back of a grubby sleeve. Her clothes looked like they had been smart once, but had long since become worn and misshapen.

"We also know that you were selling a property for Dorchester Logistics," Lesley continued. "Which is owned by a family we've come across before."

Jackie was staring at her, saying nothing.

"Is that correct?" Lesley asked.

Her phone buzzed: a message from Hannah.

Ask if she received threats.

Lesley felt her nose twitch. She didn't like being told how to do this. But if Jackie hadn't insisted on Zoe, it would be Hannah sitting next to her. It must be frustrating for her.

"Did you receive threats?" she asked. "Direct or indirect?"

Another sniff. Jackie held her hand out, and Zoe pushed a box of tissues across the table. Jackie blew her nose. Her eyes were red.

"I know this is hard," Zoe said. "Anything you can tell us, it'll help us find the people who threatened you. We want you to be safe."

Jackie shook her head. "I'll never be safe."

Lesley eyed her. This was going nowhere.

"Jackie, did the Kelvin family threaten you? Did you learn about something in the course of selling that property for them?"

Jackie's eyes widened. "Learn?"

"Read about something in a document, overhear a conversation. That kind of thing?" Lesley glanced at Zoe, remembering the work

Zoe had done, using documentation to take criminals down in Birmingham.

"No," Jackie said. "Nothing like that. It was..." She closed her eyes and shuffled her chair towards the table. Her voice was barely more than a whisper; Hannah probably wouldn't be able to hear. "I saw something. I saw them do something."

"What kind of something?"

Jackie rubbed her cheek. "They... they hurt someone. I think... I think..."

"What do you think you saw, Jackie?" Zoe's voice was gentle.

Jackie looked at her. "I saw them kill someone. I'm sure of it. In the property. I saw a man die."

CHAPTER SEVENTY

Jill sat across from Ellie Sharp in the interview room at Winfrith HQ, taking in the young woman's pale face and trembling hands. Mike Legg sat beside her, his notebook open and laptop in front of him with the case files ready.

Opposite them were Ellie and her lawyer, who wore a crisp navy suit and an air of confidence. Jill had never met her before, but then, she had been on leave for a while.

Ellie, in contrast, looked anything but confident. She was hunched over in her chair, her pale face blotched with tears, and she kept tugging at the sleeve of her blouse, which was beginning to tear.

"Interview commenced at 14:35," Jill stated for the recording. "Present are DI Jill Scott, DC Mike Legg, Ellie Sharp and her solicitor Sameena Newson."

"We should recommence this interview at a later time," Newson said. "My client is clearly in no fit state to be—"

"It's OK," said Ellie. "I'm fine. Carry on." She looked up at Jill. "Please."

The solicitor frowned and bent towards her, then thought better of it and shrugged.

"Ms Sharp," Jill began, "Ellie. What can you tell us about your visit to Peter Didson's house yesterday evening?"

Ellie's gaze darted to her solicitor, who gave a slight nod.

"I needed answers." Ellie's voice was little more than a whisper. "About my mother. About who I really am."

"And what happened when you got there?" Mike asked, his tone gentler than Jill had heard from him before.

"Sebastian came with me. He... he tried to stop me going in." Ellie wrapped her arms around herself, rocking. "I made him go back to the car. I didn't want anyone else there. But I had to know. *He* opened the door and..." She broke off, tears welling in her eyes.

"Take your time," Jill said.

"He laughed at me." Ellie's voice hardened. "When I asked if he was my real father. He told me it didn't matter. That Donald was my dad, whoever's genes I had. I said it mattered to me. And he laughed."

Jill tried to square that with the Peter Didson she'd met just twenty-four hours earlier. The Peter Didson who'd feigned surprise at Rowena's death, despite having sent her family a condolence card fifty-one years ago.

She had no idea if laughter was how he'd react. If he'd faked every reaction to her and Mike, how could she know what he was capable of?

"What happened next, Ellie?" Jill leaned forward a little, then drew back at a look from the solicitor.

"I pulled out my phone. I showed him the photos I took of my mum's diary, and the photo of the card. He stopped laughing, then. He... He had his own."

"His own what?" Jill asked.

"Letters. There were ones she actually sent. He went away and fetched them; they were in the loft or something. He left me standing on the doorstep, wouldn't even invite me in. Some father." She sobbed.

"The letters?" Jill asked. "Were they from your mother?"

A nod. "He'd put them in a shoebox. He wouldn't let me see

them. Said they were private. I told him I wanted a DNA test. Oh, God... I was foolish, wasn't I?" She looked up.

"What makes you think that?" Mike asked.

"Overreacting like that. Accusing the man of all sorts. I asked him if he'd killed my mother. He wouldn't answer me. Said something about going swimming with her." Her face crumpled. "But you found her in the harbour. So she must have drowned, yes?"

"That doesn't necessarily follow," Jill said. But she knew now that it was true; the DCI had sent a message.

"He killed her, I know he did. I had to get in. Sebbie wanted to stop me, so I told him to go back to the car. Wait for me." She pulled in a gasping breath. "I talked Peter into letting me in. I went into the kitchen with him. I was shouting. He was shouting back. And then..."

She bent over the table, her head on her arms.

Sameena put a hand on her client's back, so lightly it was barely touching. "You've distressed my client."

"I think she's distressed herself," Mike said.

Jill gave him a look. "We can give her a moment."

The lawyer glared. Ellie looked up. "No. If I don't get it all out now, I never will."

Jill swallowed. "Ellie, you were just telling us you were alone with Peter in the house. What happened then?"

Ellie drew in a shuddering breath. "I kept shouting at him. Wouldn't believe him when he said he wasn't my father." She looked up. "It's been so long, you see. So long without certainty."

"But he still denied it?" Mike asked.

She nodded. "I lost it. Started hitting him. Batting at him with my arms, not even clenching my fists. I was out of it, didn't know what I was doing. And then..."

Sameena put a hand on Ellie's arm. "You can stop now, if you prefer."

Ellie shook her head. She gave the lawyer a look of confusion then turned to Mike.

"He was bigger than me. Stronger. He might have been in his

seventies, but I'm only small. He grabbed my hands, restrained them. Said I was just like my mother, giving him trouble. Said something about how he'd managed to escape it all, forge a quiet life for himself. That I was ruining all that." Her voice cracked. "Then he grabbed my throat. Started squeezing."

Jill leaned forward, keeping her voice steady. "What happened then, Ellie?"

Ellie's eyes were wide. Jill's gaze flicked down to her throat, which did show signs of pressure. Faint red marks. Still, this was the first time she'd mentioned strangulation.

"I thought he was going to kill me," Ellie said. "I realised that if he was able to do that to me, in his seventies, then he could easily have done it to my mother, when he was young and strong." She sniffed. "I... I lost it."

Sameena leant in. "What my client is saying is that she was under threat. She acted to defend herself."

Ellie frowned at her. "Huh?"

"You were being attacked, Ellie. You had to protect yourself." The solicitor was looking into her eyes, her gaze intense.

"Oh. Yes." Ellie licked her lips. "So there was a knife block on the counter behind me." Ellie's hands trembled as she mimed reaching backwards. "I just... grabbed one. I didn't mean to... but he was crushing my windpipe and I couldn't breathe..."

There was a silence broken only by the sound of Mike's fingers on his keyboard. Jill placed a hand on his arm, and he stopped typing.

"I stabbed him." Ellie's voice dropped to barely a whisper. "He let go of me and stumbled back. There was so much blood." She looked at Jill with tear-filled eyes. "It'll be OK, won't it? I was only defending myself. He was trying to kill me, just like he killed my mum."

Sameena placed a hand on Ellie's arm. "I advise you not to say any more at this time."

"Did Peter say anything about your mother's death?" Jill asked carefully.

Ellie's face contorted. "He told me..." She slumped back in her chair. "He told me she was trying to end it. She..." a sniff. "She wanted to put her family first." Tears rolled down her face.

Jill leaned in. "Was that the night she died?"

Ellie nodded and wiped her cheek. "Yeah. He... They went swimming. He was angry. He knew..." A sob. "He knew it was their last time. That's what he told me." She looked up at Jill, her face hardening. "He killed her."

Jill fled the room still. Mike, next to her, was barely breathing. Ellie plunged a hand into her hair and wailed.

"He grabbed her, when they were swimming. He was angry. He didn't want my father to have her." She screwed her eyes shut. "He pulled her under, then swam back to his car and drove away." A pause. The *bastard*."

Jill swallowed. "He told you all this."

Ellie nodded at her, through tears. "Yes. And then... I think he realised what he'd done. That's when he grabbed me."

Jill exchanged a glance with Mike. Ellie's hand went to her throat. She winced.

"Peter grabbed you?" Jill said, her voice low.

A nod. "My throat. He..." Ellie's eyes widened. "He had me..." She put her hands around her throat, as if to demonstrate. "I thought he was going to kill me too."

The solicitor put a hand on Ellie's arm. "I think..."

Ellie pushed it away. She placed her head on the table and sobbed. "I'm sorry. I... I didn't mean to. But it was... it was just there."

Jill glanced at Mike again. They'd need forensics to confirm Ellie's account of self-defence, but the bruising on her neck gave it credence.

Ellie was sobbing uncontrollably now, tearing at her hair.

The solicitor put a hand on the table. "My client needs a break."

Jill nodded. "Interview suspended at 15:10."

CHAPTER SEVENTY-ONE

Lesley gave Zoe a nod before stepping out of the interview room. Jackie's revelation about the Kelvins meant she needed to act quickly.

She hurried to the room next door, where Hannah was watching, and closed the door behind her.

"Can we give her protection?" Hannah asked.

Lesley was already on her phone, dialling the super. "Not my call to authorise. But she and her partner will need protection if she's going to be able to help us."

The phone rang out a couple of times, then voicemail kicked in.

Shit.

She hung up and looked at Hannah. "How much of that did you catch?"

"She wasn't exactly enunciating."

"She was scared." Lesley dialled Carpenter's number again. This time it went straight to voicemail without ringing.

"Fuck."

She hung up and was about to dial Dennis, then remembered she couldn't do that anymore. She dialled Jill's number.

Jill wasn't answering either.

"Jill, it's Lesley. I need to speak to Superintendent Carpenter urgently to arrange witness protection for Jackie Kendall. Please can you go to his office and find him. Someone needs to speak to him in person."

She hung up.

"Witness protection?" Hannah asked.

Lesley nodded. "You didn't hear, did you?"

Hannah wrinkled her nose.

Lesley sighed. "Jackie's told us she witnessed a murder. In the property owned by the Kelvins, the one she was selling. The Kelvins had to be involved." She raised an eyebrow. "Now do you see why she's scared?"

"I do." Hannah frowned. "I'll call Nathan, tell him to get round to her house. You're wanting her partner to go into protection too, yes?"

Lesley nodded as she dialled Carpenter again. "Good. If they get wind of the fact she's come to us, he'll be threatened."

Hannah turned her back to Lesley, phone to her ear.

"Damn." Lesley would just have to leave Carpenter a message. "Sir, it's Lesley. I'm in Cumbria, having just stepped out of an interview with Jackie Kendall. Before her disappearance, she witnessed a murder on a property owned by the Kelvin family. She can help us, but we'll need to ensure she's safe. I'm calling to ask for authorisation to put her in witness protection."

She hung up, just as the door opened: Zoe.

Lesley nodded at her. "Sorry. I'll be right with you."

Zoe was shaking her head. "It's not that."

Lesley felt her stomach tense. What now?

"What?" she asked.

"I'm really sorry, Lesley."

"Sorry for what?"

Hannah was off the phone. She turned to them, confusion on her face. "Everything OK?"

Zoe slumped into a chair. "I'm really sorry, Lesley. But she was here of her own free will. We couldn't detain her."

Lesley stared at her. "You couldn't..." She glanced towards the door. "You couldn't what?"

Zoe looked up at her, the way she had when she was a DS in Force CID. Nervous.

"She's gone, Lesley. She decided she didn't feel safe with us, and she's left."

CHAPTER SEVENTY-TWO

MIKE PUSHED OPEN the door of the Ship Inn, the familiar smell of beer and wood polish greeting him. Johnny sat at a corner table, nursing a pint and scrolling through his phone. He looked up and waved as Mike approached.

"Alright, mate?" Johnny grinned. "Got you a pint."

"Cheers." Mike slid into the seat opposite. He eyed the drink; he was driving. "How's London treating you?"

"It's not." Johnny's smile faltered.

"No? Not a fan of the big smoke?"

Johnny sighed. "No. Look, I've been meaning to—"

Mike put up a hand to stop him. "I'm really sorry, mate, but I'm going to need a soft drink. Driving home and just got off duty. Wouldn't look good." He stood up. "You can have my pint."

Johnny flushed, something that always made his pale skin blotchy. "Oh. Yeah, er, right. Sorry, mate."

Mike went to the bar, bought a pint of Coke, and returned. "So," he said. "Tell me about London. You're not happy?"

Johnny screwed up his nose. "Cost of living's mental up there. Alice can't work because childcare's so expensive. Plus..." he hesitated. "Dad's not getting any younger. Be nice for the kids to grow up near their grandad."

"How is Eric?"

"Same as ever. Still thinks he knows everything about policing." Johnny laughed, but it sounded forced. "He's been telling me about some of his old cases. Including that Rowena Sharp you lot are working on now."

Mike looked up. "He was involved in that?"

"Not all that much. They had him doing door-to-door, processing witness statements, that kind of thing."

"Still, he might remember something."

"I doubt it, mate. Like I say, his health isn't great."

"Alzheimer's?"

"What? Oh, no. He just... I don't think he'd fancy being dragged into it."

"Fair enough. We've closed the case anyway, or near as dammit."

"You have?"

Mike leaned in. "This isn't official yet, right? But she had a lover. A guy called Peter. Looks like he killed her."

"So he's under arrest?"

"That's the kicker. He's dead too."

Johnny winced. "Well, I guess after that long..."

Mike shook his head, taking another sip of his Coke. "He was killed yesterday. By her daughter." His voice was barely more than a whisper now. The forensics weren't complete, the post-mortem hadn't been done, and he knew there would be a briefing in the morning. Whether that was to get them looking for more or to wrap things up, he didn't know.

Johnny whistled. "Well, sounds like you got a result... of sorts."

"Not a very good one, though."

"No." The two of them looked into their drinks for a moment before Johnny broke the silence.

"How would you feel about me coming back?"

Mike swallowed his mouthful of Coke, relieved he hadn't choked on it. "Coming back?"

Johnny shrugged. "Yeah. You just heard, London's crap. Or at least, it is for me and Alice. I don't know how anyone copes with being in the Met these days. I miss it here, you know?"

Mike shrugged. "I thought you were daft to leave in the first place. Career progression, I guess, but even so..."

"That was why you thought I left? Career progression?"

Mike looked at his old friend. "Well, I couldn't think of anything else. You get more varied experience in the Met, I imagine."

Johnny snorted. "Nah, mate. I'm a much smaller fish in a vastly bigger pond. I've been stuck doing the kind of gruntwork I hadn't done for years here."

"Ah. So that's why you want to come back."

Johnny eyed him. "You didn't think there was any other reason? Why I left?"

Mike looked at him. "No. Was it Alice? Has she got family there?"

"No." Johnny returned his gaze for a moment, then grinned. "Anyway, just warning you, yeah? You might be having to put up with me again."

Mike smiled. He held out his glass and Johnny clinked it. "Well, that sounds like good news to me."

He downed the rest of his Coke and made his excuses. As he got in the car, his mind went back to what Johnny had asked him.

You didn't think there was any other reason?

What was he getting at? Was there something Mike had missed?

He slid into the driver's seat and plugged his phone into the car. The important thing was, his old friend was coming back. Anything else was in the past.

CHAPTER SEVENTY-THREE

MEERA LOOKED up from the article she was reading on her phone to see headlights; a car, coming to a stop outside her and Jill's house. Their cottage was on a narrow street with just two spaces outside, neither of which were their actual property or could be reserved. Maybe today, Jill had managed to bag one of them. Sometimes Meera longed for a modern house with a wide driveway. Even a garage.

She heard the front door open and close. A moment later, Jill slumped down beside her. "Phew," she breathed. "That was a hell of a day." She looked at Meera. "Where's Suzi?"

"Fast asleep. Finally." Meera put a hand on her wife's leg. "Congratulations. I heard you closed the Rowena Sharp case."

Jill grunted. "I wouldn't say it's closed just yet. We know Ellie killed Peter, that's not in doubt. But we don't know yet what we'll be charging her with. I don't want to approach the CPS until we've got more evidence."

"You think it was self-defence?"

"That's what she's claiming, along with that clever solicitor of hers. Who works for the DCI's wife, it turns out."

Meera smiled. "Could be worse."

"True. At least it's not Aurelia Cross."

"Yeah." The woman now ran the firm that had been Nevin Cross and Short. Meera was terrified of her.

Jill looked at her. "Is it true, then? Jackie Kendall's disappeared again?"

Meera sighed. "Yeah. Hannah went all the way to Cumbria with the DCI, and then she just walked out of the station where they were interviewing her."

"She's got balls."

"She has that."

"Do you think she's at risk? Or is she just inflating things?"

Meera shrugged. "I don't know. I'm lucky, I came onto the team after Arthur Kelvin died, so I haven't seen that crew in action."

"From what I hear, you don't want to."

Meera nodded. "Anyway, I've been told to go to her partner's house with DS Strunk first thing. Find out if he's had any contact from Jackie. Maybe offer him protection, if the DCI can get it authorised."

"Good luck with that."

"Yeah." Meera leaned closer in to her wife. "Anyway, let's not be one of those couples who always talk about work."

"You're right. How was Suzi this evening?"

"Good. She ate carrots for the first time."

"Result!" Jill high-fived her. "Well done. How did you manage that?"

"I just plonked them down in front of her without comment and she ate a couple of them before she realised what I'd done."

Jill laughed. "Sometimes I think bamboozling a toddler can be harder than catching criminals."

"You haven't heard how sneaky I was. The carrots were hidden in with her chips. I cut them exactly the same way."

Jill planted a smiling kiss on her. "You're a genius."

Meera grinned. "I think so." She swallowed. "I enjoy this stuff, you know. Spending time with Suzi. Tricking her into eating vegetables."

Jill looked at her. "More than policing?"

"Right now, yes. The police is my job. Yours too, and I know you love it. But me, for now, I'm happy staying where I am. Focusing on our daughter."

Jill nodded. "You don't judge me, for being ambitious?"

Meera grabbed Jill's hand and squeezed it. "Of course I don't! The force needs more fabulous women like you."

Jill pushed back her shoulders and swept her hair aside, a glint in her eyes. "And I am rather fabulous."

"You are." Meera hesitated. Was she about to spoil a nice moment?

She was.

"Look, I need to talk to you about the damp problem."

Jill looked at her, the smile gone. "Do we have to?"

"We do. I've been reading about how those kinds of spores can affect children's lung development."

Jill's shoulders slumped. "Well, you got me there." She sighed. "I'll call someone in the morning."

"No," said Meera. "I will."

Jill gave her a long look. "You're right. We have to make this place perfect for Suzi."

Meera swallowed, wondering if they could ever make this house perfect. It looked like she'd have to try.

"But do one thing for me, won't you?" Jill said.

Meera looked back into her eyes, trying to smile. "What's that?"

"Whoever you hire, make sure the work doesn't wreck the house, will you? This place is so beautiful, I'd hate to have it... to have it sullied."

Meera felt her jaw tighten. "Of course, love. I'll make sure there's no damage. Promise."

Jill grabbed her chin and pulled her in for a kiss. Meera let herself be kissed, hoping she could live up to that promise.

CHAPTER SEVENTY-FOUR

LESLEY SAT BACK in the armchair, cradling a mug of tea. Zoe's living room was warm, a welcome change from the chill outside. Outside she'd glimpsed a hot tub, which seemed incongruous in Cumbria, even in June. Hannah was outside in the car, 'making some calls'. Getting some time to herself, more like. Not that Lesley blamed her.

Right now, rain was pattering softly at the window. It seemed like a permanent state of affairs up here.

"How's Dorset treating you?" Zoe asked, settling onto the sofa opposite.

Lesley smiled. "It's beautiful. The coast, the countryside... even the weather's not bad. Better than Birmingham, anyway."

Zoe sighed. "Sounds lovely."

Carl, Zoe's partner, wandered in from the kitchen. "You're not moving to Dorset, Zoe."

She grinned. "Too far from Nick, don't worry."

"Where is your son now?" Lesley asked.

"University of Stirling. Mo's been like a father to him, he's round there all the time, getting his washing done and being given proper food. Or at least he was; Mo's somewhere out in the sticks now." Her smile dropped. "I wish it was me, though."

Lesley looked at her former colleague. She'd all but forgotten about DS Mo Uddin, Zoe's old sidekick. Good copper, as she remembered.

Zoe turned to her. "Nick graduates in a couple of weeks though, and Mo's moving. He got a new posting in the middle of nowhere. Perthshire somewhere."

Lesley shuddered. "Sounds cold."

"Yeah." Zoe curled herself into a tighter ball and turned her gaze on the window.

Lesley looked at her. "Cumbria's not exactly ugly though, is it?"

Zoe shrugged. "It is beautiful. And it's an interesting place to work. But it's so wet."

Carl handed Zoe a glass of wine. "You'd miss the mountains."

"Maybe," Zoe said, taking a sip. "But there would still be the sea."

Lesley watched them, smiling. Zoe and Carl seemed happy, settled. They hadn't been like that in Birmingham.

"How's Sharon?" Zoe asked.

"She's good. Busy with uni. We talk most days."

"Bet she loves Exeter."

Lesley nodded. "It's a good fit for her."

Zoe nodded. "I'm glad."

Lesley shifted in her seat. "I need to ask you something, Zoe. About Jackie Kendall."

Zoe's expression turned serious. "I'm so sorry about her bolting like that. But I—"

Lesley leaned towards her. "It's not your fault, Zoe. Jackie wasn't under arrest; we couldn't hold her. She's scared, that much is clear."

Zoe nodded. "Don't blame her, if she's fallen foul of your Kelvin lot. I thought they were all dead?"

"Not the matriarch. She's stepped back in, it seems."

Zoe whistled. "Good luck with that."

"Thanks. Do you have any theories on where Jackie might have been staying? You know the area?"

Zoe grunted a laugh. "Lesley, have you seen just how bloody big Cumbria is? It takes me two hours just to get from one side to the other. Three in the summer. She could be anywhere."

"I don't imagine she's stayed nearby. She'll be worried that someone might have seen her, at your Hub."

Zoe's face darkened. "Yeah." She sipped her tea, looking worried.

"Is there something you haven't told me, Zoe?"

Zoe turned to her. "No. I can't, sorry. It's... it's an ongoing case." She glanced at Carl, who wasn't meeting anyone's eye.

Carl was a DI in Professional Standards. Lesley had worked with him enough to understand why they weren't saying anything.

But what that did mean was that there might be someone dodgy at their Hub. And that they might have seen Jackie.

She sighed. "She'll have gone to Scotland, I imagine."

"Yeah." Zoe's voice was terse. She let out a shaky breath. "What about her partner? There was a partner, wasn't there?"

"Jackie's partner?" Lesley nodded. "Yiannis Kallias. Yes. We've got officers visiting him tonight."

"Good." Zoe looked at her. "Because if Jackie's in as much trouble as she seems to think she is, he'll need you to keep an eye on him."

CHAPTER SEVENTY-FIVE

MAY 1974

JACKIE PAUSED at the door to the garage, her hand hovering over the handle. She'd heard something. A thud, maybe. Or a scrape. She couldn't be sure.

She looked back towards the house. The place was empty. She knew it was empty. She was the only one here.

So what was that noise?

Her heart thudded in her chest. She swallowed, trying to steady her breathing. It was probably nothing. Houses made noises. Especially big ones like this.

But she couldn't shake the feeling that she wasn't alone.

She took a deep breath and turned the handle. The door opened with a soft creak. She stepped inside, her heels clicking on the concrete floor.

The garage was dimly lit, the only light coming from a small window high up on the wall. Her eyes adjusted slowly. She could make out the shape of a car, covered with a dust sheet. Shelves lined the walls, filled with tools and boxes.

She listened. Nothing. Just the faint hum of the air conditioning from the house.

She took a step forward, her eyes scanning the space. The car was a sleek shape under the cover. She couldn't tell what make it was, but it looked expensive.

There it was again. A scrape, coming from the far corner.

Jackie froze, her breath catching in her throat. Her eyes darted to the corner, but it was too dark to see anything.

She took a step back, groping for the door handle. *Leave. Get out of here. Call someone.*

She didn't move. She was showing this property in under ten minutes and she had to know what was making that noise.

She took another step forward, her heart pounding. Her hand brushed against something on the shelf. A torch. She picked it up and fumbled with the switch.

Its beam cut through the darkness, illuminating the corner. She swept it across the floor, her hand shaking.

Nothing. Just a stack of boxes.

She was being stupid. There was nothing here.

As she turned to leave, she heard it again. A low moan.

Jackie's limbs stiffened. She swung the torch back to the corner, the light shaking.

A pair of eyes stared back at her, reflecting the beam. She gasped, stumbling backwards into one of the shelves. She caught herself on a toolbox, and it fell to the floor with a crash.

She pointed the beam back towards the corner. She had to be wrong. She was imagining things.

She wasn't.

The torchlight illuminated a man, slumped in a chair, his face pale. Blood pooled around the chair, seeping into the concrete. A strap – a belt? – secured his wrist to the chair.

Jackie's breath hitched.

She took a step back, her heel catching on the edge of the dust sheet covering the car.

The man shifted, the chair leg scraping. Was he alive?

She looked back at the man's face. He had a deep gash, running from above his eye down to his cheek. The eye was closed, the sight of it making her gag. The right eye. Or the left?

Her brain wouldn't function.

Then she caught movement. To the side.

A second man, standing. He turned towards her, his face half-hidden in shadow. He wore a dark suit, and even in the poor light, Jackie could tell it was expensive, probably tailored. His hair was slicked back, his expression calm.

He held a phone to his ear.

"Yes, Mrs Kelvin," he said, his voice low. "It's done."

Jackie's heart pounded. She took another step back, her hand gripping the torch so tightly her knuckles ached.

The man's gaze shifted to her. He didn't look surprised. More... annoyed.

"Looks like we've got company," he said into the phone.

Jackie's instincts kicked in. She turned, her heels slipping on the concrete. She stumbled and caught herself on the doorframe.

She had to get out. Now.

She bolted, the torch clattering to the floor behind her.

CHAPTER SEVENTY-SIX

JUNE 2025

MEERA STOOD outside Yiannis Kallias's house, eyeing the overgrown front garden. The weeds were worse than last time. Rubbish was piled next to the bins, spilling onto the driveway.

"Doesn't look like he's been keeping up with the gardening," DS Strunk said, joining her.

"Or the bins," Meera added. Not that she could blame him, with his partner missing. "Let's see if he's in."

They walked up to the front door. Meera knocked, listening for movement inside. Nothing.

The DS tried the doorbell. Still nothing.

"Looks like he's out," he said. "Let's come back later."

Meera shook her head. "I think we should have a look around. Just in case."

He gave her a funny look, but nodded. "Good idea."

They moved around the side of the house. The side gate was open. Meera glanced at the sarge, who gave her an approving nod. She opened it and went into the garden. It was just as overgrown as the front.

Through the back windows, she could see the living room was a mess. Papers and empty coffee mugs littered the table. The suit she'd seen on the back of the door was gone, just an empty coat hanger in its place.

"Same as last time," Meera said. "Doesn't look like he's tidied up."

The DS frowned. "Or he's left in a hurry."

Meera moved along the back of the house, looking into the kitchen. The sink was full of dirty dishes. The bin was overflowing.

"He's not been here for a while," she said.

"Or he's just not been taking care of the place." He looked up at the first-floor windows. "Let's see if we can get inside."

Meera raised an eyebrow. "You think we should?"

"A house in a state like that," the sarge said. "He might be in trouble."

"You think he's dead in there?"

"I don't think anything. But let's check."

They moved back to the front of the house. Meera tried the door handle. It was locked.

"Figures," she muttered.

The DS beckoned for her to follow him round to the back. "I saw an open window. Just a top one, but you're small."

She looked at him. "Really?"

"Let's take a look."

Meera followed him back to the garden, shaking her head. The overgrown grass brushed against her ankles. She surveyed the house, spotting the open window he'd mentioned.

"You're serious about this?" she asked.

He nodded. "We need to know if he's in there. You up for it?"

She sighed. "Fine. But you owe me."

Strunk gave a small smile. "I'll buy you a coffee."

She grunted. *Is that all?*

She moved to the wall, eyeing the window. It was a top window, above the kitchen sink. Just above head height. She'd need a boost.

"Give me a leg up," she said.

The DS crouched, lacing his fingers together. Meera stepped onto them and steadied herself against the wall.

"Ready?" he asked.

"Go on."

He lifted her, and she reached for the window ledge. It was a tight fit, but she managed to wriggle through, landing awkwardly on the kitchen counter.

"Made it," she called down.

She'd broken into houses when she was in uniform. Without the bulky uniform and kit, it was surprisingly easy.

"Well done," he said. "Let me in."

She hopped off the counter, careful not to knock over the stack of dirty dishes. The smell was rank. She wrinkled her nose and moved to the back door, unlocking it.

The sarge stepped inside, looking around. "Nice work."

"Thanks."

They moved through the kitchen into the living room. It was even worse than she'd expected. Papers and old photos were scattered everywhere, and the coffee mugs had grown mould.

"Nice," she muttered.

The DS picked up a piece of paper. "Bills. Unpaid."

Meera glanced at the sofa. The laptop was gone. The one thing that Yiannis had seemed interested in, the campaign to find Jackie. "He took his computer."

He nodded. "Let's check upstairs."

They climbed to the first floor. The bedroom door was open. Inside, the bed was unmade, but the wardrobe doors were open, hangers empty.

"He's cleared out," Meera said.

Strunk nodded. "Clothes, laptop. He's done a runner."

She checked the bedside table. No phone charger. "He's taken his essentials."

The DS looked around. "Why now?"

"Maybe he heard from Jackie."

"Or from someone else."

Meera felt her chest constrict. She looked at the open wardrobes. "At least he's not been taken."

The DS nodded. "No one nicks all of someone's clothes and electricals after abducting them."

She shook her head. "Especially not when they're as vile as his were."

The DS sighed. "I'd better call it in. Nice work, Meera. You did alright."

She'd been proud of herself, getting in the window like that. But now, she was just sad.

CHAPTER SEVENTY-SEVEN

JILL STOOD at the front of the briefing room, her team gathered around the table. The morning sun streamed through the windows, casting a warm glow over the room. She felt a sense of optimism, a welcome change from the tension that had clouded her personal life. Things were better with Meera, and it made everything else seem more manageable.

"Right, let's get started," she said, looking at each member of her team. "We do have one concrete fact, and that's that Ellie Sharp's confessed to killing Peter Didson."

Mike leaned back in his chair. "She claims it was self-defence, though."

"That's what she's saying," Jill replied. "She claims Peter attacked her after admitting to killing her mother. But we need to wait for more evidence before we can draw any conclusions."

Katie tapped her pen against her notebook. "Do we believe her?"

Jill shrugged. "Forensics are working on it. We're waiting for their report."

Mike shook his head. "Any chance the Ring doorbell might have picked up sound? It got Ellie leaving the house, it might have picked up Peter's voice, if he was still alive."

Jill shrugged. "Forensics are still analysing the footage. If there's anything useful, we'll know soon."

Stanley leaned forward. "If Peter did kill Rowena, why confess to Ellie?"

"People do stupid things when they're scared," Jill told him. "Or when they think they've got nothing left to lose."

The door opened and Gail Hansford entered, a folder tucked under her arm. The Crime Scene Manager looked tired, but her jaw was set. Jill hadn't worked with the woman before, but she knew the DCI thought highly of her.

"Gail," Jill said. "Thanks for coming in. What have you got?"

Gail took a seat. "We've finished the preliminary analysis of Ellie's injuries." She looked up. "It took a while, as she had to be accompanied to Poole Hospital for examination by a specialist nurse."

Jill nodded. "And?"

"Ellie's got defensive wounds," Gail said. "Broken fingernails, some bruising to her neck. It looks like she was attacked."

"Can you tell when she received those wounds?" Jill asked.

Gail nodded. "The bruising hasn't yellowed yet. It's recent. And the fingernails... Harder to tell."

Jill turned to Katie. "What were her nails like when you went to her flat the afternoon before it happened?"

Katie shrugged. "I wasn't really looking, guv. But I'd have noticed if they were damaged."

Gail took out a photo of Ellie's hands and passed it across the table. Katie looked at it, then across at Stanley.

"Stan?" she said. "I don't think her hands were like that when we spoke to her. Do you?"

"I don't think so." He rubbed his chin. "But then, it's not something I'd be looking for."

Jill nodded. Katie was diligent, and had short, tidy nails herself.

She was confident this was the kind of thing that would snag her attention. "So it's likely the damage to her nails was sustained during an altercation with Peter. Could she have been the one who instigated it?"

Gail shrugged. "I can't tell you that, sorry."

Jill pursed her lips. It was enough for Ellie to claim self-defence. And if she had a good lawyer...

Elsa Short's firm were representing her. That gave her an advantage.

She sighed. "Is it enough to suspect excessive force?"

"Manslaughter," muttered Stanley.

Gail shrugged. "I'm not the CPS, but I've got a report here detailing Peter's wounds. There's only one cut, just below the ribs. No practice cuts, no sign that she struck again after the first blow."

Jill raised an eyebrow. "So she didn't go overboard."

Gail shook her head. "You can try for murder, but I don't think the forensics will help."

Jill sighed, looking around the room. "Well, thanks, everyone. It was never going to be an easy case. But we do know at least that Rowena Sharp died of drowning. And it looks like Peter Didson was her killer."

She allowed herself a small smile. "We'll be releasing Rowena's body soon, and Ellie and Sebastian will be able to hold a funeral for her. At least the family has closure now."

Stanley grunted. "Funny kind of closure."

Jill turned to him. "Look, this was only our second case. We cleared up the first one within days, the Lyme Harbour body. Largely thanks to Mike." She gave him a nod. "This one was never going to be easy. We did what we were asked to do: we pieced together the story behind Rowena's death. That's all we could do, under the circumstances."

Stanley grunted again, unconvinced.

There wasn't much more Jill could say to make them feel better about it. "Now take some time off. You've all earned it."

They sat in their spots, staring at her. She made a gesturing movement towards the door. "Go."

Stanley and Mike headed out with Gail, but Katie lingered. She approached Jill, twisting her hands together.

"Can I help piece together any evidence against Ellie?" she asked.

Jill shook her head. "No, Katie. Take some time with your colleagues. Ellie killed Peter, but he attacked her. That's all there is to it."

Katie hesitated, then nodded. "Right, guv."

Jill watched her go, pushing back her own disappointment. The DCI would be back soon, and she'd have to update her. She wasn't looking forward to it.

CHAPTER SEVENTY-EIGHT

LESLEY GLANCED at the satnav as they passed Sutton Scotney heading south. Another hour, at least. She shifted in her seat, trying to find a comfortable position. The stop at Cherwell Valley had helped, but the drive was still dragging.

Hannah sat beside her, focused on the road. They'd barely spoken since leaving the services. Lesley wasn't sure if that was a blessing or not.

"Shall I put the radio on?" Hannah broke the silence.

"Um. Yes, OK." She braced herself for something loud, or perhaps something ridiculously erudite.

Hannah turned on the radio and pressed the advance button till it landed on Radio 2; Sara Cox. Was it really that late?

She checked the clock on the dash. It was just gone 4pm. She'd barely have time to speak to the team, at this rate.

She opened her mouth, about to ask Hannah if she could put her foot down, then thought better of it. They'd make up some miles once they were on the M3. She preferred not to think about what the A31 would be like towards Ringwood.

Silence again. Lesley checked her phone. No messages. She'd expected something from Elsa by now.

Her phone buzzed just as she'd put it away. She pulled it out again, glad of some relief. It was Sadie Dawes.

She frowned, glancing at Hannah. There was no way she was taking this call on speaker.

She deactivated Bluetooth on her phone then answered the call. "DCI Clarke."

"Very formal, today."

"Sadie. How can I help you?"

Sadie would be sniffing around Peter Didson's death, trying to find the 'human interest' story behind it. There was certainly one of those, but not one Lesley was about to discuss with the press.

"Lesley," Sadie said. "I've just had a call I think you should know about."

Lesley sighed. "What now?"

"Jackie Kendall."

Lesley sat up straighter. "Jackie?" She glanced at Hannah, who frowned.

"You're still looking for her, right?" Sadie asked.

"What did she say?"

"She told me to leave her alone. Said she's safe, she's got her fella, Yiannis, with her."

Lesley looked at Hannah. She mouthed *Yiannis is with Jackie.*

"And you believe her?" she asked Sadie.

"She sounded... scared. But she insisted she's fine."

"Did you record it?"

"No. And before you ask, the number was withheld, and she told me not to bother tracing it because it was a burner."

Lesley rubbed her forehead. "Of course it was."

"Lesley, she said she wants us to leave her alone."

"Us?"

"You know what I mean. The media. The police."

"Did she specifically say police?"

"She mentioned you by name. And your mate Zoe, in Cumbria. Keen as ever."

Lesley ignored that comment and reactivated Bluetooth, putting the call on the car's speakers. Hannah gave her a tight smile.

"Did she say where she was?" Lesley asked.

"You're not listening, Lesley. She doesn't want us looking for her. You. Whoever. She didn't say where she was, of course she didn't. Just that she's safe."

"And you really didn't record it or try to trace the call?"

"Like I said, it was a burner. She probably threw it away as soon as she hung up, if she's got any sense." A pause. "Lesley, what is it Jackie's so scared of? What happened to her, last summer?"

"You know I'm not going to answer that."

"No. Confidential. Well, I just hope that whoever it is she's so terrified of doesn't find her. Looks like you can't help her there."

"And you," Lesley reminded her.

"Of course." Sadie hung up.

Lesley didn't much appreciate Sadie telling her how to do her job. But for Jackie to have disappeared from Zoe's police station like that, and now this...

"Boss?" Hannah asked.

"Mm-hmm?"

"Did I catch that right? Jackie's been talking to a journalist, making her pass on the message to leave her alone."

"Pretty much."

"Why? I mean, why not contact us herself?"

Lesley rubbed her forehead. "Because she doesn't trust us."

"She should."

"I know that, you know that. Jackie doesn't."

"So she thinks Sadie Dawes is more trustworthy than the police."

"Not us," Lesley said. *The people we work with*, she thought, but didn't say aloud. Hannah had been in Devon when the truth had come out about DCI Mackie's death; she didn't need the full detail.

"So what are you going to do?" Hannah asked.

"I don't have much choice."

"You're going to find her. You need evidence, after all."

Lesley shook her head. "No, Hannah. I've seen what happens when vulnerable witnesses get caught up in this kind of thing. She's not reporting a crime. There's nothing we *can* do. I'm going to respect her wishes and leave her alone."

CHAPTER SEVENTY-NINE

JACKIE KENDALL PULLED the coat she'd found in a charity shop tighter against the Edinburgh wind. The city was bustling, tourists and locals weaving through the streets. She kept her head down, blending in.

She reached into her pocket, feeling the burner phone. It had served its purpose. She stopped by a bin, looked around, and tossed it in. As she walked away, it started ringing.

She didn't look back.

The crowds thinned as she moved away from the city centre. The buildings grew more worn, the streets less inviting. She knew where she was heading. Yiannis would be waiting.

She crossed a road, avoiding eye contact with a group of teenagers hanging around a bus stop. She'd learned to be cautious. She'd learned a lot since leaving Bournemouth.

The wind picked up, carrying the distant sound of sirens. She ignored it, focusing on her steps. *Head down.* She turned down a narrow alley, her footsteps echoing.

She paused at the end, checking her surroundings. It was quiet here. She stepped out, heading towards a block of flats. The entrance was grimy, the door slightly ajar.

Inside, the lift was out of order. She took the stairs, her footsteps heavy on the concrete. Second floor. She stopped outside a door, listening.

Nothing.

She knocked, a pattern they'd agreed on. The door opened a crack, then wider. Yiannis stood there, his face tense.

"Jackie."

She stepped inside, the door closing behind her.

CHAPTER EIGHTY

Lesley stepped inside Dorset Police HQ, the familiar hum of activity surrounding her. The building's modern design, all glass and metal, felt clinical, but she was growing used to it. She gestured to Hannah to follow her and they made their way to Jill's office.

Jill was at her desk, papers spread out in front of her. She looked up as they entered.

"Boss. How was the journey?"

Lesley shrugged, ignoring the pain in her back from having spent at least fourteen of the last forty-eight hours sitting. "Good as can be expected at this time of year. How was your day?"

Jill sighed. "I'm sorry, boss. We don't have enough to charge Ellie Sharp with Peter Didson's murder. We don't even know for sure that Peter killed Rowena."

Lesley sat down opposite her. "Slow down. Why don't you have enough?"

"Because the evidence points to it being self-defence."

"Peter attacked her?"

"Mm-hmm." Jill yawned, then put a hand in front of her mouth. "Sorry."

"It's fine. I'm pretty knackered myself. Look, Jill, This case was never going to be easy. A body that's been in the water for fifty-one years, we—"

"Fifty-two."

"Fifty-two years. A body that's been in the water that long, we were lucky she'd even been preserved the way she was."

"The mud."

Lesley nodded. "Don't beat yourself up. It wasn't your fault that Ellie decided to take the law into her own hands."

Hannah was standing next to Lesley, watching. Lesley looked up at her. "We've been unlucky too, haven't we, Hannah?"

"I wouldn't say unlucky."

Lesley shook her head. "Jackie Kendall gave us a few scraps of information about something she witnessed at a property she was selling. It's over a year ago, but it's worth visiting the property, seeing if there are any forensics." She looked up at Hannah. "It's not a complete dead end."

Hannah grunted.

Jill looked between them. "Won't Jackie tell you any more?"

Lesley shook her head. "She ran. Decided she was too scared, and left the police station in Cumbria."

Jill winced. "Ouch."

"But at least we know she's OK. Well, we think we do."

"I wouldn't be so sure," Hannah muttered.

Lesley frowned at her. *Be positive, woman.* It was like having Dennis back.

But without the swear jar and the tweed, at least.

"We need to respect her wishes," she said, looking from Hannah to Jill and back again. "Jackie is no longer a missing person. She's told us she's safe and that she doesn't want us to look for her. There's no case."

"What about the Kelvins?" asked Hannah.

Lesley forced calm into her face. "We need to tread carefully there. The Kelvins are dangerous people, the kind who surround themselves with the best lawyers money can buy, and make themselves almost impossible to take down. Not to mention the fact that they almost always have someone else do their dirty work for them."

"But I can visit the property," Hannah pointed out. "Take a look around the garage."

"You can. We'll have to come up with a cover story for it; we have no way of knowing if the new owners are associated with the previous ones."

"That's something, then."

"It is," Lesley said. "But don't expect too much from it."

Her stomach rumbled. She hadn't eaten since a large latte and a muffin somewhere around Stoke. She was starving, and tired. She just wanted to get home.

But first, there were two teams to speak to. They'd be disappointed. Her job was to buck them up.

Lesley sighed. *God, sometimes I bloody hate being a DCI.*

CHAPTER EIGHTY-ONE

LESLEY LED the way two doors along to the MCIT team room, Jill and Hannah flanking her.

"I gave my team a few hours off earlier," Jill said. "But they're all back now. Wanted to know what was happening with the Jackie Kendall case."

Lesley nodded. "Good. Are they all together?"

"Yes."

Lesley nodded. There were connections between these teams that ran deep. Some of them had worked together for years. Others were married.

Inside, everyone was gathered, the space too small for both teams. Mike sat in the chair that normally belonged to Tina, peering at the desk like his wife might suddenly appear from it. Katie perched on the front of Meera's desk, repeatedly smoothing down her skirt. Meera stood by the window, staring out. Nathan and Stanley were in a corner, speaking in hushed tones that made Lesley frown.

And there was an extra person. Johnny Chiles, standing next to Mike at Tina's desk and looking awkward. He kept pushing his hair back; it had grown.

Dear God. Was that a mullet?

Lesley cleared her throat as Jill and Hannah slid in behind her. The room quieted.

"Right folks," she began. "I know things have been... tricky. But you've all done a good job."

Johnny stared back at her, unblinking. How many people here knew who he was?

Better deal with the elephant in the room.

"Some of you will know DC Johnny Chiles," Lesley said, gesturing towards him. He gave a small bow. "Johnny used to be a member of the MCIT, until he took a transfer to the Met three years ago. Now he's decided he'd much rather be in the sunny climes of Dorset than the mean streets of the capital."

There was nervous laughter. Mike gave Johnny a clap on the back.

"Johnny will be joining the Cold Cases team when Mike goes on his parental leave," she said. "At which point Tina will return to the MCIT."

Meera gave a little cheer. Lesley looked at her and cocked her head.

"Sorry, boss. Just... Tina's good."

"She is." Lesley swallowed. "And so's Johnny. For the weeks before Tina returns, Johnny, I want you to work with the MCIT. The work will be more familiar to you anyway. Hannah will be your DI, I'm sure she'll brief you."

Hannah gave Johnny an appraising look. He grinned at her, and when her stare didn't soften, he dropped the grin.

"Boss," he said to her.

"Hannah," she replied. "You can call me by my name."

"Oh." Johnny glanced at Mike, who nodded. "Hannah. Pleased to be part of the team."

"Alright, that's enough of that," Lesley said. "I want you all to know you shouldn't feel down. Yes, we don't know for sure who killed Rowena Sharp, but it looks very likely that it was Peter

Didson, and at least the family now has a body so they can hold a funeral."

"What about Ellie Sharp?" Katie said. "Isn't she going to prison?"

Lesley nodded at Jill, who stepped forward.

"The evidence points to Ellie killing Peter Didson in self-defence. She didn't use excessive force, and her claim is that he was attempting to kill her, or at least do her serious harm. It's a convincing defence. There's no case against her."

"Not a strong enough case for the CPS, anyway," Stanley muttered. Jill shot him a look.

"What about Jackie?" Nathan said. "You spoke to her, right? Found out what she was so scared of?"

"We have a good idea," Lesley said. "But not enough to launch any kind of investigation. But the good news is that Jackie is safe, even if she doesn't want to speak to us. We've cleared up a missing persons case, and that's not nothing."

"It's not really something though, is it?" said Hannah. "Not unless we can get something from that house she was selling."

"Tread carefully with that," Lesley said. "I already warned you."

Hannah's gaze dropped. "Of course."

Lesley stepped back, allowing the hum of voices to fill the room. Johnny approached her, his voice low.

"Thanks, boss," he muttered. "For letting me back in."

Lesley tensed. She hadn't exactly had a choice. She gave him a curt nod. "Just do your job, Johnny."

He nodded and moved away. Lesley watched him, unease prickling at her.

Hannah was at her side. "Everything alright, boss?"

Lesley forced a smile. "Fine."

Hannah didn't look convinced. "If you say so."

Lesley turned her attention back to the team. Were this lot ever going to gel? Would Johnny's return make things harder, or easier?

Truth was, she had no idea.

CHAPTER EIGHTY-TWO

Mike sat at the kitchen table, watching Tina as she fed Daisy. The baby gurgled, her tiny hands reaching for the bottle.

"How was your day?" he asked.

Tina smiled. "Quiet. Well, apart from Mum's usual nonsense. She bought Daisy a new pram. I told her she's got a perfectly good one already, and she needed to be saving her money. She's a pensioner, Mike. Why does she want to spend all her money on things we don't need?"

"It's just her way of showing you she loves you." Truth was, Annie Abbott could be stifling at times. She doted on Tina and the kids and liked to show it with presents. Lately, she'd been distracted by her mates in the swimming club she'd formed in Lyme Regis, but now it seemed she'd reverted to retail therapy.

Tina grunted. She looked down at Daisy with wide eyes. "Your nanny's bonkers, you know that?"

Mike smiled. Annie was eccentric, yes. Bonkers, not so much.

"Johnny's coming back," he said, changing the subject.

Tina looked up. "Johnny Chiles?"

"Yeah. Wants to transfer back to Dorset."

"I thought he was after career progression, joining the Met."

Mike shrugged. "He's skint. London's too expensive, on a DC's salary. And his dad's not well."

"Fair enough. It'll be weird having him back." She looked down at Daisy, making cooing noises.

Mike leaned back, watching them. He could hear Louis in the next room, singing along with something on the TV. He should get up and take him to bed, but it was nice just sitting here, him and Tina.

And Daisy. He was getting used to that. To four of them in this poky house.

Tina looked up. "Why'd he leave in the first place? Johnny? Always seemed odd, him going to the Met like that."

Mike shrugged. "It's his life."

She didn't look convinced. "Still."

He licked his lips. "We wrapped up the Rowena Sharp case. Sort of."

"I know. It's all over the news."

He nodded. "Yeah. It's been... intense."

"What about Jackie Kendall?"

He hesitated. "She turned up. But then disappeared again."

Tina frowned. "Did she say why she disappeared?" She shook her head. "I always thought she was going to turn up in a ditch."

"Sorry, love. I don't know. I'm not in the MCIT. It's a sensitive case."

She nodded, looking thoughtful. "I'll find out soon enough."

"In three weeks," he reminded her. "When we swap."

She kissed Daisy's forehead. "I'll miss her."

He could see it in her eyes, though. She couldn't wait to get back to work.

CHAPTER EIGHTY-THREE

LESLEY SAT across from Elsa in the dimly lit restaurant. She'd forgotten about the dinner reservation until getting home to find her wife sitting in the kitchen in her favourite blouse and the earrings Lesley had bought her for her birthday. She didn't have the heart to cancel.

The place was new, all straight lines and muted colours. Not her usual choice, but Elsa seemed at home.

Their main courses arrived. Lesley poked at her grilled sea bass and looked across at Elsa.

"I hear your new team's getting involved in my cases."

Elsa looked up, a faint smile on her lips. "If you mean Sameena representing Ellie Sharp, then yes." She leaned in and stroked Lesley's hand. "But I bet you're relieved it's not me."

Lesley turned her hand over to hold Elsa's. "I won't be facing you across the table anymore. Carpenter wants me behind a desk, not interviewing suspects."

Elsa's gaze was sharp. "And you hate it."

"I..." Lesley considered. "I don't hate it. I'll just have to get used to it." She sighed. "It's what I did in Birmingham, after all. I had four teams there, four DIs."

"And a dodgy boss."

"And a dodgy boss, indeed. So things are better here all round, wouldn't you say?" Lesley put on a broad smile.

Elsa laughed. "You don't have to pretend."

"I'm not pretending." Lesley swallowed a mouthful of her fish. It was good. "I'm happy. I've got you, our beautiful new house—"

"Not all that new anymore. It's been six months."

Lesley shrugged. "Our beautiful newish house. And Sharon's happy in Exeter."

"But you're bored."

"I'm not bored. I got to go to bloody Cumbria to speak to a witness today. That's not boring."

"Sitting in a car for however many hundred miles? Sounds pretty dull to me." Elsa cut off a corner of her steak and put it in her mouth.

"OK," Lesley admitted. "It is dull. A bit. But I'll find a way to make it less so."

Elsa smiled. "I'm sure you will."

Lesley nodded and picked up her fork. They ate in silence for a moment.

"By the way," Lesley said, "your associate did a good job."

"Sameena? Good." Elsa cocked her head, studying Lesley's face. "Maybe we will find ourselves across the table from each other anyway. I hear your team have been sniffing around the Kelvins again."

Lesley felt her stomach dip. "Surely you're not representing them?"

Elsa laughed. "God, no! Of course not. But these things have a way of coming back to haunt us, don't they?"

Lesley swallowed her fish before she could choke. "I bloody well hope not."

I hope you enjoyed reading *The Poole Harbour Murders*. You can read a bonus novella, *The Lyme Regis Murder*, for free via my website. The Cold Case Team's first case takes Tina and Nathan to the beautiful town of Lyme Regis to investigate a mystery that turns out to be closer to home than Tina expects. Get your free copy in ebook or audio at rachelmclean.com/lymemurder. Happy Reading!

Rachel McLean.

READ A FREE NOVELLA, THE LYME REGIS MURDER

DCI Lesley Clarke is back, and she's got not one, but two teams to head up.

When the body of a prominent local business owner washes up in Lyme Regis Harbour, Lesley must lead her new team through a murky investigation revealing the darker side of the picturesque town.

As she navigates betrayal, secrets, and the challenges of managing two teams without her old sidekick, Lesley grapples with her own past while racing against time to uncover the truth. Can she filter through the evidence to sort fact from fiction and find the real killer?

Read *The Lyme Regis Murder* in ebook or listen to the audiobook for free by downloading from rachelmclean.com/lymemurder or buy the paperback from book retailers.

READ THE DORSET CRIME SERIES

The Corfe Castle Murders

The Clifftop Murders

The Island Murders

The Monument Murders

The Millionaire Murders

The Fossil Beach Murders

The Blue Pool Murders

The Lighthouse Murders

The Ghost Village Murders

The Poole Harbour Murders

The Chesil Beach Murders

...and more to come

Buy from book retailers.

ALSO BY RACHEL MCLEAN

The DI Zoe Finch Series – buy from book retailers.

Deadly Wishes

Deadly Choices

Deadly Desires

Deadly Terror

Deadly Reprisal

Deadly Fallout

Deadly Christmas

The McBride & Tanner Series – buy from book retailers.

Blood and Money

Death and Poetry

Power and Treachery

Secrets and History

The Cumbria Crime Series by Rachel McLean and Joel Hames – buy from book retailers.

The Harbour

The Mine

The Cairn

The Barn

The Lake

The Wood

The Port

...and more to come

The London Cosy Mystery Series by Rachel McLean and Millie Ravensworth – buy from book retailers.

Death at Westminster

Death in the West End

Death at Tower Bridge

Death on the Thames

Death at St Paul's Cathedral

Death at Abbey Road

The Lyme Regis Women's Swimming Club Series by Rachel McLean and Millie Ravensworth – buy from book retailers.

The Lyme Regis Women's Swimming Club

A Brush with Death

The Mystery of the Runaway Reindeer

...and more to come